GRAND SLAM

THE WINNING ACE SERIES (BOOK 3)

TRACIE DELANEY

For Louise - my rock

1

You're not my goddamn type. Never were, never will be.

Tally squeezed her eyes closed as the memory of Cash's hurtful words came tumbling into her mind. A deepening ache grew in her chest. She slowly breathed in through her nose and blew out a shuddering breath. A few weeks earlier, she wouldn't have imagined he could be so cruel, but ever since a car had mown him down and left him with a severe brain injury, he hadn't been the same person. God, she loved him—desperately—but he'd made it all too clear he no longer felt the same way.

Before the accident, they'd been planning on getting married. Now all she had left to remind her they'd ever been engaged was a slight indentation on her ring finger where, for a few short weeks, her engagement ring had nestled.

Winter had arrived early in Northern Ireland, even though it was only mid-October. The wind howled, and rain streamed horizontally across the windows as she sat on the runway, waiting for the plane to depart. For the moment, she'd stopped crying, and her insides felt numb, hollow, empty.

The captain finally announced they'd been cleared for take-off. As the plane accelerated down the runway, Tally ached for the familiarity of Cash sitting beside her, clinging to the seat and muttering curses under his breath. He hated flying. It didn't frighten her in the least. A much scarier prospect was the reason for this trip. Rather than being snuggled up in bed next to Cash, she was heading back to London, where she'd have to relive the last few hideous hours as Pete and Em grilled her until she spilled every single detail.

Little more than an hour later, the plane landed at London City Airport. Tally wrenched her bag from under the seat in front and queued with her fellow passengers to disembark. Her luggage was almost last off the carousel, and when she turned around to leave, the arrivals hall was virtually empty.

She joined an enormous line for taxis but had little choice. The DLR would be rammed at this time of the morning, full of keen city types pretending they couldn't wait to get to work. In truth, like her, they'd all prefer to be at home in bed.

When she reached the front of the line, she sank into the back of a black cab. Fortunately, she'd lucked out. The taxi driver was also morose, allowing Tally to slip into despair in peace without having to pretend to be interested in someone else's mindless chatter.

Forty-five long minutes later, she arrived at Em's new place. When Tally moved to Northern Ireland, Em had given up their old flat. She now lived a few streets away in a one-bed apartment that was cheaper on rent.

The taxi driver barely waited for Tally to slam the boot before he sped off, no doubt in search of the next lucrative fare. *Damn. What if Em isn't at home? Only one way to find out.* With her luggage trailing behind her, she walked up the narrow path. She pressed the bell for flat four and waited.

"Hello?"

"Em, it's me."

"Tal?" Em said, her tone full of surprise. "What the fuck? Hang on."

Less than thirty seconds later, the door opened. Em took one look at Tally's face, her eyes flickering to where Tally was clutching her luggage, fingers red from the wind and cold, and surprise turned to concern.

"You're freezing. Get in here." Em plucked a suitcase from Tally's hand and led her upstairs to the flat. "In there, babes," she said, pointing to the living room before she disappeared into the kitchen.

Tally dropped onto the sofa and pressed her fingertips to her temples. Exhausted and overwrought, all she wanted was to sleep, to wish away the nightmare of the past five hours and wake up next to Cash.

"Here you go," Em said, passing her a steaming cup of coffee. "What's the matter, babes?"

Tally took the mug from her. "I don't know where to start."

"Wherever you need to."

"He's kicked me out."

Em's mouth fell open. "He's fucking *what*?"

Tally's eyes welled up, and despite furious blinking, the tears spilled over. "He said he doesn't love me anymore," she said, dashing the back of her hand across her damp cheeks.

Em frowned. "Of course he loves you. The man worships the ground you walk on."

Tally shook her head. "Not anymore. He's different since the accident. It doesn't matter what I do, Em. I can't reach him."

Em wrapped her fingers around Tally's and squeezed. "How did all this come about?"

"I found him watching the Singapore Masters early this morning. God, Em, he looked so broken." Her breath caught on a sob. "We started rowing. Well, he did really. And then he threw a vase at me."

"He *what*?"

Tally reassuringly patted Em's hand. "Not *at* me. He didn't aim for me. His anger flares up from nowhere, and he reacts. After he threw it, he told me to go. He said he didn't want me anymore." Her voice cracked. "He said I wasn't his type. That I never had been."

Grief and desperation surged through her, taking her breath away with its intensity, and her whole body trembled with the effort of dragging in the air her lungs demanded. Em pulled her close.

"Babes, this can't be right. There must be a reason. Cash loves you."

Tally eased her fingers from beneath Em's tight hold and rubbed her eyes. "You weren't there. His face... Em, he looked as though he *hated* me."

Em scratched her cheek, a deepening frown pulling her brows low. "I don't get it."

Tally's shoulders dropped. Her whole world had crashed around her, and she felt as though she was floating above her body, looking down on the shell of a person who used to love and be loved. This had to be a terrible nightmare.

"I know you don't have the room, but can I sleep on the sofa until I get myself sorted?"

Em's warm hand rubbed soothing circles against her back. "For as long as you need, babes."

"Love you," Tally whispered as more tears fell.

"Want me to cancel work today?"

"No. To be honest, I'd welcome a bit of time on my own."

"Does Pete know?"

"Not yet." Tally clamped her eyes shut. "I need to work out what to say before I go to see him."

"This is the place to do that." Em glanced at her watch. "Shit. I'm late." She wheeled out of the room and, after a lot of clattering and banging, returned fifteen minutes later carrying four bags, her back curved from the weight of them all.

"Today's client thinks I can make a silk purse out of a sow's ear. Clearly, I'm going to need every fucking trick in the book."

Despite the hollow ache in her chest, Tally laughed. "If anyone can, you can."

Em grimaced. "We'll see." She gave Tally a forlorn stare. "We'll talk properly later. Everything will work out. I promise."

The silence that enveloped Tally when Em left was almost oppressive. She lay down on the sofa and curled her knees into her chest then closed her eyes and slept.

TALLY WOKE a few hours later with a stiff neck. She drew the back of her hand across her mouth, wiping drool from the corners. The sun had dipped low in the sky, casting a weak shadow into Em's living room. She pushed herself to a seated position and massaged the tight muscles in the back of her neck. The sofa was comfy enough, but it didn't come close to her bed at home. Except she didn't have a home anymore.

A wave of despair crashed over her as she faced her new reality.

No Cash.

No home.

No future.

She trudged into the kitchen and flicked the kettle on. After opening several cupboards, she managed to locate a jar of instant coffee. She spooned a heaped amount into a mug in the vain hope caffeine would make her feel better. It wouldn't, of course. There was no cure for a broken heart.

The kettle had just boiled when the front door slammed.

"Tal?"

"In here."

The sound of several bags being dropped on the floor was followed by Em appearing in the doorway to the kitchen. "Make that two." Em flopped into one of two chairs pushed up against the kitchen wall.

She added slightly less coffee to Em's mug and put it on the table in front of her. Tally remained standing, blew on her drink, and took a cautious sip. "How's the sow's ear?"

Em made an exaggerated motion with her hands. "I tell you, babes, I'm a fucking genius. 'Course, it's a lot easier when you start with a better canvas, but still, I impressed myself."

Tally chuckled. "You always were a miracle worker. I should know."

Em snorted. "Hardly. Comparing you to her is like comparing a Van Gogh to some production-line picture you can pick up at Ikea." She kicked her shoes off, and they thudded against the kitchen cabinets. A relieved sigh spilled from her lips. "Enough about me. How are you doing?"

"Not great."

"Has he been in touch?"

"No." Tally gave a short, bitter laugh. "I don't expect him to."

"So what's the plan?"

"You don't give a minute, do you?"

Em leaned back. She crossed one foot over the opposing knee and began massaging the sole of her foot. "I don't mean to push, babes, but I know you. The last thing you need is time to think. Keeping busy—that's the key."

Tally blew out a soft sigh tinged with defeat. "I guess the best thing would be to ask Pete for my job back. If he'll have me."

"Of course he'll have you."

Tally sighed. "I'm dreading having to tell people and watch them pity me."

"Then don't. Tell them to mind their own fucking business."

As another wave of hopelessness and loss washed over her, she covered her face with her hands. "I don't know what to do."

Em rose from her chair and wrapped her arms around Tally's shoulders then gently rocked her back and forth like a mother soothing a distressed child. "You don't have to rush into anything, but at least make the beginnings of a plan. Don't let the days slide by, Tal. That's when depression sets in."

"Yeah. I know."

"Right," Em said gruffly. "I can't be arsed cooking. Let's get pizza." She grabbed a bunch of takeout menus from the drawer beside the sink and began riffling through. After reaching into her bag for her phone, she swiftly brushed away a tear.

"I'll be okay," Tally said, her voice small and tinged with defeat.

Em turned to face her. "As if you haven't been through enough, what with Cash's accident and everything."

Sorrow squeezed her heart. "I wouldn't change a single thing, even if I knew how it ended."

"This isn't the real Cash. You know that, right?"

A headache began to pound behind Tally's eyes, and she dug her fingertips into her temples. "After his accident, I read everything I could get my hands on about head-injury victims. It changes people, Em. Changes their personalities. I couldn't find one case where the victim wasn't different in some way. And seventy-five per cent of couples split up following severe head injury." She sighed wistfully. "I was certain we'd be in the twenty-five per cent. Shows how wrong you can be."

"So you've given up on him?"

Tally expelled a frustrated breath. "No. He's given up on me."

"But—"

She put her hands in the air, warding off any further comment. "Let's talk about something else, please. Order the pizza."

∾

WHEN TALLY CLIMBED into her makeshift bed later that night, she allowed her mind to wander. Her chest ached with despair. If she weren't careful, depression would join the party, as Em had warned. Tally hadn't considered a future without Cash, not for a long time. In the beginning, she constantly waited for him to dump her, but she hadn't suffered those feelings for a long time. He'd made her feel secure wrapped in his love, and she'd planned a whole life, with him at the centre of it. Marriage, career, kids. Now she had to walk in a different direction. Alone.

Hot tears sprang to her eyes, but she wouldn't let them fall. Not this time. She needed to toughen up, and quick. The next few weeks were going to be hell. If she allowed the pain to suffocate her like last time they'd split up—after Kinga had sent the photographs of Cash kissing Gracie, his mother's nurse—the road back would be torturous.

Sleep, when it came, was fitful, and as the first rays of daylight seeped through the blinds, Tally flung off the covers and stiffly got to her feet. She showered and dressed as quietly as possible, left Em a note telling her where she was going, and slipped out of the flat. It was barely past six, but Pete had always been an early riser, and Tally wanted to catch him before he left for work. She couldn't face talking to him at the paper, not with all those curious eyes raking over the dying embers of her life.

The tube was quiet—the hour being too early for most commuters—and Tally easily got a seat. Pete's place was only a few stops from Em's, and at six thirty, Tally found herself standing outside. The blinds were open, meaning he was up, but he wouldn't have left for work yet. She took a deep breath and rang the bell, its peal sounding hollow in the hallway.

Pete's grumbles seeped through the door, and she couldn't help a small smile from creeping across her lips. He'd be pissed off, assuming she was an early cold caller, and he'd be getting ready to give her a piece of his mind.

The heavy mahogany door swung back, showing Pete's mouth already open in readiness to berate the poor sucker. When he saw Tally, surprise flashed across his face.

"Tally? What are you doing here?"

"Can I come in?"

"Sure, sure." He stepped back and drew her into his arms as he kicked the door shut. "What's wrong? Is it Cash? He's okay, isn't he?"

"Let's go and sit down, Uncle Pete."

She ignored the look of confusion he gave her at the word *Uncle*—a moniker she rarely turned to these days—and brushed past him into the living room. She sank into her favourite chair.

Pete sat opposite, a deep frown knitting his eyebrows together. "What's going on?"

Tally steadied herself. "Cash and I... we've split up."

Pete's head flinched to one side as though he'd been slapped across the face. "What?"

"He... I... he doesn't want me anymore. Told me to go. So I did."

Pete's eyes widened, his posture stiffening. "Tally, the man's not in his right mind. He won't have meant it. Have you called him?"

"He meant it. You didn't see his face. He's not the person he was."

"When was this?"

"Yesterday."

"Oh, sweetheart." He held out his arms. "Come here."

Tally rose from her chair and nestled next to Pete on the sofa. His warm, comforting embrace was exactly what she needed, and he held her without saying a word as she cried. It was one of the many things she loved about him. He knew when to talk, and he knew when to be quiet.

Spent and exhausted, she finally sat up. She reached into her pocket, pulled out a tissue, and blew her nose. "You need to change your shirt."

Pete glanced down and rubbed at the wet patch her tears had created. "It'll soon dry."

"At least dab it with some water. The salt will make the fabric go stiff."

"Are we really sitting here talking about my bloody shirt? What do you need me to do?"

She took a breath and met his gaze. "Can I have my job back?"

"No."

Tally blanched, a sudden coldness striking her core at his harsh and instantaneous refusal of her request. "Why not? It's what I need."

"No, it isn't. What you need is space. Time to get your head around what's happened. Coming back to work, with the resultant stress, is the last thing you need."

Tally repetitively rubbed her forehead. "I'm not earning enough freelancing yet. I need a steady income. I can't afford to take a break or wallow in self-pity. I know I've messed you about, but please, Pete. I'm begging you."

Pete chewed his lip and didn't answer. She needed him to agree. If he didn't take her back, she didn't know what she'd do for money. She couldn't expect Em to subsidise her living expenses. Em barely earned enough to keep herself afloat.

"You have money," Pete finally said.

Tally frowned in confusion, and then her eyes widened. "I will *not* be using Cash's credit card, if that's what you mean. I'm cutting it up as soon as I get home."

"No, that's not it. You have your own money." When Tally stared in utter bewilderment, Pete continued. "Your dad had an insurance policy that paid out when he died. The money went into a trust. I'm the trustee."

Almost robotically, Tally raised a hand to her head. "Why am I only hearing about this now?"

Pete shrugged apologetically. "Your dad insisted I was to let you have the money only when a real need arose. That time is now."

It took a second or two for the information to sink in. When it did, her relief was tinged with annoyance at the collusion. "I can't believe this."

Pete patted her hand. "I did what I thought was best. I was planning to give you the money on your wedding day, but now..."

"How much money?"

Pete rocked his head from side to side. "About one hundred and fifty thousand."

Tally's mouth dropped open. "A hundred and fifty thousand *pounds*?"

He cracked a small smile. "Yes."

"Holy shit." Tally rose from her seat and paced across the room. This was unbelievable. *Unbelievable.* Her dad had died right before the credit crunch hit, and by the time she'd recovered enough from the shock to agree to sell the house, the proceeds had barely covered the mortgage. And now this bombshell. That amount of money would bring her freedom, choice. It would give her space to sort out her screwed-up life, not to mention her screwed-up head.

"I-I don't know what to say."

"You don't have to say anything."

"Oh, Uncle Pete, thank you." She flung herself at him, and as his arms came around her once more, a wave of unconditional love brought tears to her eyes.

"I still think you should call Cash," Pete said when they finally broke apart.

"He hasn't called me." Tally winced as the hollow ache in her chest made a comeback.

"Do you really want to play that game?"

She got to her feet. "It's over. Let it lie."

"Why don't I call him? Have a chat. Man to man."

"No." Her hands formed into fists. "I'm not a child. Leave it, please."

Pete made a frustrated noise. "All relationships go through bad times, Tally, although you and Cash have had more than your fair share. You need to remember, the ones that survive are where both sides fight, and fight hard."

She exhaled on a sigh. "I would fight if Cash would let me, but he's given up—on himself and on us. What else can I do?" A pang in her heart made it difficult to breathe, and she rested a hand against the fireplace to steady herself.

Pete's face softened. "Look, go back to Em's and have a think about what you want to do, but my advice, for what it's worth, is to take your time. There's no need to do anything rash."

Tally chewed over Pete's revelation as she rode the tube back to the flat. As she walked up to Em's building and let herself in, a wave of nostalgia brought a smile to her lips. Although Dad was no longer alive, he'd still managed to save her.

2

Cash listlessly reached for his phone when the damned thing pinged again with an incoming message. Seven missed calls, twenty unanswered texts, multiple WhatsApp notifications.

None of them from Natalia.

He tossed his phone beside him. He'd made his feelings perfectly clear, and she'd listened—thank fuck. If she'd stayed, it would only be a matter of time before he hurt her, and he couldn't allow that to happen. Doing the right thing didn't ease his pain, though.

His phone rang, and regardless of the internal conversation he'd just had, hope spiked within him. He glanced at the screen —and came crashing back to earth. Mum calling again. He needed to answer it, put her mind at rest, but he couldn't face the questions she would undoubtedly ask about Natalia. He'd have to explain how he'd thrown her out in the middle of the night with nowhere to go.

He squeezed his eyes shut. God, he was a fucker. He'd told her that on their first date, but she hadn't listened. She wanted him anyway, and for a time, he truly believed they could be happy, that he could have a normal life like everyone else.

How wrong he'd been. He could blame the accident, but it was a catalyst really, a way for the universe to readjust to how things were meant to be.

He scraped a hand through his hair. He missed her. It had only been three days since she'd left, and he missed her more than he ever thought possible.

Cash wandered aimlessly around the house, catching sight of himself in the hallway mirror. He looked like shit—hair unkempt, beard in desperate need of a trim. He had dark circles under his eyes, an outward sign of an internal battle.

The buzzer sounded, telling him someone was at the front gates. Well, they could fuck off. He didn't want to see anyone.

"Cash, it's Mum. Is everything okay?"

Not even her.

"I don't care how long I have to stand here before you let me in, but you should know it's raining. Do you want me to catch cold?"

He grimaced as guilt pinched at his insides. *Of course not. What does she take me for?*

"Tally, open the gates, darling, or so help me, I'm climbing over."

Fuck.

He pressed the buzzer, estimating it would take his mother about two minutes to walk up the drive. He had two minutes to get his shit together and try to find a way to explain why Natalia wasn't there.

He didn't get two minutes. Sixty seconds later, Mum knocked at the door.

"You should have called." Cash opened it, ignoring her shocked face as she got a good look at him.

"I did. Several times." Rachael closed the door behind her and followed him into the living room. Her eyes fell on the broken vase he still hadn't dredged up the energy to tidy since he'd smashed it three days earlier. He hadn't aimed for Natalia. Had he?

"What's going on? Where's Tally? And why aren't you answering your phone?"

"That's a lot of questions," he muttered, dragging a trembling hand through his hair.

"So take them one at a time."

"Fine," he snapped. "I'm losing my fucking mind. Natalia isn't here because I threw her out, and I'm not answering my phone because I don't fucking want to talk to anyone."

He sank onto the sofa and glanced at the floor because he couldn't stand to look at the stunned expression on his mother's face. Silence lay thick between them. It was his responsibility to speak first, but the words of apology stuck in his throat.

The sofa dipped as his mother sat beside him. Her fingers wrapped around his, and she squeezed. "Do you want to tell me what happened?"

"No."

"Is she okay?" she asked gently.

He flashed her a black look. "You mean have I turned into my father?"

"That isn't what I meant," she said in an indignant tone. "Don't put words in my mouth, Cash."

"Sorry," he mumbled. "She's fine. But she won't be if she stays with me."

"What does that mean?"

He faced her, hot tears burning his eyes because he refused to let them fall. "I don't know what's happening to me. I get angry over nothing, and I have no control over it. I can't turn into him, Mum."

"Oh, Cash." She put her arms around him. For a few seconds, he remained stiff, but as she hugged tighter he gave in, sinking against her. She stroked his hair and whispered comforting words in his ear.

"I had to make her go, because if I didn't, I couldn't be sure I wouldn't hurt her."

She gently cupped his face, giving him no choice but to look at her. "You need help, sweetheart."

He jerked his head back and folded his arms across his chest. "I'm not seeing a shrink."

A resigned sigh spilled from her lips. "Then there must be someone you can talk to. Someone who understands what you're going through."

He pinched his nose between his thumb and forefinger as he contemplated his mother's idea. There was someone, but Cash hadn't seen him in a long while. Far too long.

The time had come to build bridges.

CASH MANAGED to find a space in a cramped Dublin side street. He locked the car and yanked up the hood on his coat. The wind whipped, chapping his face. He bent his head against the driving rain and tucked his hands into his jeans. It only took him about ten minutes to get to the house, but he still cursed the fact he'd been unable to find a space right outside. By the time he knocked on the door, his hands were frozen, he was drenched, and he could barely feel his feet.

As the door opened, Cash ducked his head.

"Hi, Louisa," he said, his tone full of sorrow and regret.

Louisa gave him a warm smile and stood back so he could get out of the rain and cold. "Come on inside. It's lovely to see you."

"I'm sorry," he said. "I haven't exactly been the best friend."

Louisa made a tutting sound. "Now now, none of that. You'll find no judgement here." She helped Cash out of his wet coat.

"Hey, you made it."

Cash glanced around as Rowan Murphy appeared on the far side of the hallway, his wheelchair squeaking on the tile as he trundled over. He thrust out his hand. Cash made an attempt to shake it, but his grip was limp and lifeless.

"Fucking thing," he said with a grimace. "I'm sorry I haven't been around as much as I should have, Rowan."

Rowan rolled his eyes. "Don't start with the guilt tripping. Fucking freezing, isn't it? Let's get you warmed up." He tilted his head back and smiled at his wife. "Thank you, angel."

Louisa gave him a fond look and swept her hand down his arm. "I'll leave you boys to it."

Rowan spun his chair around and headed back down the hallway. Cash followed. The doorway at the end opened up into a large living room where a fire burned in the grate.

"Have a seat," Rowan said, waving his arm at the sofa.

Cash sat and leaned forward, warming his hands in front of the flames. "Not even winter yet."

"Gotta love living in Ireland," Rowan said with a grin.

Cash sighed. "I really am sorry, mate. I should have made the time to come and see you after your accident."

Rowan waved a hand in the air. "Forget it. If anyone knows how much being a professional sportsman takes over your life, it's me. Come on, Cash, talk to me. I'm here to help."

"How much do you know about what's happened?"

Rowan wrinkled his nose. "How about you tell me in your own words."

Cash swept a hand over the back of his head. "I'm not coping very well. I thought it would be a good idea if I talked to you about how you managed, the difficulties you had—how you came out the other side with your sanity intact."

Rowan paused while his housekeeper brought coffee. Once she'd retreated, he turned to Cash and chuckled. "Not sure Louisa would agree with the sanity bit. But honestly, what other choice did I have? Couldn't exactly let myself fall apart. I had a wife and two kids who relied on me."

"I've split up with Natalia," Cash blurted. Saying the words aloud bored a fucking great hole in his stomach.

"Shit. I'm sorry. That's rough. When?"

"A week ago. I was watching the Shanghai masters, and I could feel the anger building inside me as I watched the match. It should have been me out there competing, and yet I have this useless thing." He waved his right hand in the air. "Can barely grip a cup, let alone a tennis racket. Natalia tried to comfort me." He shrugged. "I should have told her to leave me alone. I wasn't in the right headspace to be comforted, but instead, I let the anger spew out, and she caught the brunt of it. I threw a vase at her."

Rowan sucked in a breath. "Shit."

Cash grimaced. "Fortunately, it missed. I've been trying to convince myself it was because I didn't aim at her, but the only reason I missed was because I had to throw with my left hand."

He hung his head as guilt threatened to drown him, although after living with remorse for so long, he should have been used to it. He didn't notice Rowan had moved closer until a warm hand landed on his arm.

"What you're feeling is completely normal. The anger, the frustration, the pushing against everyone you love. Go ahead— beat yourself up. Wallow in self-pity. You're allowed to do all those things, Cash. Rail against the unfairness of it all. Why you, right? Then when you've done all that, ask yourself one question: why not you? What makes you so special that you're protected from the shit life throws around? The answer is, you're not, and once you realise that, once you figure out you're just as human as the rest of the population, *then* you'll be ready to face the long road to recovery."

Cash stared at Rowan. He had said those words to himself hundreds of times since he woke from the coma. *Why me?* But

Rowan was right. Why not him? Who the fuck was he to avoid fate, chance, a random accident that changed the course of his life forever?

"How did you manage?" he eventually said.

Rowan briefly smiled. "Badly. At least in the beginning. Louisa went through hell the first few weeks. Remember, I was exactly like you—a successful sportsman at the top of my game. After winning individual and team gold at the Olympics, I thought I was fucking invincible. Then my life falls apart on a stupid hack with a horse that, until then, had been bombproof."

"But aren't you angry you're confined to a wheelchair and can't ride anymore?"

"Confined?" Rowan scratched his cheek. "If it wasn't for my wheelchair, I'd be bedridden, unable to get around by my own steam. And I still ride. I need help to do it, but I get up there, strap my legs onto the saddle, and away I go. I ignore the things I can't do and focus on the things I can. You should try it."

"But what if I never play tennis professionally again?"

Rowan gave a wry smile. "Can I give you some advice?" When Cash nodded, he continued. "Don't let others limit what you're capable of or tell you something's impossible. You're stronger than that. And competitive. Use those traits to your advantage."

"I don't feel strong. Not anymore." Cash swept a hand over his face. "It's the anger that scares me. I have no control over it."

Rowan wheeled himself over to a desk in the corner of the room. He returned with a business card and handed it to Cash. "Call this guy. Dr Bauer. He's got a facility in Hamburg that specialises in anger management. I spent some time with him after my accident when the voices in my head became too destructive."

Cash stared at the card. "You think there's hope?"

"I know there is."

A shrink. Jesus. "Thanks. I'll think about it." Talking to strangers about personal shit—was he even capable of that?

"Don't think too long," Rowan said as Cash stood to leave. "The mind doesn't heal like the body."

Louisa walked Cash to the door. "Come back anytime," she said as he stepped outside. "You're always welcome here."

He bent down and kissed her cheek. "Thanks, Louisa."

Sleet and rain froze his skin on contact as he ran back to the car. Once inside, he shrugged out of his wet coat and stared at the business card for several minutes. Rowan had made a good point. If Cash left things as they were, he had zero chance of getting his life back.

He reached for his phone and made the call.

Tally opened the online banking application for what felt like the tenth time. Her balance read £152,473.56. As promised, Pete had transferred the money. It was hers to do with as she pleased. With the money in her account, she could move forward and plan for her future.

Her mind was all over the place. The money had brought choices, which in turn had brought confusion. Should she stay in London and work on building her network and her freelance reporting business? Or should she get away as Pete had suggested?

As boredom set in, she browsed through Facebook. Her news-feed was full of happy, happy, and more happy. Tally closed it down and opened her emails instead. She deleted most of them and was about to cast her phone aside when one email caught her eye. Or rather, the sender did. Joe Martinez— a snake and a curse against *real* journalists. What the hell was he doing contacting her? She thought about deleting without reading, but the subject—"You're going to want to see this"—made her curious.

She sighed in defeat and clicked on the email. It contained an attachment and one line of text:

I see Gallagher is up to his old tricks again.

Her pulse jolted, and she clicked on the attachment. A picture appeared, clearly taken with a long lens but detailed enough to show Cash pressing his lips to a woman's cheek. Several other pictures followed, showing him with his head bowed against the weather, coat collar up, sprinting down the street.

Sorrow surged through her. A little over a week had passed since she'd last seen him, and he was already moving on. The photo of him with the woman was Martinez stirring things up. She'd made that mistake once before and wasn't about to fall for it for a second time. The kiss was chaste. There was nothing even remotely sexual in it. But the story the pictures told were not of a man sitting at home, pining for what might have been. No, he was out and about, visiting friends, living his life.

Unlike her.

Anguish clawed at her stomach. She had to face facts. Cash wasn't going to come knocking, begging her to take him back, pleading for forgiveness. She needed to follow his lead and make a new start. She'd wasted enough time.

"ARE you sure you've got everything?" Em was dashing about, opening drawers and cupboards, creating chaos in her wake.

Tally rolled her eyes. "Anything I've forgotten I can buy. I'm hardly travelling to the back of beyond. We're going to be late if you don't get a move on."

Em cursed as Pete honked the horn for the fourth time. "Jeez, chill out."

"He has a job to get to, and I have a flight to catch. Now, will you hurry up?"

"Okay, okay. Right. Keys, phone, bag. Ready."

Em slammed the door, and the two of them made a dash for Pete's car.

"Sorry, Dozer," she said with a cheeky smile that belied her apology as she clambered inside.

"You'll be late for your own funeral," he grumbled as he pulled out from the kerb.

"Had to make sure my girl's got everything. She's not going to the corner shop, you know."

"Nor the moon," Pete said.

As Pete pulled into the drop-off area at Heathrow airport, Tally glanced at her watch. A little less than two hours until take-off. She had plenty of time.

Pete lifted her suitcase from the boot and pulled out the extending handle. "Come here," he said, wrapping his arms around her. "Call me when you land."

"I will. Thanks for everything."

Tally turned to Em, who had started to cry.

"I don't want you to go," she said, wiping her nose on her sleeve.

"I've got to, Em."

"Doesn't mean I have to like it."

"It's only for a few months. Once I get settled, you can come out for a holiday."

"Try and stop me." Her hug, when it came, was brief. "Take care, you."

Tally watched the car disappear around the corner, trying to ignore a nagging sense of being totally alone in the world. She dragged her suitcase into Departures and checked in. Once she was through security, she grabbed a latte at the nearest coffee shop and finally allowed her mind to wander. Everything had moved so fast since she'd decided to get away, which was just as well. With more time to think about how crazy this was, she might have changed her mind. She'd always been risk-averse, and heading to a foreign country for a few months when she couldn't speak one word of the language was probably the riskiest thing she'd ever done.

As she walked down the gangway to board her flight, fear clutched at her stomach. She was scared out of her mind. She almost turned back but then remembered something her father had said when he was teaching her to swim. He'd been in the water, trying to get her to jump in. She must have been about six. She could still vividly recall how terrified she'd been as she shivered on the side of the pool.

"I'm scared, Daddy. I'm so scared."

"Be scared, my darling girl," he'd replied. "Be scared, and then do it anyway."

Tally got on the plane.

A few hours later, she arrived in Athens. As she stepped outside the terminal building, the weak sun warmed her skin. It was a lot warmer than London at this time of year, though it wasn't hot. She stood in line for a taxi and managed to make the driver understand where she needed to go. One night at a hotel was all she'd booked. By the next day, she needed to decide on her final destination. She had a half-baked idea to write an article about the refugee crisis. After talking to the barman at her hotel, who was extremely knowledgeable about the plight of the migrants, she decided to focus on Safome, a small island that had received its fair share of refugees seeking a new, safer life in Europe. Recession had hit the locals hard, yet rather than turn them away, the residents of the little island had welcomed the newcomers with open arms.

She popped down to the business centre and booked a flight to Rhodes for the following morning. From there, she'd be able to get a ferry to Safome.

Her new life was about to begin.

4

Cash jogged down the airplane steps to his waiting car. He handed his bag to the driver, got the formalities out of the way, and climbed into the back seat. Five minutes later, they were speeding down the autobahn towards Dr Bauer's offices for Cash's interview to see if he'd be a suitable candidate for the treatment programme.

Interview. He'd laughed when the receptionist had told him that, until he realised she wasn't joking.

After making the decision to follow Rowan's advice and seek proper treatment from an expert, he'd almost caved and called Natalia. He was desperate for her to know he hadn't given up on their relationship, but as his finger had hovered over her number, he hadn't been able to send the call. He was amazed Pete or Emmalee hadn't rung to give him a mouthful. He'd certainly expected it in the days after he kicked Natalia out. But as time passed without hearing from them, he'd stopped jumping every time the phone rang.

He touched her engagement ring, which hung on a chain around his neck. It was his one connection to her, a constant reminder that he'd better work his fucking nuts off to try to recover. If he succeeded, maybe one day he'd be able to slip it back onto her finger.

Dr Bauer's office was on the outskirts of Hamburg, a modern-looking facility, all glass and wood and chrome. It looked expensive and exclusive, which was not surprising, considering he was being charged a wedge for a one-hour consultation. And if the doctor deemed Cash suitable for his programme, that fee was a mere drop in a very big fucking ocean.

Cash slipped his phone into his jacket pocket and left his overnight bag in the car. His legs were heavy as he trudged up the path to the front of the building. Anyone would think he was heading for the gallows rather than meeting a man he hoped would help him get his life back.

The doors opened automatically, and Cash stepped inside. The reception area was empty—as per his instructions—apart from the receptionist who sat behind a large oak desk, her fingers flying over her keyboard.

"Mr Gallagher, welcome." She stood and waved at a row of chairs lined up against the wall. "Take a seat. Dr Bauer will be with you shortly. Can I get you something to drink?"

"No, thanks."

He sifted through the obligatory magazines, but none piqued his interest. He tidied them back into a pile and tapped his foot impatiently. He didn't have to wait long for Bauer to arrive. He looked German, if there was such a thing—sandy hair, thinning on top, compensated by a very bushy beard. He wore horn-rimmed glasses and a tweed jacket with leather patches on the elbows. Cash almost laughed. The man was a walking cliché.

"Mr Gallagher," he said in heavily accented English. "I'm Dr Bauer." He shook Cash's hand, his grip firm yet warm. "Please come through."

Cash followed him down a thickly carpeted hallway, which resembled a decent Hilton as opposed to a mental health facility. Bauer's office was at the very end and looked out onto well-trimmed gardens with regimented borders filled with multi-coloured plants. Cash inwardly groaned. He was definitely losing the plot if he'd begun to notice flowers.

"Sit, please." Bauer waved to a comfy-looking chair that was a far cry from a psychiatrist's couch. *Perhaps not the full cliché package, then.* Cash sat down, his legs jiggling of their own accord.

"You seem nervous."

Cash grimaced. "Been a long time since I had an interview that mattered, Doc."

Bauer chuckled. "Try not to think of it like that. It's more of a getting-to-know-each-other session."

"So how does this work exactly? I spill my guts, and you decide whether I'm a candidate for your programme?"

Bauer leaned back in his chair, fingers steepled under his chin. "Do you want to spill your guts?"

"Not particularly. But we're not going to get very far if I don't, are we?"

"Aren't we?"

An uncomfortable feeling stirred in Cash's chest. Was this guy taking the piss?

"Are you feeling angry now?"

Cash glared across the desk. "You some kind of mind reader?"

"A reader of body language perhaps."

Cash glanced down at his fisted hands and unclenched them. "Sorry," he mumbled. "This isn't exactly comfortable for me."

"I'm sure it isn't." Bauer picked up a pad and pencil. He crossed his legs, resting the pad on one knee. Pencil poised, he fixed his gaze on Cash. "How long has it been since your accident?"

Cash counted backwards. "A little over three months."

"And you were in the coma for how long?"

"Fifteen days."

Bauer scrawled on the pad, the pencil making a scraping noise that began to get on Cash's nerves.

"And apart from the rage, any other symptoms? Headaches, eyesight problems, loss of memory? Impotence?"

Cash's lips twitched, despite the churn in his gut. "I have no memory of the moments right before the accident until I woke up two weeks later, but apart from the crush injury to my hand, everything else works just fine, Doc."

Bauer almost smiled, but Cash got the feeling the man didn't possess an active sense of humour.

"Have you noticed any patterns in what causes the rage? Places, people, events?"

Cash hesitated. "Only one. Every time I think about not being able to play tennis again." Flames of anger licked at his insides, and he breathed in slowly through his nose.

"Has that been medically confirmed?"

He met Bauer's steady gaze. "Your lot never say never, right?"

"My lot?"

"Doctors. They've used words like *challenging* and *difficult*, but no one has said I'm definitely screwed, even though I am."

Bauer tilted his head to the right. "And why would you think that?"

Cash leaned forward and picked up a glass of water. It instantly slipped through his fingers and smashed on the floor. "Lost my best wanking hand, Doc."

Bauer gave the first genuine smile Cash had seen, but it disappeared as quickly as it had arrived. "Are you still having physio?"

"On and off."

"I suggest more on and less off. I can recommend someone if you'd like. Local to here."

"And what use would that be to me?"

Bauer dropped the pad onto his desk and held out his hand once more. "Welcome to the programme, Mr Gallagher."

Half an hour later, Cash opened the door to his hotel room and dropped his bag on the floor. He flopped onto the bed. He'd made it onto the course for nutjobs. He wasn't totally sure how he felt about being accepted into Bauer's programme, but at least he was doing *something*. Bauer seemed confident Cash had a good chance, maybe not of a cure but of finding coping mechanisms to help manage the mental changes brought about by his accident. And if he learned to control his anger, then he had a chance of winning Natalia back.

Right then, he made a promise to himself. Whenever this road got tough—and it would—he'd keep her at the forefront of his mind. He was doing this for himself, for her, and for their future together.

Looks like I'm moving to Germany.

5

The ferry moored in Safome's harbour, and Tally gathered her things as she waited for the captain to tether the ship to the quayside. The hotel staff in Athens had been brilliant, helping her book a hotel on the island for the next seven nights, which would give her time to find a more permanent place to stay. Her dad's legacy wouldn't last long if she spent it on hotels. She needed to find an apartment to rent as soon as possible.

She already loved this place and hadn't even seen much of it yet. Blue water lapped over golden sand, and the hillside was dotted with white buildings. For the first time in months, a calm settled over her. This was the place to heal her ravaged heart and broken life. She'd never get over losing Cash, but he'd made his feelings perfectly clear, and she had enough self-respect not to beg.

After a short walk from the harbour, she arrived at her hotel. Check-in was easy, and minutes later, she walked into her room, a lovely traditional space with whitewashed walls and light furniture. It even had a small balcony with a couple of plastic chairs and tables and a lovely view of the sea.

She dug out her phone and put in a quick call to Pete. He worried too much, and she didn't want to be the cause of more concern. Once she'd put his mind at rest, she settled on the balcony and rang Em. At first, she thought her friend wasn't going to pick up, but right before the call went to voicemail, Em's breathless voice sounded on the other end.

"Don't hang up!"

"I'm here," Tally said. "Where were you?"

"In the bloody shower. I'm standing in the middle of the living room, starkers and dripping wet."

"Lovely. Go and get dressed. I'll hang on."

Em was back two minutes later, her girly giggle making Tally terribly homesick. "Think the guy across the street got more than an eyeful. The blinds are open."

"He'll probably be your next boyfriend."

"Ew, no. He's about fifty, fat, and bald. I might be desperate, but I'm not quite that desperate yet."

Tally laughed. "Good to know."

"Where've you landed anyway?"

"Safome."

"Where's that?"

"Not too far from Rhodes. A short ferry ride away from an airport. It's quiet and quaint. Exactly what I need."

"At least you've arrived safely. What's the plan?"

"I don't know yet," Tally said, unwilling to discuss her idea about the article until she had it firmed up in her mind. "The hotel I stayed at in Athens got me sorted with a hotel here for the next week. I guess I'll decide over that time whether I'm staying, which I probably will, and then I'll get an apartment."

"As long as it has a sofa bed or somewhere for me to kip."

"Of course it will." Melancholy swept over her, and she forced brightness into her voice. "Miss you already."

"Miss you too, babes."

"I'll call you in a couple of days."

"You'd better."

As Tally ended the call, she gave herself a virtual slap. This was an exciting opportunity, one afforded to her by Dad, and she wouldn't waste it feeling sorry for herself.

When her stomach rumbled, she decided to go for a walk, get her bearings, and grab something to eat. She headed down to the harbour. Along the seafront were a couple of tavernas. Tally seated herself at one of them and waved to catch the waiter's attention. All the concerns she'd had about not being able to speak the language were unfounded. Everyone spoke excellent English, especially compared to Tally and her nonexistent Greek, and they were thrilled to have someone to practice on, insisting she correct them whenever they mispronounced anything or couldn't find the right word.

When the waiter brought her food, she asked him if he had time to sit with her for a while. As it was off-season and the restaurant was virtually empty, he agreed. They chatted as she ate, and after she'd finished, she decided to raise the subject she was most interested in.

"Tell me about the refugees," she said, sipping her Coke.

Sadness crossed his face. "It is so terrible. Such a tragedy."

"Are there many here?"

"Yes. About two thousand. It is all the camp can take. The refugees, they wait here until papers come through, and then they travel to the mainland."

"Two thousand?" Tally raised her eyebrows. "That's a lot for a small island."

"It is." He gave her a pained look. "The government cannot cope. That is when a group of us decided we had to help. We do what we can, although we don't have much."

The more he shared, the more excited Tally became. This would make a great story, not only from the point of view of the refugees. She'd be able to offer a slant on how those with so little were willing to give what they could to those who had even less.

Maybe if she shone a light on what was happening there, more help would come.

She thanked him for his company and went for a wander around. Behind the harbour, the streets were narrow with one-of-a-kind shops, a couple of cafés, and an ice cream parlour serving many varieties she'd never even heard of. She peered in the windows of a few of the shops and went inside one or two. Only when her shadow became longer did she notice the sun was beginning to dip behind the buildings.

She set off for the hotel but must have taken a wrong turn because nothing looked familiar. As darkness descended, she dug her phone out of her bag and switched on the torch app. Along the street, a warm glow shone from a shop window. *Thank goodness. It must still be open.* Surely whoever was inside would be able to give her directions back to her hotel?

Her sanctuary turned out to be a small café. She opened the door, the bell above dinging to alert the staff to her presence. The place was empty, and after a minute or so when no one appeared, she called out. Still no one came. Behind the counter was a doorway to what she presumed was the kitchen. Feeling a little cheeky but needing directions back to the hotel, she ducked behind the counter and pushed open the door.

The kitchen had clearly been cleaned down for the day, ready for the next day's trade. Tally began to wonder whether the owner had left without locking up.

"Hello," she called out. "Is anyone here?"

Greeted with nothing but silence, she ventured farther inside. At the far end was another door. That one was ajar, allowing a light breeze to waft through Tally's hair. Tentatively, she pushed it open. It led onto a small courtyard. Sitting at a table, silently sobbing, was a girl who couldn't have been more than twenty.

"Are you okay?" Tally asked.

The girl's head snapped up. "Who are you? How did you get in?"

She spoke English with barely an accent, although her appearance was Greek.

Tally pointed behind her. "The front door is unlocked, and the lights are on. I'm lost, and you seem to be the only place open."

"Shit." The girl brushed past Tally and walked into the shop. She grabbed a set of keys from behind the small counter and waved her hand at the open door. "Thank you for telling me."

"Wait. I'm looking for directions back to the harbour. I'm staying at a hotel close to there."

The girl sighed. "Turn left at the end of the street. Walk about fifty yards, then turn right. Follow that road all the way, and it will take you to where you need to go."

"Thanks." Tally began to leave, and then she stopped. "You were crying."

She huffed. "So?"

"Can I help?"

"I don't know." The girl rested her hands low on her hips and gave Tally an exasperated look. "Do you have twenty thousand euro?"

Tally smiled. "I do, actually."

Surprise flitted across the girl's face before she painted her aloof mask back on. "I'd be careful who you tell that to. People round here are poor. It's been tough since the recession."

"What's your name?" Tally said.

The girl paused. "Nerissa," she eventually replied.

"I'm Tally. Today is my first day on the island."

"Good for you. Now, can you go? I need to lock up."

Something about this girl called to Tally. Maybe it was Nerissa's obvious despair, which she hid behind a stiff, proud posture, or maybe Tally was more attuned to heartache since her own experiences.

"I'd like to help, if I can."

Nerissa let out an exasperated sigh. She marched across to the door and locked it. "Sit down," she said, directing Tally to a table. "I'll make a drink."

Tally took a seat by the window at a table covered in a blue checked cloth. Nerissa came across with two hot chocolates. She sank into the seat opposite Tally and rubbed her eyes.

"You speak really good English. I mean, everyone I've met so far does, but I can barely detect your accent."

Nerissa reached for a packet of sugar and tipped the granules into her drink. "My grandmother is English. She moved to Greece after meeting my grandfather. She schooled me from a very young age."

"She did a good job," Tally said, feeling the need to set the girl at ease.

Nerissa shrugged.

"Why do you need twenty thousand euro?" Tally said.

Nerissa smoothed her skirt, a threadbare, tatty affair. "I don't even know you."

"Sometimes, it's easier to talk to a stranger."

Nerissa laughed, but the sound was hollow. "This place," she said, waving her hand around. "I run a soup kitchen with my grandmother for the refugees. We were doing okay, but then she was taken ill, and she can't help out anymore. And now, more come. I can't keep up with it." She angrily dashed away her tears, almost as though she was embarrassed to show any weakness. "I need more space, a bigger kitchen. More help. But it's hopeless."

"Don't say that." Tally squeezed Nerissa's hand and half expected the girl to shake her off, but she seemed too exhausted to bother.

As they sat in silence, an idea began to form in Tally's mind. It was insane. Totally and utterly insane. But after what she'd been through, a bit of crazy would do her good.

"Look, I'm going to be sticking around here for a few months. Why don't I pay for the extension? I'll help out here, too, if you like."

Nerissa's mouth dropped open, and she blinked several times, a look of astonishment mingled with hope on her face. "Why would you do that?"

Tally shrugged. "Let's just say I've had my priorities reorganised recently. Made me want to take a few more chances."

And helping those much worse off than me might put my own problems into perspective.

Nerissa paused, and then she thrust her hand out. "You're mad, but I'm desperate. Okay, you've got yourself a deal."

6

"I'll be over next weekend," Rachael said as Cash zipped up his suitcase.

Cash ignored her. He was having trouble holding his emotions in check, and the last thing he needed was to lose it in front of his mother.

He glanced around his bedroom, the one he'd shared with Natalia. So many memories. So much love. He bit his lip. He had to find the person he'd been before the accident. *Would* find the person he'd been. Dr Bauer had explained how it all worked. Brain injuries like his changed things forever, but the doctor had given him hope. He'd told him about cases where miracles had happened.

Cash was going to be one of those fucking miracles.

He startled when his mother laid a hand on his arm. "You're doing the right thing."

He scrubbed a tired hand over his face. "Yeah."

"You are, Cash. I know you're scared, but—"

"For Christ's sake, stop fussing."

"Sorry," she mumbled.

He raked a hand through his hair, taking deep breaths as the doctor had told him to whenever he felt the horrible churning in his stomach—the one he was feeling at the moment. "No. I'm sorry. I shouldn't have snapped."

"It's okay," Rachael said with a tentative smile.

He wanted to scream, *No, it fucking isn't*, but he said nothing as he heaved his suitcase off the bed and started down the stairs.

Isaac was already waiting outside with the car. He rushed forward and tugged the bag from Cash's clenched fingers. The rear door of the car was open, and Cash slipped inside, followed by his mother. He'd prefer she didn't come to see him off, but he'd hurt her too much already, so he bit his tongue and let her have her way.

The trip to the airport only took twenty minutes, but the atmosphere in the car was thick and heavy, making the journey seem twice as long. Rachael made two attempts to speak, both of which Cash shot down with a glare. She spent the rest of the time fiddling with the strap on her handbag and staring out of the window.

He was a shit. A useless good-for-nothing shit of a son, lover, friend. Good job he was taking off for the next few months. They all needed a break from him. It was a shame he couldn't get a break from himself.

The car pulled to a stop, and Cash quickly climbed out. And then he groaned. "What the fuck are you doing here?"

Rupe gave him a goofy grin, the one that used to make him laugh. Now it got on his nerves. "To see you off."

"I told you not to bother."

"And I ignored you."

Cash stepped up close, getting right in Rupe's face. "Well, take a good look. Because you won't be seeing my ugly fucking mug for a while."

Rupe's brow creased as his eyebrows shot in the air. "Is that right?"

"Yep. I don't want you coming to see me in the loony bin. Or you," he said, glancing over his shoulder at his mother.

"Cash..." she began.

Rupe held up his hand, stopping her. "Two things." He stood up straight to give himself a little more height but was still an inch or so short of being able to stare Cash squarely in the eye. "One, it's not a fucking loony bin, and if I hear you describe it like that once more, so help me, I'm going to kick you in the balls." His cheeks coloured with frustration and annoyance. He reached behind Cash, clasped Rachael's hand, and gently pulled her forward. "And two, I am your best friend, and *this* is your mother. We *will* be coming to see you whether you fucking like it or not."

A sharp retort was on the tip of Cash's tongue until he caught sight of his mother's face. Her watery gaze signalled she was close to tears, and she kept pulling on the strap of that damned handbag. Cash turned his back and, for the second time that day, took a few deep breaths. He *hated* being like this.

"Fine," he said, facing them once more. "But don't expect me to be dancing on the fucking tables."

Rupe gave a half laugh, half snort. "Thank Christ for that."

Cash smiled then, his dark mood momentarily lifting. "You're a bastard."

"I know."

Cash wrapped his arms around his mother. "Step one of a million," he whispered.

Her head bobbed against his chest. "Step one," she repeated. "But that means you've started the journey." She moved back, her palms cupping his face. "I love you. You can yell, scream, shout, punch walls. None of it will ever change the fact that you're my son, and I will always love you."

Cash slowly blinked. "I'll call you." He walked towards the metal steps leading into the cabin of the plane. "Look after her," he muttered in Rupe's ear as he passed by.

Rupe nodded and clapped him on the back. Cash took off up the stairs and didn't look back.

7

"Go on—hit it."

Tally glanced over her shoulder at Nerissa, who'd plonked herself on top of an old washing machine. "What if the roof falls in?"

"It won't." Nerissa rapped her knuckles against the peeling plaster. "Solid building, this. Been here for hundreds of years. Go on. It's only an internal wall. Good for getting out your aggression."

Tally grinned. She swung the sledgehammer and slammed it against the wall. A small crack appeared.

"Terrible," Nerissa said. "Go on, Tally. Give it all you've got."

Tally swung again and again until a hole appeared in the wall. She dropped the sledgehammer and peered through. "Wow, there's tons of space back there. It's going to make an amazing room."

Nerissa jumped to the floor and picked up the sledgehammer. "We'll be here all day. Move aside, weak little English girl. Let the tough Greek girl have a go."

Tally laughed. "I can't wait to see this."

Nerissa took hold of the sledgehammer, one hand firmly gripping low on the handle, the other right behind the head. She twisted her body as though preparing to throw a discus. The sledgehammer smashed into the plaster. A large portion of the wall fell away, revealing the room behind.

Tally was about to make a joke about tough Greeks and weak English when a loud creak sounded above her. She glanced up in time to see an enormous crack speeding across the ceiling, almost like an upside-down earthquake, and then a huge chunk of plaster came crashing to the ground.

"Shit." She covered her head with her arms as debris peppered her and Nerissa.

Once the dust cloud settled, their eyes met. The two girls fell about laughing.

"You're a mad bitch," Tally said. "You told me the roof wouldn't fall in."

"The roof is intact. That's the ceiling." Nerissa was still laughing as she shook the dust out of her hair. "Besides, you love being around a mad bitch."

"You're right, I do."

Nerissa turned on the tap above the old, rusty sink. Brown, sludgy water spluttered before eventually running clear. She dampened a cloth. "Here," she said, passing it to Tally.

Tally wiped her face and hands and ruffled her hair, coughing when she breathed in dust particles. She passed the cloth back to Nerissa then walked over to the huge hole in the wall and peered inside.

"Definitely the right decision to knock through, even though I'm wearing half the ceiling."

"And I'm wearing the other half," Nerissa said with a grin. "But you're right. It will be a great space once we've finished with it."

"Better get onto your builder friend and tell him the job is a little bigger than we first thought."

"I'll call later after I've cleaned myself up."

Tally giggled. "Think they'll let me in the hotel looking like this?"

Nerissa nodded. "This is a small island. Anything out of the ordinary will be talked about for weeks. Maybe months in your case."

"Better get it over with then."

"Want to come for dinner tonight?" Nerissa reached for a brush and began sweeping the floor.

Tally swiped her bag off the floor and shook the dust from it before slinging it over her shoulder. "Thanks, but no. All I want is a bath, a quick catch-up with Em, and bed." She was halfway out of the door when she hesitated. "Nerissa?"

Her friend looked up from her vigorous brushing. "Yeah?"

"Thanks for everything. For letting me help with the refugees. For this place. It's a bit of a building site, but once it's done up, it will be a perfect little apartment."

Nerissa shook her head. "It's me who should be thanking you. If you hadn't come along when you did, well, I'm not sure what I would have done. This place has been lying empty for years. Probably because it's a death trap." She grinned, and then her face fell. "Will you tell me how you ended up here? One day?"

Tally crossed the room and pulled her new friend into a warm hug. "I will. See you in the morning, partner."

It took Tally ages to get all the dust and pieces of plaster out of her hair, leaving her hotel room a mess, but finally, she was able to sit on the balcony with a cup of tea and a sandwich. The last three weeks had been a whirlwind of activity. Getting the extension to the café underway. Meeting Nerissa, who was fast becoming a close and wonderful friend. Finding out that she also owned the space above the café, which Tally could move into once they'd renovated it to liveable standards.

She was so busy that most days she managed not to think about Cash. But once she had time alone, her mind inevitably turned to him, and she would allow herself five minutes to cry. Five. Not a second more.

She put her laptop across her knees and opened Google, typing the same words into the search bar that she had every night since she'd arrived on Safome: "Cash Gallagher."

Several pictures of Cash appeared on the right-hand side of the page, underneath which was a short biography, all terribly familiar:

"Cash Gallagher, Tennis player. cashgallagher.com

"Cash Gallagher is a tennis professional from Northern Ireland. Formerly ranked number one, a recent car accident led to him retreating from public view."

Underneath that were his date of birth, height, and number of Grand Slam victories.

Tally scrolled down the page.

"People also search for Miroslav Ilic, Anatoly Mishnev, Rachael Gallagher, Rupert Fox-Whittingham, Natalia McKenzie."

The first time she'd seen her name there three weeks earlier, she'd almost had a heart attack, and the sight of it still caused her to snatch a breath. She'd clicked onto her name to find she had her own Wikipedia page in exactly the same format as Cash's. The amount of information in the public domain had been shocking, although in hindsight, she shouldn't have been surprised.

She ignored her own name this time and clicked onto the news tab. Nothing new. There were still no sightings of Cash. It was as if he had truly disappeared, removed himself from the world. There was lots of speculation, though. He'd died. He'd fallen back into a coma. He'd been abducted by aliens. Anything to fill up the web pages and sell newspapers, and all utter rubbish. Tally had no doubt that if Cash had died, she'd have heard the news directly one way or another.

Her thoughts turned to Em, and she reached for her phone.

They hadn't managed to catch up for a couple of days, and she missed their nightly talks.

"Hey, Shirley Valentine," Em said when she answered the phone. "Thought you'd forgotten me."

"Who on earth is Shirley Valentine?"

"It's a cheesy eighties movie about a bored housewife who runs off to Greece to find herself. It was on some obscure TV channel the other night."

Tally chuckled. "You really need to get out more. And I'm hardly here because I'm a bored housewife."

"How are the renovations going?"

She peeled back the cellophane on her sandwich and took a bite. "Great. The extension to the café should be finished next week, and the apartment is coming along. We knocked down the wall between the living room and the kitchen today, and then the ceiling fell in. Nerissa and I got covered in dust and plaster."

Em laughed. "Only you, Tal. But it's going okay?"

"Yeah, it is." A wave of empathy swept over her. "There's something about helping those worse off than yourself that puts things into perspective."

"Amen to that."

"Do you know when you'll be able to come over?"

"Going to be difficult this side of Christmas, babes," Em said in an apologetic tone. "Party season and all that. It's my busiest time."

"Sure, I understand," Tally said, swallowing a huge chunk of disappointment.

"But if we leave it until the new year, I should be able to come for a week. January is always shit for beauticians. Everyone's skint and covered in unwanted body hair."

Tally laughed. "Sounds good."

"Rupe came round last weekend," Em said

Tally sucked in a quick breath. "He did? How is he?"

"Same old Rupe. Was good to see him, though. I miss the old bugger."

"Me too." She sighed. "You didn't tell him where I was?"

"What do you take me for? No, of course I didn't tell him. He asked, though, several times. Seriously, I think I could stand up to torture after his grilling."

"Did he mention Cash?"

"No. Bet he's as miserable as you, though."

"I'm not miserable."

"Why don't you call him?"

"No."

Em exhaled a breath of frustration. "You two are both as bad as each other. Neither wants to be the one to blink first. And you know where that gets you? Singleton city."

Tally rubbed her eyes. "It's not that simple, Em. You weren't there the night he threw me out, or when we got back from Paris. He would flip out over nothing." She allowed the memories to slip into her mind. "One minute, he'd be unbelievably loving and attentive, the same Cash as always. The next, he'd be furious. Throwing things. Punching walls. Yelling at everyone, including his mother, Anna, Rupe. Me."

"He's hurting, babes. Must be so confusing for the poor sod."

"Since when were you his biggest fan?" Tally said, trying to keep her tone calm. "It doesn't matter anyway. According to the Internet, he's disappeared."

"What do you mean?" Em's voice shifted up a notch.

Tally tossed her half-eaten sandwich in the waste bin and flopped onto the bed. "He hasn't been seen in public for weeks."

"So you're still looking, then?"

Tally sighed. "Can't help myself."

"Give it time. If you do want to know where he is, I can ask Rupe."

"No. Cash would have called me if he wanted me to know."

"You changed your number."

"That wouldn't stop him. Remember how quickly he found me in Brighton? If he wanted to, he could. Like that." She clicked her fingers even though Em couldn't see her.

"Do you want him to?"

Tally frowned. "What makes you ask that?"

"Honestly, babes, I'm confused. This is Cash, your child-hood obsession, adult reality, and the man you were going to marry. Yes, he clearly has anger issues, and you probably did right to leave that night, especially after he threw the vase, but maybe if you talk to him, you could persuade him to get some help."

"I left because he doesn't love me anymore," Tally said, her voice breaking up.

"If you love him, you'll fight for him."

"There's no point. I can't make him love me." She inhaled a shuddering breath. It didn't matter how many times they had this conversation—she couldn't make Em understand. "When the feeling has gone, it's gone."

Em paused. When she spoke, her voice had a slight tremor. "I'm worried how quickly you've put down roots in a place you barely know, hundreds of miles from home."

"I know it sounds crazy, but I needed somewhere to ground me. Somewhere I could come to terms with losing him." As tears threatened, she bit down on her lip. "It wouldn't work in London. Not the way I'm currently feeling. I don't plan on staying here forever, but right now, it's good for me."

"I only want to make sure you're doing the right thing."

"I am," Tally said gently, smiling to herself at Em's sigh of surrender.

"I just want you to be happy, babes."

"Give me time. It's so tranquil here, and the people are lovely. Once you come and see for yourself, you'll understand."

"I'll need the break after a mad London party season," Em said with a laugh.

"Speaking of parties, how's David?" Tally said, jumping onto the change of subject.

"He's fine," Em said in a dreamy tone.

"Oh, come on. How long have you been seeing him now? Two weeks?"

"Three."

"Exactly. A Fallon record."

Em chuckled. "You make me sound like a right tart."

"Nah. Just picky."

"You've got that right."

"But it's going okay?"

Em hesitated. "I'm scared to jinx it, but I really like him, Tal. I can't wait for you to meet him."

"Don't bring him out in January," Tally said, inwardly cursing her selfishness.

"Not a chance. January is girl time. There will be plenty of opportunities for you two to meet."

Tally yawned loudly. "I'm off to bed. Early start in the morning. I'm on breakfasts. I'll call you in a day or so."

"Make sure you do, Shirley," Em said. Tally heard her giggle before the phone went dead.

She changed for bed and climbed under the covers. She reached for her phone, opened the photos app, and scanned through the hundreds of pictures of her and Cash—personal pictures that weren't on social media or the Internet.

A searing pain speared her chest. She retrieved his number from her contacts, her thumb hovering over the eleven digits. What she wouldn't give to hear his voice, the tone of his soft Northern Irish lilt causing a flash of desire to speed through her as he spoke her name.

She pressed the number but hung up before the connection was made. The craving to speak with him was overridden by fear. What if he repeated the horrible things he'd said? The longer she avoided calling him, the more she could keep hope alive that one day he'd realise he'd made a huge mistake and beg her to come back.

"Idiot," she muttered to herself. Switching off the bedside lamp, she turned onto her side. Tomorrow was another day. She'd feel better after a good night's sleep.

Of course she would.

8

"It's definitely improving," Dieter said as he scrawled notes onto a chart. "What do you think?"

Cash flexed the fingers on his right hand. "I agree. More movement, less pain and stiffness."

"You're still doing the daily exercises in between our sessions?"

"Religiously," Cash said. "You're pretty bolshie for a physio. I wouldn't dare skip a routine."

"Good. That'll be why you're seeing so much improvement." Dieter stood and opened the door to his office. "Come on," he said, cocking his head.

Cash narrowed his eyes. "Where are we going?"

Dieter smiled. "You'll see. I want to try something."

Cash tried not to groan. Dieter had some outlandish ideas, and very few of them were fun, but Cash couldn't deny the results he was getting. He'd only been in Germany six weeks, and already, his hand had massively improved. It hadn't completely recovered—nowhere near that—but it was much better.

He'd set two goals: to win back Natalia, and to play competitive tennis once more. He wasn't about to compromise on either, no matter what it cost him.

He followed Dieter towards the back of the facility, immediately guessing where they were going when Dieter turned left at the end of the corridor. Fear grabbed Cash by the throat as his confidence plummeted. "Wait," he called out.

Dieter stopped and glanced over his shoulder. "You're not bailing."

"I'm not ready for this."

"Yes, you are." Dieter set off walking again, but Cash's feet might as well have been nailed to the floor. When Dieter reached the door that led to the gardens, he rested his hand against it and paused. Without turning around, he said, "Move your fucking arse, Cash."

"What if I can't do it?"

"Only one way to find out." Dieter pushed at the door, and weak winter sun seeped inside the artificially lit hallway. Without another glance at Cash, he walked through, letting the door swing closed behind him.

Cash expelled a resigned sigh. He'd known this day was coming. Dieter had hinted a couple of times after Cash's grip began to gain strength, but he'd chosen to ignore his physio's insinuations.

Cash followed him outside. Dieter was already several feet in front, purposefully striding towards the tennis court on the far side of the gardens, behind the gym. The cocky bastard didn't even look behind him to see whether or not Cash was there.

By the time Cash reached the tennis court, Dieter had already set up. Two tennis rackets—shit makes—were propped against the fence, and he was uncorking a tube of tennis balls.

"If I'm playing, I want my own racket."

"Fine," Dieter said. "Go and get it. You've got five minutes, so run."

Despite himself, Cash grinned. Dieter was a hard taskmaster, which was exactly what Cash needed. He reminded Cash of Brad. Christ, he missed Brad and Jamie. They'd been like family, an unbreakable team. Except that team had been broken by a fuckwit of a drunk driver. Even though Cash knew Brad and Jamie had no choice but to leave him, to go and work with other players, it didn't stem the ache and the emptiness in his chest as he thought about how complete and perfect his life had been before the accident.

He was back within the allotted five minutes, albeit out of breath, and he lightly tossed the racket from hand to hand. It felt good to hold it again.

"Now, remember." Dieter took up position at the far side of the court. "I'm not a bad tennis player, but I'd get killed by number two hundred in the world, let alone former number one."

Cash tried not to wince at the word *former*. "I'll go easy on you," he said with a smile he wasn't feeling.

Dieter stood on the baseline, bounced the ball on the ground, and then hit it over the net. The ball landed in the deuce court, and Cash tightened his grip and swung his racket. An intense joy swept through him as they hit the ball back and forth. There was no power behind the shots, but nonetheless, it felt so bloody good.

"Go on," Dieter said after they'd been playing for a few minutes. "I know you're dying to tell me I was right."

"Take a pew, buddy, coz you'll be waiting a while for me to admit that."

Dieter threw his head back and laughed. "More?" he said, holding a yellow tennis ball in the air.

"Yep."

After half an hour playing, Cash's hand began to ache, and Dieter suggested they stop. Cash could barely keep the grin off his face. It was the first time he'd even held a tennis racket, let alone hit a ball, since he lost in the Wimbledon final back in July. Almost six months.

"Don't forget to do your exercises tonight. We need to make sure your fingers don't stiffen up."

Cash clenched and unclenched his right hand. "I will. See you day after tomorrow."

He jogged back to his on-campus apartment. For the first time since he'd arrived in Germany, optimism stirred within him. Perhaps his former life wasn't completely out of reach after all. Dr Bauer seemed happy with his progress in managing his anger, although Cash wasn't, and Dieter was confident that with the correct treatment and commitment, Cash would get back the full use of his right hand. Until that day, he hadn't really believed it, but after the short stint on the tennis court, he was starting to come around.

Alone with nothing but his thoughts, Cash yearned to speak with Natalia. He wanted to share his news, to tell her he was working his bollocks off to find the person he'd been before. Rupe hadn't been able to get anything out of Emmalee when he'd visited the other week, although one thing was certain—Natalia wasn't living with her best friend. There'd been no sign of her, and Emmalee had stubbornly refused to tell Rupe anything about her whereabouts.

With a fear of rejection weighing heavily on his shoulders, he picked up his phone and dialled her number. His heart thundered in his chest as he waited for the call to be connected.

"The number you are trying to reach is no longer in service."

Cash frowned and redialled.

"The number you are trying to reach is no longer in service."

What the fuck did that mean? He opened the Google app and typed the message into the search bar. After reading about three responses on various forums, his heart headed south. She'd changed her number. He couldn't exactly blame her. He'd been far too convincing that night in October, and she'd believed him.

If she wanted nothing more to do with him, why was he bothering with all this? His recovery only had meaning if they had a chance of a future together. Without that hope, he might as well give up. And even if he did carry on, maybe she wouldn't want the damaged Cash. What if she had this perfect image in her mind that she'd harboured all those years, and when he deviated from that...

No. Nope. Not going there. He wasn't giving up.

She'd loved him once. He could make her love him again. He had to treat this recovery process like training for a Grand Slam —all in, one hundred per cent, because he couldn't risk trying to rekindle his relationship with Natalia until he had enough coping mechanisms to curb his anger. He had to be confident he wouldn't hurt her.

Pain tore through his gut as he realised that he hadn't recovered yet, but he clung tightly to the belief the day would come.

Because if it didn't, there was fuck all to live for.

9

Tally rolled over in bed and hit the snooze button. Cracking open one eye, she confirmed that she could afford another five minutes, although the way she was feeling, another five hours still wouldn't cut it. She was absolutely knackered all the time lately. She shouldn't have been surprised, considering she hadn't stopped to rest since meeting Nerissa. Renovating the flat and then moving in had taken its toll.

At least working the soup kitchen and writing the article—which she'd decided to turn into a series of articles—gave her little time to think. That suited her perfectly. Thinking led to regretting—and regretting led to hankering.

The alarm went off for a second time. Tally groaned and forced herself out of bed. She shoved her feet into her slippers and trudged into the bathroom. As she caught sight of herself in the mirror, she grimaced. Dark circles framed her eyes, and she looked closer to thirty-five than twenty-five. She'd need a ton of concealer to avoid the sympathetic looks and kind words of the refugees, who constantly told her how she should be taking better care of herself. Considering their lives had been completely destroyed by war and they faced an uncertain future, their thoughtfulness always brought her to the brink of tears.

Christmas Eve had arrived, and they were closing at three. Based on how hard it was to wake up, she'd be back in bed by three fifteen. At least she didn't have a shift the next day or the day after. Nerissa had roped in some help from a couple of her neighbours to work over the festive period to give them both a break. Normally, Tally would have insisted on working, but she'd actually been relieved when Nerissa had organised the time off. Her plans for Christmas Day and Boxing Day started and ended with catching up on sleep.

Unable to face breakfast, she made a strong cup of coffee, added a good dollop of cream, and sank into a chair at the tiny kitchen table. Feeling lightheaded and nauseous, for a brief moment she thought about telling Nerissa she was too sick to work. But skiving never had been her style, regardless of how unwell she felt.

She swilled out her cup and set off downstairs. It was still dark outside as Tally began prep for the day. She hadn't been there long when Nerissa arrived. She gave Tally a horrified glance and immediately pulled out a chair.

"You look *terrible*. Sit down, please. Why didn't you call me?"

Tally waved her away. "I'm fine. Stop fussing."

"I'm not kidding, Tally. You really don't look well. Have you eaten?"

"Can't face it."

Nerissa placed her hand over Tally's forehead. "You're a little warm but nothing excessive. Shall I call Clio?"

"I don't need a nurse. I need a good night's sleep."

Nerissa frowned. "You're not sleeping?"

"Fits and starts, but I haven't slept through the night for weeks." Tally pressed her fingertips to her temple. "I keep having these weird dreams. They wake me up, and then it takes me ages to drop off again."

Nerissa tilted her head to one side. "What are you dreaming about?"

"All sorts of things. Driving a bus that tips over and kills everyone on board. A tsunami hitting the island and wiping everyone out. The other night, I dreamt I was working in a car factory and I was in charge of fitting the engine. I don't know a thing about cars."

"You're right," Nerissa said with a laugh. "Very strange. No wonder you're so tired. What was last night's treat?"

Tally's face heated, and she stared at the floor. "Sex," she mumbled. "Lots of sex."

Nerissa grinned. "Lucky you. Was the guy hot?"

"Very. My ex."

"Ah." Nerissa nodded. "You don't say much about him, but I'm guessing he's the reason you're here, because he's an ex?"

"Yes," she said, ignoring the bite of pain in her chest. "He was hit by a car on the same night he proposed to me. He was in a coma for over two weeks, and when he came around, everything had changed. He'd changed. We had a row one night, and he told me he didn't love me anymore and threw me out. I haven't seen him since."

Nerissa whistled through her teeth. "That's rough."

"Yeah, it was." Tally lurched to her feet. "Right, let's get prep done. Otherwise, we'll have a riot on our hands in about thirty minutes."

Nerissa picked up Tally's cue to move on from discussing Cash, and the morning passed quickly, but by midday, Tally was barely clinging on. Exhaustion swamped her, and every single action took a momentous effort. She was reaching into one of the top cupboards for some gravy granules when a severe dizzy spell hit her. The tub clattered to the floor, and Tally grabbed the counter top, barely keeping herself from tumbling after it.

"Tally!" Nerissa caught her as Tally's knees buckled. Rhea,

one of the other helpers, pulled out a chair, and Nerissa eased Tally into it.

"Go and get Clio," Nerissa said to Rhea.

"No, I'm fine," Tally said, wearily waving her hand in the air. "I'm overtired, that's all." But it was no use. Rhea was already pushing past the long queue that snaked out of the door and down the street, her small figure wrapped in an oversized coat as she disappeared around the corner.

"Humour me," Nerissa said, pressing a glass of water into Tally's hand. "Let Clio give you the once-over, and then I'll stop nagging."

"Promise?" Tally said with a wry grin.

"Don't be silly," Nerissa said. "I'm lying. You know how I love to nag."

"Yeah. I pity your grandmother."

"Don't. Where do you think I got it from?"

Tally laughed. The dizzy spell had passed, and she was feeling much better already, but that didn't stop Nerissa continuing to fuss, nor did it remove the concerned looks on the faces of several of the refugees. A couple of them scooched behind the counter and began to serve ladles of stew into plastic bowls to keep the line moving. Tally gave them a grateful smile.

Rhea had been gone about fifteen minutes when she returned with Clio in tow. Tally sat back and accepted her fate as Clio took her temperature, pulse, and blood pressure. Then she made Tally stand up and sit down. She asked questions until Tally was hoarse from answering.

"Okay, let's get you upstairs," Clio said. "Bed rest for you, at least for a day or so."

"But the—"

"I've got it," Nerissa said, rubbing her arm. "You do as Clio says. I'll come and see you when I close up later."

Bone-weary, Tally reluctantly agreed. She leaned on Clio as

they negotiated the narrow staircase to her apartment above the café.

Clio ordered her straight to bed. She disappeared into the kitchen and five minutes later returned, holding a cup of camomile tea. "Here, drink this. It should help you sleep."

Tally took a sip. "So what's the verdict?"

Clio met her gaze but didn't speak. The longer Clio remained silent, the more worried Tally became. What if something was really wrong with her, like cancer? She'd assumed she'd caught a virus, something that would be gone in a few days, but the way Clio was staring shot her brain into overdrive.

"Tally," she said finally. "Is there a possibility you could be pregnant?"

A sudden coldness hit her core, and her heart began to race. "No," she croaked. "It's not possible. Not possible at all."

"When was your last period?"

Tally frowned, counting back the days, weeks. "I-I can't remember. I've been so busy."

"When did you last have sex?"

"Ages ago. My boyfriend and I split up in October, and there hasn't been anyone else. Surely if I was pregnant, I'd have had signs. Morning sickness or something. But I haven't. I'm just tired."

"Why don't I pop down to the pharmacy and pick up a pregnancy test kit."

Tally opened her mouth to protest.

"Just to rule it out," Clio added.

Tally's head flopped against the pillow. She didn't have the energy to argue. "If you must."

Once Clio had left, Tally reached for her phone and opened the calendar. The last time she and Cash slept together was the Friday before he threw her out. The ninth of October. That was more than ten weeks earlier. She lifted her pyjama top and placed the palm of her hand on her abdomen. She'd never had a washboard stomach, but it certainly wasn't any bigger than usual. If she was more than ten weeks pregnant, there'd be a sign, a bump. No, it was going to be fine. Clio was being thorough, that was all, systematically ruling things out until she identified the real reason for Tally's illness, which was more than likely a winter bug. There were plenty of them going around this time of year.

Clio returned after half an hour, clutching a brown paper bag. Tally would take the test, but it was a waste of time. There was no chance of her being pregnant. She and Cash had always been extremely careful. Neither of them had been ready for the responsibilities of parenthood.

"So how does this work, then?" Tally removed the white plastic stick from the box.

"You pee on that part," Clio said, her index finger pointing at the stick. "Nothing more complicated than that."

"Aren't you supposed to wait until the morning?"

"Old wives' tale. Off you go." Clio waved in the direction of the small bathroom situated off Tally's bedroom.

Tally was back a minute or so later and handed the stick to Clio. "How long do we have to wait?"

Clio glanced at the instructions. "Two minutes."

"Great." Tally paced back and forth. She didn't know why she was so on edge. In two minutes, the test would show up as negative, and Clio would have to try to find another reason for why Tally felt so unwell.

"Ready?" Clio said when the two minutes were up. She held the stick in Tally's direction.

"You do it."

"You're sure?"

"Yep."

Clio glanced down, her face giving nothing away. After a few seconds, she lifted her head, her steady gaze meeting Tally's.

"Merry Christmas, Tally. You're going to be a mama."

10

Tally stared at Clio as her jaw dropped. *Pregnant?* She couldn't be. But Clio said she was. Unless Tally had peed on the stick wrong. Could you get the peeing-on-the-stick bit wrong? She didn't know, but one thing was certain: she was going to freak.

Having suffered panic attacks in the past, Tally recognised the signs—sweaty palms, heart palpitations, dizziness, nausea, and an overwhelming sense of being choked. Her hands clutched at her throat, and she began to pant.

"Okay, Tally," Clio said, gently tugging Tally's hands away from her neck. "Take it easy. Slow breaths. In and out. In and out. Come on, breathe with me. Forget everything else."

It took a while, but after listening to Clio's calm voice and her reassuring demeanour, Tally eventually calmed down. Her breathing returned to normal as the realisation swept over her that nothing was ever going to be normal again.

"Are you sure?" she whispered, a tiny nibble of hope rippling to the surface.

"We should get you properly checked out, but in my experience, these home tests are extremely reliable."

Tally thrust the heels of her hands into her eyes. "Oh God," she muttered.

"It's not the end of the world," Clio said.

Of course it's the end of the world. "Do you mind giving me some space? I need to sort my head out."

"No problem." Clio began to walk out of the room, glancing back at the last minute. "I'll arrange for a trip to Leros."

Tally frowned. "Why?"

"You need to see a doctor. Get a scan and a blood test. We don't have the correct facilities on the island to give you the proper prenatal care."

Fear congealed in Tally's chest. She'd never thought about how difficult medical care would be on such a remote island. Why would she have?

"So I'll have to travel to Leros for everything, including the birth."

Clio nodded. "Yes."

"How long does it take to get there?"

"Twenty minutes or so by ferry. I'll let you know when your appointment is."

Clio gave her a warm smile and left. Once Tally was sure Clio was out of earshot, she turned on her side and wept. She wanted kids, of course she did. Someday. But not like this. Not when she was alone, emotionally scarred, barely able to take care of herself day-to-day.

But this was Cash's child.

She curled her hands around her belly. She couldn't abort Cash's child. A part of him and a part of her. A precious life to be protected at all costs. She'd manage, somehow.

God, she wished he were there.

On impulse, she picked up her phone. She found his number and hit Dial. Her heart hammered in her chest as the phone began ringing out. With absolutely no idea what to say, she waited for him to answer. And waited. After eight rings, the call went to voicemail.

"Hey, it's Cash. Leave a message."

Same voicemail he'd always used. Same voice that made her stomach clench with need. She hung up, her mind running riot. What was he doing? Visiting his mum perhaps, or having dinner with Rupe. Or in bed with another woman.

She winced. The thought of him with someone else... she closed her eyes, overwhelmed with the unexpected turn her life had taken. There'd been too much change in too short a time, and her brain was struggling to process everything. She was exhausted, scared, and lonely. She and Cash were supposed to be together, to raise a family together, to grow old together. She missed him with every cell in her body and missed the wider family she had to give up when he'd kicked her out.

Rachael, a perfect substitute for the mother she'd never had.

Rupe, the best brother anyone could ever wish for.

Anna, Brad, Jamie—the whole gang.

How could she have this baby alone? The thought of giving birth on a strange island, miles from home, horrified her. What if she went into labour at a time when there weren't any ferries? She was sure ferries from Safome were only once per day to neighbouring islands. Oh God, she could end up giving birth without any medical assistance.

Her mouth flooded with saliva, and she made a dash for the bathroom. Once the retching stopped, she rinsed a flannel under cold water and dabbed her face. She squeezed some toothpaste onto her toothbrush and scrubbed her teeth to get rid of the gritty acid taste. She hated being sick, and maybe she'd be one of those pregnant women who wouldn't suffer too badly.

Exhausted, she staggered back to the bedroom and collapsed into bed. She needed to get a grip. She was young and healthy and wouldn't be the first single mother in the world. Okay, it wasn't exactly the dream route to motherhood, but she'd have to play the hand she'd been dealt.

Tally lifted her head at a light tapping on the door. "Come in," she said, pushing herself upright when Nerissa poked her head around the door.

"Hey, how are you doing?"

"I'm okay. Tired, but okay."

Nerissa perched on the edge of her bed. "What did Clio say?"

Tally frowned. "She didn't tell you?"

"No."

Tally scrubbed her face. "I'm pregnant."

"Oh."

She could see Nerissa searching for the right thing to say. Taking pity on her friend, Tally squeezed her arm. "It's okay. A bit of a shock, that's all."

"That's why you've been so tired?"

"It seems so. Clio's arranging for me to have a proper check-up on Leros." She leaned over to the bedside cabinet and picked up the stick. "See for yourself."

Nerissa took it from her and stared at the blue vertical lines. "Could be wrong."

"Highly unlikely, according to Clio."

"So how do you feel?"

"I don't know. I need time to think."

"But you're keeping it, yes?"

Tally nodded, a small smile tweaking at her lips as Nerissa sighed in relief. "Good. Everything will be fine. We'll all pitch in. That's the beauty of this island. We're like one big family."

"I don't know whether I'm going to stay now."

Nerissa's eyebrows shot up. "Whyever not?"

"I'm not sure. Another decision I need to make, but none of them need to be made today."

"Have you told your ex?"

Tally sighed softly. "I called earlier, but it went to voicemail.

And even if he had answered, I'm not sure I would have told him."

"You need to tell him," Nerissa stated firmly.

"And I will. But not yet. I have to get my head around this before I completely blow his mind. I don't want him to think I'm trying to trap him into us getting back together. He made his feelings about me perfectly clear."

"He has a right to know he's going to be a daddy."

Tally nodded without committing to anything. Now wasn't the time to make rash decisions. She rested a weary hand on Nerissa's arm. "I'm really tired. Do you mind going?"

"Not at all." Nerissa rose from the bed, giving Tally a warm smile before disappearing.

As the bedroom door clicked shut, Tally closed her eyes. Nerissa's feet echoed on the wooden staircase before silence fell. She should call Em, but she didn't have the energy to face the type of questions and demands her best friend would have. Em and Pete could wait for another day. Better to find out for sure that she was pregnant before scaring those she loved. She was scared enough for all of them.

She must have fallen asleep, because the next thing she knew, her phone was ringing. Barely conscious, she couldn't work out whether it was a call or her alarm. With her eyes still shut, she reached out and located her phone. She squinted at the screen and sat bolt upright.

Cash was calling her.

The phone slipped through her fingers and landed in her lap. Snatching at it, she managed to answer before the call was diverted to voicemail.

"H-Hello," she said tentatively.

"I got a missed call from this number. Who is this?"

Tally sucked in a breath. Hearing Cash's voice after so long was like putting soothing lotion on a nasty burn. She closed her eyes as though that would somehow make it easier to speak.

"Don't mind me, love. I've got all fucking day," he said, forthright as ever.

"It's Natalia."

Her hands shook as she was met with a stony silence.

"Are you okay?" he finally said, although his tone held no warmth.

"Yes. I-I'm sorry for calling."

"What do you want?"

Tally flinched at his bluntness. "To hear your voice," she said, her vision blurring with unshed tears.

"There's hundreds of videos on YouTube."

A flash of pain shot through her chest. "This was a mistake." She pulled her phone away from her ear.

"Wait! Don't hang up. Are you still there?"

"Yes," she whispered.

"How are you?"

"Good. I'm good."

"You changed your number."

She closed her eyes. "Yes."

"But you kept mine."

"Yes."

"Don't live on false hope, Natalia."

She fisted her hands into her pyjamas as another burst of pain shot through her. His coldness reaffirmed her decision not to tell him about the baby.

"It's late. I'm going now."

"Natalia?"

"Yes."

A pause. "Take care of yourself."

11

C ash ended the call. The ache in his heart at hearing Natalia's voice caused a physical pain so sharp he found it difficult to breathe. He strode into the bathroom and swilled his face with cold water as he stared at himself in the mirror. He should have told her. *Why didn't he?* What a fucking idiot. Prime opportunity to tell her everything—about the help he was getting to manage the anger caused by his head injury and the fact that he'd begun playing tennis again, albeit poorly. And he could have explained why he'd pushed her away.

Shit, he'd thought he was making progress. And yet his response to hearing her voice had been fear that if he told her he wasn't fixed—that he might never be fixed—all hope that they stood a chance would disappear.

He lashed out, his arm sweeping everything off the bathroom shelf. Glass bottles shattered, the contents spilling over the floor.

"Fuck." His left hand slammed into the mirror. It splintered into several large pieces. He glanced down. His hand was covered in blood, and a two-inch shard of glass was embedded in the flesh. He gritted his teeth and pulled it out, causing blood to splatter into the sink. He wrapped his hand in a face cloth, but after ten minutes, when the bleeding hadn't stopped, he picked his way through the broken glass on the bathroom floor and called for help.

Half an hour later, the on-call nurse had stitched and bandaged his hand, and the maintenance guy had cleared up and replaced the mirror. Cash certainly couldn't fault the service, although considering he was paying far more than a five-star hotel would cost, it was nothing less than he should expect.

Alone in the dark, Cash closed his eyes and allowed himself to think about the conversation with Natalia. She'd called him. That had to mean she missed him—that she wasn't over him—although after his cold response, she wouldn't be calling again. He wanted so badly to see her, be with her, touch her. But the fact that he had four stitches in his hand and an urgent need to visit a pharmacy to replace all his stuff was a red flag. He didn't have this anger shit anywhere near under control. Definitely not enough to consider begging Natalia to take him back.

Hit with an overwhelming urge to hear her voice once more, he picked up his phone and almost dialled. Almost. Mustering every ounce of willpower, he switched off his phone and tossed it into a drawer. No doubt, he'd be made to examine every single detail of the last couple of hours at his next appointment with Bauer, who would scribble notes in his pad, sagely nod in all the right places, and tell Cash he was making progress.

What utter bollocks. He wasn't making any fucking progress.

His hand throbbed, and he threw back a couple of ibuprofen and climbed into bed. He craved the oblivion of sleep after the disastrous call with Natalia. No such luck on this night, though. He was still awake when dawn arrived. He crawled out of bed and drew back the curtains. It was raining again. It rained a lot in Northern Ireland, but Germany wasn't too far behind.

"Merry fucking Christmas," he muttered.

He glanced at his watch. Rupe and Mum would be arriving in a few hours. Despite his reticence, they'd insisted on spending the next couple of days with him. When he refused to return home for the holidays, he'd wrongly assumed they'd relent and leave him alone. Instead, his mum had got all excited about visiting Germany. Not the response he'd hoped for at all.

He made a protein shake and took it with him to the gym. To give himself a chance of getting through the day, he'd need to exhaust his body and hope his mind would follow suit. He loved his mum more than the world, and Rupe had been his best friend and wingman forever, but he could have done without their untimely visit. Rupe had made it clear he thought Cash was punishing himself by separating from everyone and everything he held dear and living in a kind of purgatory. Cash didn't disagree.

Ninety minutes later, he staggered into his apartment. Every muscle ached, and his damp shirt clung to his body, but he felt calmer than he had in several weeks. Job done. He showered, changed, and settled on the couch to read. The author had also written the book Cash had read to Natalia during their holiday to the Maldives. The memory of Natalia curled into his side on a white, sandy beach while he read aloud made his heart clench.

He opened the bedside-cabinet drawer and took out his phone. The minute it booted up, he had an overwhelming need to call Natalia again. Now that he knew her number, it was as if a switch had been flicked, and he constantly wanted to meddle with it. From very early on in their relationship, he'd thought his attraction to her was as strong as heroin would be to a narcotic addict. Despite him being the one to push her away, that compulsion hadn't abated. In fact, it had strengthened in the time they'd been apart, and hearing her voice the previous night had filled the syringe. All he had to do was plunge it into his arm.

After the fifth time of pressing Call and End in quick succession, he phoned Rupe instead. His call went to voicemail, and when he checked his watch, he groaned. They'd only just landed, so Rupe's phone would still be switched off. Antsy despite the gruelling workout, he paced up and down, looking at his watch every five minutes. When he estimated Rupe and his mum would be off the plane, he tried again.

"Jesus, have you got a camera on me or something?" Rupe said when he answered.

"Yeah. I hired some dick to follow you around."

Rupe snickered. "You okay, man?"

Cash forced a smile, hoping it would seep into his voice. "Yeah. What time are you getting to the hotel?"

"We should be there in half an hour."

"Good."

"What's up?"

"Nothing."

"Bollocks."

Cash sighed. "I spoke to Natalia."

Rupe inhaled a sharp breath. "You did?"

"Didn't know it was her. She's changed her number. I got a missed call, and when I called back to find out who it was, she answered."

"How is she?"

"I miss her." Cash's voice caught, and he kicked himself for showing weakness.

"Did she say where she was?"

"No."

"Did you ask?"

"No."

"Useful conversation, then."

"Fuck you."

Rupe laughed. "Look, head on over to the hotel. Let's get your mum a few gin and tonics, and then you and I can have a proper talk. Man to man."

"Man to man? You lying to yourself again?"

"Fuck you right back."

Cash chuckled, a lightness lifting his spirits. "I'll meet you there."

Despite his initial reticence at their visit, he couldn't wait to see them. He opened the wardrobe door and checked the bag of presents, grabbed his overnight case, and set off.

The roads were empty, and it didn't take long to drive to the hotel. He parked and walked into a reception area decked out with Christmas decorations and an enormous tree covered in twinkling lights. At least they'd made an effort. The hotel was definitely more festive than the residential facility.

He made his way up to the suite of rooms he'd booked on the top floor. He only had to knock once before the door flew open and his mother threw herself into his arms.

"Easy, Mum," he said, kissing her on both cheeks.

"Merry Christmas, sweetheart," she said, tugging him inside. "I was worried you wouldn't come."

"Wouldn't miss it for the world," Cash said, deciding not to tell her how close he'd been to bailing. "Flight okay?"

"Yes, lovely." She looked him over, her keen gaze missing nothing. "What happened to your hand?"

Cash shrugged. "I had an accident. It's fine. It'll be good as new in a few days."

She narrowed her eyes. "What type of accident?"

Cash expelled a breath. "Let's not ruin the day, Mum. I'm making progress—so Dr Bauer says."

"And what do you say?"

He wandered over to the minibar and grabbed a juice. "Some good days, some not so good."

"What was the trigger for that?" she said, pointing her chin at his hand.

Cash inwardly groaned. "Do you mind if we don't go into the details?"

A flicker of sadness crossed her face. "Of course not."

"I'll go and get Rupe," he said. "And then we can open presents before lunch."

CASH KICKED off his shoes and flopped onto the couch. After a long and stressful day, the stirrings of a migraine had him reaching for his painkillers. He poured a glass of water and threw two back.

"You still get a lot of headaches?" Rupe asked.

"Not nearly as many as I used to."

"Do you want me to go?"

"No." Cash massaged his temples. "It'll pass."

Rupe's gaze became shuttered. "I know you didn't want us to come for Christmas. I'm sorry if we've made things harder."

"It was more that I didn't want to go home."

"Why not?"

Cash teased at his beard. "Because I wouldn't have come back."

Rupe frowned. "You've been here seven weeks. Surely that's enough?"

Cash waved his bandaged hand in Rupe's face. "Yeah, I've totally got everything under control."

"I think you're being way too hard on yourself. But then again, you always have been."

Cash expelled a sigh. "You don't get it."

"Then explain it to me."

Rupe's insistent questioning started to irk him. Cash lurched to his feet and began to pace. "You want to know what I'm most afraid of?" he said, his voice increasing in volume with every word spilt. "That I'll end up like *him*."

Rupe clenched his jaw. "You are nothing like your father."

"What the fuck do you know?" Cash poked a finger into his temple. "You're not inside my head."

"Thank Christ for that," Rupe said with a grin.

His anger began to grow at Rupe's cavalier responses. He leaned down, his face inches from that of his best friend—and the man he badly wanted to punch. "Fuck you."

Rupe gave a brief shrug. "If it makes you feel better, go ahead. Curse at me all you like. But remember, I've known you for eighteen years. You've always had a quick temper. But physically abusive? Come on."

"But that was before!" Cash yelled in Rupe's face, his hands curling into tight fists. "Before that pissed-up bastard ruined my life."

He launched himself upright, closer than he wanted to admit to headbutting the supercilious fucker who was imitating his best friend. He laced his hands together and cupped the back of his neck as he began to pace once more. Rupe, meanwhile, didn't say a word. He sipped his wine, one leg crossed over the opposing knee, and watched Cash storm around the room. Rupe didn't even flinch when Cash shot the occasional venomous glare his way. In fact, he looked bored and at one point even yawned.

Dredging up every ounce of self-control, Cash forced himself to cross over to the window. He focused on the people below going about their business. He took several deep breaths and rolled his shoulders. After a few minutes, he managed to pull himself together. He turned around and perched on the window ledge.

"Sorry," he said to a still-silent Rupe, who was thoughtfully rubbing his chin.

"How come you didn't hit me?"

Cash frowned. "What?"

"How come you didn't hit me?" Rupe repeated.

"Why would I hit you?"

"Exactly," Rupe said, shooting Cash a triumphant stare.

Cash scratched his cheek. "What the hell are you going on about?"

"Jeez, dickhead. You may have the looks, but I've definitely got the brains."

The last remnants of Cash's anger dissipated, and he grinned. "Are you going to explain what you mean, or sit there insulting my intelligence?"

"You were furious with me. I could see it in your eyes. You really wanted to give me a good hiding, didn't you?"

"Yes."

"So what stopped you?"

"I don't know," Cash said.

"Sure you do." Rupe refilled his wine glass and took a sip. "Think about it."

Cash stared at the ground, his teeth gnawing on his bottom lip. He'd come so close, his fists clenching of their own volition, but then he'd chosen to walk away. He'd taken a self-imposed time out and called upon the coping techniques Bauer had been teaching him all these weeks.

He lifted his eyes to Rupe's. "Because you're the closest thing to a brother I've ever had, and the thought of hitting you... I'd rather cut my hands off."

Rupe spread his arms out wide. "And my genius status remains firmly at number one."

"As does your arrogance."

"I'd say we're neck and neck on that score."

Cash's lips twitched. "I'm not sure you've actually proved anything."

"Yes, I have. Only you're too dumb to figure it out."

"Okay, wise one. Fill me in, then."

Rupe touched his tongue to his teeth and grinned. "In a straight-out fight between me and Tally, who do you care about more?"

Pain lanced through Cash at the mere mention of her name. "No offence, but I'll never love anyone as much as I love her."

Rupe rose from his seat and clapped his hands around Cash's upper arms. "And there you have it, numbnuts. If you couldn't hit me, despite my provocation, why are you so sure you'll hurt Tally?"

Cash expelled a curt breath. "I threw a vase at her head."

Rupe shook his head. "Remember when you broke your right arm jumping off that wall in the second year of high school?"

Cash gave him an exasperated look. "Relevance?"

"You still played cricket that weekend. You bowled with your left hand and were still faster and more accurate than anyone else on the field. If you'd wanted to hit Tally with that vase, you would have."

Cash rubbed a hand over his mouth. "I can't take the risk."

Rupe raised his eyes heavenward. "You infuriate me, Cash. This all comes down to your determination to punish yourself because you don't think you're deserving of her love. Or anyone's for that matter. And yet she loved you with everything she had, so you had to find a way to ruin it. Face it, all this stems from the fucking guilt you're still carrying around about your father."

"I didn't ask to be hit by a drunk driver."

"No, but you were past that. On your way to recovery. The whole breakup with Tally was engineered by you."

Cash snorted. "Don't be ridiculous. I love her. I was going to marry her. More than anything, I want her back, but I also wouldn't be able to forgive myself if I hurt her."

"And I've proved that is highly unlikely. If you can't smack me, despite my best efforts to rile you, there's no way you would *ever* hurt her. You'd call on one of those self-help-strategy things you've been learning about and do exactly what you did with me today."

"I'm not fixed yet," Cash said.

Rupe cursed under his breath. He grabbed Cash's jacket and reached inside to grab his phone.

"You're fixed enough," he said, thrusting the phone into Cash's hand. "Call her."

Cash hung his head. "I can't," he whispered.

The phone slipped out of his hand and thudded onto the floor.

12

Tally stood by the quayside and pulled her coat closer around her. A chill wind was blowing off the Mediterranean Sea, and she shivered as she watched the ferryboat draw ever closer. Though the day was cold, the sun shone brightly, and she held up her hand to shield her eyes. Five more minutes, and the boat would dock.

Her stomach was tight with nerves and her mouth uncomfortably dry. She licked her lips and swallowed. It didn't matter how many times she played events over in her mind. She couldn't second-guess the outcome. Em was unpredictable at the best of times. It was one of the things that made her such a fun person to be around. No one quite knew what she was going to do next.

Except this time, Tally needed her reaction to be thoughtful and measured, rather than the usual knee-jerk response. "Speak first, think later—if at all," was Em's motto.

Tally touched her fingers to the crisp envelope nestled in her pocket. The contents of the envelope held the precious scan of her unborn child. She'd had it done a week earlier but still couldn't wrap her mind around the fact that she was going to be a mother. She must have looked at that grainy picture twenty times a day, hoping the more she did, the more real her situation would become. And yet every day the thought of motherhood grew more surreal.

As the ferry docked, the first mate threw a rope onto the quayside and jumped out to secure the vessel. Safome didn't get many visitors this time of year, and there were only a handful of people aboard. She spotted Em and waved, more anxious than ever to get this over with. Many times over the past week, she'd almost spilt her news over the phone but had refrained. She needed to do this face to face, where she'd be able to read Em's reaction.

Em was first off the boat, and she ran towards Tally, dragging her suitcase along the slippery gangway. The two girls fell into each other's arms.

"God, I've missed you," Em said with her head buried in the collar of Tally's coat.

"Missed you more," Tally said, hooking her arm through Em's as they set off walking. "Come on. My place isn't very far from here. Let's get out of the cold."

"Cold? This is positively tropical compared to London. Minus three when I left."

Tally grinned. "It's amazing how quickly you get used to the temperature here. What feels mild to you is bloody freezing to me."

"I can't wait to see the place. How's the refugee thing going?"

"Great. I love working in the café. Feels like I'm doing some real good in the world, you know? Seeing how gracious and grateful the refugees are, it sort of puts my shit into perspective."

Em nodded. "I can imagine. What about the first article?"

"I sent it over to Pete a couple of days ago. I'm hoping he'll agree to publish soon. It's so sad, Em, what's happening here and across Greece."

"Well, if anyone can do a story like that justice, it's you, babes."

When they walked into Tally's apartment, Em parked her suitcase by the door and drifted over to the window.

"Blimey. What a view. Look how green the water is from up here."

"Yeah, it's pretty special."

"And we have to take a walk along that beach. It's stunning."

"Definitely," Tally said.

Em glanced over her shoulder. "No wonder I can't persuade you to move back to London."

A slug of homesickness hit Tally. "I do miss it."

"Yeah, but this place is tranquil. Exactly what you need."

Deciding now wasn't the time to voice her thoughts about moving back home, Tally nodded. "Why don't I put the kettle on?"

Em flashed her an incredulous look. "Kettle? I haven't seen you in weeks. Please tell me the fridge is full of wine?"

Tally chuckled. "I've not been very well, so I think I'll stick to the tea." Not exactly a lie, but certainly misleading.

Em narrowed her eyes. "Why, what's wrong with you?"

"Nothing serious. I'll be fine."

"You never mentioned it."

"Because I'm okay."

Em frowned. "Come to think of it, you do look a bit peaky. Here, you sit, and I'll make the tea."

"That would be nice."

Tally shrugged off her coat and threw it over the back of the couch. She was going to let Em make the tea, and then she would tell her. Nausea flooded her stomach. She began to fidget as Em faffed about. When Em finally handed over her tea, Tally was almost at bursting point.

"What the hell is wrong with you, babes?" Em said, settling into the chair by the window. "You're jumpy as fuck."

Now that the time had come, Tally couldn't find the right words. No matter where she thought about starting, she knew it wouldn't come out right. Instead, she handed over the envelope containing the scan picture.

"What's this?"

"Open it," Tally whispered. She wiped clammy hands on her jeans.

"Is it a letter from Cash?"

"Just open it, Em."

Em reached inside and removed the ultrasound picture. Her brows knitted together, and then her head jerked backwards. Her stunned gaze found Tally's.

"You're pregnant?" she said in an incredulous tone.

"Yep."

Em gasped, her eyes wide as her mouth opened and closed, even though no words came out.

"Say something," Tally said.

"Is it Cash's?"

"Jesus, Em. Yes. For Christ's sake, what do you take me for?"

Em nodded. "Yeah. Silly me. Cash ruined you for anyone else."

"Please don't," Tally said.

"Does he know?"

"No."

"When are you going to tell him?"

Tally rested her head against the back of the sofa and closed her eyes. "I'm not."

"Yes, that's probably best," Em said.

Surprised, Tally's eyes snapped open. "I didn't think you'd agree with my decision not to tell him."

Em shrugged. "Well, if you're not keeping it, there's no point shaking the tiger's tail."

Tally cocked her head to the side. "What makes you think I'm not keeping it?"

Em's body stiffened. "You can't be seriously considering keeping this baby."

"I *am* keeping it."

Em pressed closer. "Why would you choose to ruin your life?"

"I don't see it that way. Lots of women have babies alone. They cope. So can I."

"It's not about that," Em said, gesticulating wildly. "Don't you see? If you have this baby, every time you look at him or her, you'll see Cash. And your heart will break. If you're still determined you're not going to try to make things right with him, then please think about what you're doing."

"But it's Cash's kid," Tally whispered, her eyes filling with tears.

"Babes." Em moved next to her on the couch and hugged her tightly. "I know how much you love him, but you have to think this through. Please make sure you're looking at this not romantically, but practically, because when that kid has been screaming for three days straight, and you're knackered and alone, reality is going to bite you in the arse."

Tally recoiled. "Are you saying you won't support me?"

"Of course I'm not," Em said, horror etched on her face. "I'm there for you whatever you decide. But I wouldn't be your friend if I didn't make you look long and hard at this decision."

"I'm keeping it." Tally plucked the ultrasound picture from between Em's fingers. "This is *my* baby. Mine."

Em blew out a soft sigh and took back the picture. She stared at the grainy image. "I can't believe it."

Tally gave a bitter laugh. "Try being in my head."

"When's it due?"

"Sixteenth of July."

"You need to tell Cash he's going to be a father."

"No." Tally's response was instantaneous and firm.

"If you are keeping this baby——"

"I *am* keeping it."

"Okay, *as* you are keeping this baby, Cash has a right to know.

And maybe, just maybe, that will be the catalyst to bring you two back together."

"I called him."

Em's eyebrows shot up. "When?"

Tears welled in Tally's eyes. "The day I found out. Christmas Eve. I wanted to share the news with him."

A frown drifted across Em's face. "But you didn't?"

Tally blinked several times as the memory of Cash's harsh words and even harsher tone came rushing back. "It went to voicemail, and then he rang me back. He didn't know it was me when he called. We spoke for a minute or two, and then I knew I couldn't tell him."

Em tilted her head to the side. "Why not?"

"He was... aloof. Cold. When I said I'd called because I wanted to hear his voice, he told me there were plenty of YouTube videos knocking about and that I shouldn't live on false hope."

Em sucked in a breath. "The arrogant fucker."

When a tear spilled onto Tally's cheek, Em's arms curved around her neck. Tally rested her head on Em's shoulder and gave in to her sorrow.

THE MORNING EM was due to go back to London, Tally sat in silence, her mood sombre as she watched Em pack. Acute loneliness swept through her as she realised she'd soon be alone once more. Safome was great, and Nerissa had become a dear friend, but it wasn't the same. Not like with Em, whom she'd known most of her life.

Or Pete. She hadn't even told him she was pregnant. It didn't seem right to tell him over the phone. He deserved better than that.

"Right, that's the last of it, I think," Em said, scanning Tally's bedroom.

"Did you get your hair straighteners from the bathroom?" Tally asked.

"No. Shit. Imagine this mane without them," she said, pointing to her perfectly straight bob, a look she achieved by clamping her hair between two hundred degrees of ceramic plates for twenty minutes.

"I'd rather not. There are things the eyes should never see," Tally said, ducking when Em threw a cushion at her.

Em returned from the bathroom and stuffed her hair straighteners into her suitcase. She zipped it up and heaved it off the bed, where it thudded onto the floor. "I think I may be over the weight allowance for the flight," she said with a grimace.

"I'm not surprised, with the amount you've bought this week."

"I've been on holiday," Em said with a pout. And then she chuckled. "Although I never need an excuse to shop."

When Tally didn't join in with her laughter, Em sat on the edge of the bed and tucked a lock of hair behind Tally's ear. "Talk to me."

Tally met Em's gaze, her vision blurring as her eyes filled with tears. "I want to go home."

13

A week later, Tally's plane touched down in Heathrow, and the moment it did, she knew this had been the right decision. She'd been wrong to think running away was the answer to her problems. The baby had brought everything into sharp focus. She didn't need tranquil. She needed London, with its fast-paced lifestyle, overcrowded streets, and general buzz.

Nerissa's teary face drifted into Tally's mind. Her friend had bawled like a baby when Tally told her she was leaving, but Tally reassured her they would definitely stay in touch. Running away might not have been the right thing, but she'd achieved great things—a serialised story that highlighted the plight of millions, a new and dear friend, a café that was better set up to help those in need. And an apartment she'd be able to rent out.

She disembarked. Icy air bit into her skin as she walked up the jet bridge, and she was relieved when she reached the warmth of the terminal building,

As luck would have it, her bags were amongst the first off the carousel. She loaded them onto a cart and set off towards the

Nothing to Declare lane, which didn't have a customs officer in sight.

Tally exited through the automatic doors into the arrivals hall and glanced around. She spotted Em about three rows back, waving madly. She weaved through the crowds of arriving passengers, eventually reaching her friend. The two girls hugged as though they hadn't seen each other for months.

"You made it," Em said, kissing her cheek. "This place is nuts."

"Everyone's heading home after the New Year's holidays."

"I've had to park in the multistorey," she said, taking the trolley away from Tally.

Tally planted her hands on her hips. "I am capable of pushing my own trolley."

"I know," Em said, completely ignoring Tally's attempts to take it back. Em set off at a clip, catching the ankles of a few shufflers. With a muttered apology, she steered the baggage trolley around them.

Em refused to allow Tally to put her suitcases in the boot, even going so far as to open the passenger door and help her inside. But when Em grabbed the seatbelt and tried to clip it in place, Tally snatched it away.

"I'm pregnant, not an invalid. I had enough of this when we were in Safome."

"Still grumpy, I see," Em said, dismissively waving as she walked around the car to climb into the driver's seat.

"Please tell me you're not going all mother hen for nine months," Tally said, giving her a hard stare.

"If you think this is bad, wait until you tell Dozer. That uncle of yours won't let you lift a finger."

Tally swallowed hard. "Do you think he'll be mad?" she said, glancing sideways at Em.

"What right does he have to be mad? You're not sixteen."

"Still..."

"I think he'll be worried, but once he sees you're okay, he'll be thrilled."

"I hope so," Tally murmured.

"We can find out tomorrow," Em said.

"Why tomorrow?"

"Because I've invited him over for dinner."

"Emmalee!"

"Oh, come on, Tal. You think I'd actually be able to keep him away. You know how delighted he is you've decided to move back home. He hated the fact he couldn't get over to see you at Christmas. He might come across as a grouchy old bastard, but he loves the bones of you. He's missed having you around."

"I know. He told me every time I called," Tally said, grinning. "I thought I'd have more time to prepare, that's all."

"Rip the plaster off, babes. Easiest way."

As Em drove through the grimy London streets towards her flat, Tally's excitement grew. Ten weeks wasn't long, but she'd missed home. Having this baby on the way meant she needed her family around more than ever.

Her palm settled on her stomach, and she absentmindedly rubbed it. Cash might not want her any more, but she still loved him desperately. If this baby was all she had left of their relationship, there wouldn't be a child more wanted, more cherished, more precious.

By the time Em parked up outside her flat, Tally could barely keep her eyes open. A ferry, two flights, and an hour scrambling across London in heavy traffic had finished her off. This time, she didn't argue when Em insisted on carrying her bags inside.

"Do you mind if I take a bath?" Tally said.

Em rolled her eyes. "Please don't tell me you're going to be asking if you can do this or do that or if it's okay to make a cuppa every five minutes, because that will get on my bloody nerve pretty quick."

Tally laughed. "Nerve? As in singular?"

"Yep. I didn't have many left after the week I've had, and the drive from the airport eroded the last few away. A bowl of pasta, a glass of wine, and a good night's sleep, and the others will grow back."

"Here's hoping," Tally said over her shoulder as she pushed open the door to the bathroom. She turned the hot tap on full. While the bathtub filled up, she rummaged through her suitcases, eventually locating her toiletries and a warm set of pyjamas.

She stripped off and turned sideways to look in the mirror. The slight bump was easily detectable, although anyone not in the know would probably think she'd eaten too much bread.

She sank down into the bath and closed her eyes. The hot water soothed her aching muscles, and her body began to relax for the first time since she'd found out she was pregnant. She was so glad to be home. She needed those she loved around her, especially now.

But the one she loved the most was missing.

14

Tally paced between the sofa and the window while she waited for Pete to arrive. She'd convinced Em to leave her to it. She needed to do this alone, not with Emmalee prodding her in the back every five minutes. Her friend meant well, but Tally wanted to gauge Pete's mood so she could approach her news in the right way.

She jumped when his three-rap knock sounded on the door. Taking a deep breath, she opened it.

"Hi, Pete," she said, giving him a warm hug. "Come on in. That wind is bitter."

"It's great to see you, Tally." Pete closed the door behind him and wiped his feet on the mat. "I'm glad you decided to come home."

"Me too," she said with a warm smile. "It was definitely the right decision. I can't keep running from my problems. Time to face up to them."

"At least it turned out to be weeks rather than months." He followed her into the kitchen. "Where's Emmalee?"

"She's gone to the cinema."

Pete frowned. "Oh. I thought she was joining us for dinner."

"I asked her to go," Tally said, stirring the pasta. She dipped a spoon into the sauce and held it up for Pete to taste.

"Perfect," he said, licking his lips. "You always were a fabulous cook."

"Sit down, then," she said, nodding at the small kitchen table. She filled two bowls with food and pushed one in front of him. "I wanted it to be just us tonight."

"Why's that?" he said, stabbing at the spaghetti with his fork.

"I haven't seen you since I left for Greece. I saw Em last week."

"Fair enough." Pete slurped another mouthful of spaghetti, splattering his shirt with bolognaise sauce. "Dammit. Every time."

She giggled. "Here," she said, passing him a damp cloth.

"Good job I have a fabulous dry cleaner," he said, laughing at his own clumsiness. "I need a bib."

"You always did get more spaghetti sauce on you than in you," Tally said.

A warm glow spread through her veins as the familiar scene unfolded in front of her, and she couldn't wait any longer. "I'm pregnant," she blurted.

His hand froze halfway towards his mouth, his fork full of spaghetti. He glanced up, eyes wide. "What did you say?"

"I'm having a baby. In July." She reached across the table and clasped her fingers around his. "I know it's a shock. It was to me too when I found out." She shrugged. "But I'm slowly getting used to the idea."

She could see him working backwards. "It's Cash's?"

"Yes. Not planned, obviously."

"What has he said?"

"I haven't told him."

Pete patted her arm. "Good. Because I want to be there when you do."

Tally shook her head. "No need. I'm not telling him."

Pete's mouth set in a firm line. "You have to tell him."

"Why? Cash has made his feelings perfectly clear. He doesn't want me, and I'm sorry, Uncle Pete, but me and this baby come as a package deal."

"Tally..." Pete's head dropped, and he slowly shook it.

"I've made my decision."

"You can't have a man's child and not tell him he's a father. Look, you know how I feel about Cash. I hate how he's hurt you. But whether he wants to be involved or not, that isn't your decision to make."

Tally set her jaw and met Pete's unwavering gaze. "I am not telling him. And if you do, I swear I will never speak to you again."

His mouth creased in thought, and for a minute, Tally feared he was going to call her bluff. Then he leaned back in his chair and beamed. "I'm going to be a great-uncle."

Letting out the breath she'd been holding, Tally returned his smile. "This baby is going to be one lucky dude or dude-ess."

"Of course it is," Pete said. "It will have you as a mother."

TALLY STARTED WORKING at the paper again, and apart from the reminder of her ever-growing belly, everything was pretty much as it had been before she'd ever met Cash Gallagher.

Her pregnancy was progressing well, and she was into her fifth month when Pete beckoned her into his office one Monday at lunchtime. He wore a grave expression as he waved for her to sit.

A growing sense of dread made her skin tingle. "What's wrong?"

"I'd like to hide this from you," Pete said with a grim twist to his mouth as his gaze flicked between her and his iPad. "But you're bound to stumble across it one way or another."

Instinct told Tally this had something to do with Cash. A horrible, sick feeling churned in her stomach. She held her hand out. "Let me see."

Pete hesitated and then slowly pushed the tablet across the desk. Tally picked it up... and her heart dropped through the floor. In front of her was a picture of Cash with a skinny blonde coming out of the Dorchester. She'd recognise those green arches anywhere.

He was dressed casually in jeans and a crisp white shirt open at the neck, revealing smooth golden skin. He looked so goddamned handsome she wanted to cry, but the real killer was the expression on his face as his eyes connected with the woman's. She knew that look. It was one he'd often wear before he met her—the one that said he'd been up all night screwing and didn't care who knew.

She flicked onto the next picture. In this one, he had his arm around the blonde's waist and was whispering in her ear. The final one had captured the woman's adoring look perfectly, her eyes shining as she gazed lovingly at him, a sexy smile gracing her perfect face.

Tally dropped the tablet on the desk. "He's a free agent," she said in a dull tone.

"Tally—"

"Can I go now?" she snapped, already out of her seat before Pete could say another word. She spun on her heel and left his office. As she passed her desk, she swiped her coat off the back of her chair and slung her bag over her shoulder. Ignoring Danny's concerned look, she ran into the hallway and sped down five flights of stairs to the street below. By the time she got outside, she could barely catch her breath. With no idea where to go, she turned left and began walking.

She must have wandered around for about an hour before

she stumbled upon a GBK restaurant Cash had once taken her to. She hesitated with one hand on the door. Knowing her decision would probably give rise to more tears, she pushed the door open and walked in.

The hostess greeted her with a warm smile. "Table for one, is it?"

Tally glanced across to the table she and Cash had sat at all those months earlier. A young couple occupied it. They had eyes only for each other. The man was rubbing his thumb back and forth over the back of the girl's hand, and she was coyly glancing at him from beneath long eyelashes that graced her cheeks every time she blinked.

"I'm sorry," she mumbled to the hostess. "This was a mistake."

After stumbling back onto the street, she pulled up the collar of her coat and set off walking again. She'd known this would happen eventually. Cash was a highly sexed male, the type who couldn't be without a woman for very long. If anything surprised her, it was how long he'd taken. They'd split up almost five months ago, and even during that one phone call, he'd shown no inclination for them to get back together.

Why shouldn't he be with other women?

She bent over double as pain tore through her insides. She leaned on a lamppost as she waited for the pain to recede. Never again would Cash's lips softly press against hers. Never again would his calloused hands explore her body. Never again would she feel him moving inside her.

As a dull ache spread throughout her chest, the baby kicked for the first time.

Tally held her breath, unsure whether it had been a kick at all. She waited, and then it happened again, like a muscle twitching in her stomach. She couldn't stop a smile spreading across her face. It was as though her baby knew she'd needed a pick-me-up right at that moment and had provided it in the most wonderful way possible.

She dug around in her bag, desperate to tell someone. Her fingers trembled as she called up Em's number.

The call went to voicemail, and she cursed as she waited for the automated message to finish. "Em, it's me. You'll never guess—"

Her arm dropped to her side as her gaze fell on a familiar figure across the road.

Rupe.

Her feet were frozen to the pavement, and before she could move, he began to jog towards her. In a panic, she buttoned up her coat. She could *not* let him see the bump. It didn't take a genius to put two and two together, and Rupe wasn't exactly the slowest off the mark.

"Tally, my darling girl." He reached out to hug her, frowning when she pulled away and held out her hand instead.

"Nice to see you, Rupe," she said formally.

"What the fuck is this?" he said staring at her outstretching hand. "A handshake, like I'm some stranger."

She shrugged. "I guess you are now. I haven't seen you in five months."

He winced. "I deserved that, but in my defence, you disappeared."

She shrugged again.

"I asked Emmalee several times where you were. She refused to tell me."

"Probably because she thought you'd run straight off to tell Cash. Not that it matters. He's hardly come running after me. Too busy moving on, reverting to type."

Rupe frowned. "What's that supposed to mean?"

"Check out the *Daily Mail*," she said, unable to stop the bitterness leaking into her voice. "They sure do seem to get the best snaps."

"Tally—"

"I've got to go."

She dashed off, and as she rounded the corner, a black cab was dropping off a passenger. Tally threw herself into the back and urged the driver to hurry as Rupe made a lunge for the door handle. He missed by inches. Tally twisted in her seat and stared at his confused expression until he'd disappeared from view.

15

Cash opened one eye, cringing at the carnage inside his hotel suite. Cans and bottles were strewn everywhere, and at a brief glance, he counted eleven pizza boxes. He shouldn't have agreed to the party, but Suze had started calling people before he could stop her, and in the end, he hadn't given a shit. It wasn't worth the hassle to argue.

He staggered off the bed and managed to make it past several unconscious bodies into the bathroom. Fortunately, it was empty, and he locked the door and sat on the rim of the bath, desperately trying to remember more than flashes from the previous evening. He'd taken Suze out to dinner as a way to test whether he was human enough to be around people again, but then she'd started banging on about getting the old gang together and how great it would be to rock the house, like old times.

He grimaced as a sharp pain shot through his temple. They'd rocked the fucking house all right. So much so that he'd have some serious grovelling to do if he wanted to stay at this hotel anytime in the future.

He filled the sink with water and swilled his face. After vigorously scrubbing his teeth, he felt better. If only the splitting headache pounding at his temples was as easy to shift. As he wandered back into the main area of the suite, he counted seven bodies. Five he definitely recognised, including Suze, who was curled up on the right side of his bed wearing nothing but a very tiny thong.

A cold blast shot through him. *Oh no.* He couldn't have. He had enough trouble getting it up when sober since his split with Natalia. Totally pissed, he would have had to swallow five Viagra to have any chance of getting a hard-on. And even then, he'd need to have totally lost his marbles to stick it into Suze.

Before he had a chance to delve into possibilities that were too horrendous to contemplate, someone banged like hell on the door. A couple of the bodies on the floor began to stir as Cash stepped over them. He pressed his eye to the peephole and groaned.

He flung the door open wide, allowing Rupe to step inside. "Don't."

"What the fuck is going on?" Rupe scanned the hotel room. He tripped over an empty bottle of champagne, cursed loudly, picked it up, and slammed it down on the nearest table. Cash was surprised the bottle didn't smash.

"Had me a little party," Cash said with a sheepish grin.

"I can see that. Okay, okay," Rupe said, poking his toe at prostrate bodies lying on the floor. "Party's over. You can all fuck off."

The various groans and moans of still-drunk revellers didn't stop Rupe. He kept kicking and prodding until he'd corralled the majority into the corridor as they staggered and muttered curses under their breaths.

When he spotted Suze lying on Cash's bed, Rupe flashed him a look of pure loathing. "You fucking idiot."

Cash threw his arms out to the side. "I didn't." He frowned. "I couldn't have."

Rupe crossed to the bed and gently shook Suze. "Time to go, my lovely," he said, scooping an arm under her and tugging her off the bed. He helped her into her clothes and walked her towards the door.

"Wait, my bag," she mumbled, clearly still half-pissed from the night before.

Rupe checked around and eventually spotted it hanging off the back of a chair. "Here we are," he said, slipping the strap over her head.

"Stop!" she shouted as he began to close the door. "I haven't had my goodbye kiss. Come here, baby." She reached for Cash. He instantly recoiled.

"Okay, bye-bye." Rupe deposited Suze in the hallway, slammed the door, and deadlocked it. "Sometimes, I fucking hate you," he said as he fixed Cash with a hard stare.

"I didn't bang her."

"If I asked you to swear on Rachael's life, could you?"

Cash stared at the floor. "No."

"I saw Tally today," Rupe said.

Cash's head snapped up. "Where?"

"Near Marble Arch. She looked as though she'd been crying. Wouldn't even let me hug her. Muttered something about the *Daily Mail*."

"What does that mean?"

"Let's find out, shall we?" Rupe lifted his phone from his pocket. A minute later, he handed it over to Cash. "You fuckwit."

Cash stared at the pictures on Rupe's phone and then met Rupe's fearsome glare. "I didn't screw her," he said, the horror of his potential fuck-up more than he could bear. If he had slept with Suze, he could kiss goodbye to ever getting back together with Natalia. "It was supposed to be an experiment."

Rupe expelled an exasperated breath. "An experiment in what?"

With legs that felt as if the bones had been removed, Cash sank into the nearest chair. "You know my history with Suze. Before I met Natalia, she was my London go-to gal for when I needed a quick lay, but out of the sack, she always annoyed the hell out of me. I thought if I managed to spend a night in her company without lamping her, then I had enough coping mechanisms to allow myself to be around Natalia again. And maybe, just maybe, if I explained all this to Natalia, she'd consider taking me back."

Rupe blinked slowly. "For fuck's sake," he said, scrubbing a hand over his face. "You are a total arse."

"I need to call Suze." Cash unsteadily climbed to his feet and scanned the room, looking for his phone. When he spotted it over by the window, he trudged across and picked it up.

"What for?"

"If I fucked her, I've probably screwed up my chances of ever getting back with Natalia. I need to know."

"You think she'll tell the truth?"

Cash grimaced. "We're about to find out."

He dialled her number and listened as the hollow sound of the ring tone played in his ear. After the fifth ring, she picked up.

"Why did Rupe throw me out?" she said in a slightly petulant tone.

"Hey, Suze," Cash said smoothly. "Sorry about that. He needed to speak with me urgently."

"Well, tell him he's off my Christmas-card list." A girlish giggle erupted from her.

Cash's jaw clenched as he fought down annoyance. "I will."

"Last night was great, yeah?"

"Like old times," Cash said, cringing as he spoke the words aloud. Reliving a slice of his past had reaffirmed how much he wanted his future to be with Natalia.

"I've missed those crazy parties of yours, although I do have a little bone to pick with you."

"Is that right?"

"I'm not too mad, because I know it's been tough since the car accident, but really, baby, next time you invite me out on the promise of wild sex at the end of the night, I expect you to deliver."

Cash's heart started to beat double time. "So we didn't..."

"No. I tried, believe me," she said with a harsh cackle. "But you kept pushing me away."

Without saying another word to Suze, Cash hung up. He glanced over at Rupe, a slow smile spreading across his face. "I'm only in the goddamned clear."

16

The cab pulled up outside Em's flat, and Tally jumped out, feeling excitement because her baby had kicked for the first time and sadness at the way she'd dealt with Rupe. He'd always been like a brother to her, and she shouldn't have treated him with that level of contempt. But shock at seeing him across the street, mixed with fear that he'd figure out she was pregnant and go running to Cash, had made her behave pretty badly.

She unbuckled her shoes and wandered into the kitchen, hoping to see Em, but the flat was empty. Desperate to share her news with someone, she dug her phone out of her bag with the intention of calling Pete. Spotting five missed calls and two texts from him, plus a whole bunch of WhatsApp messages from Danny, she cursed. She should have called after she'd torn out of the office. *Wow, I'm on a streak. First treating Rupe like a leper, and now this...*

She clicked on recent calls and returned one of Pete's, her heart plummeting when she heard the concern in his voice.

"Are you okay, honey?"

"Yes, I'm fine. Sorry for running out on you. It was a bit of a shock."

"Where are you now?"

"At home. I know I should come back to the office, but––"

"Don't be silly. You need to take care of yourself. Stress isn't good for someone in your condition."

Tally grinned. "Speaking of which, the baby just kicked for the first time."

Pete took a sharp intake of breath. "It did?"

"Yep. Weirdest feeling ever."

"But pretty wonderful, I bet."

"Yeah," she said, her voice catching in her throat. "Pretty wonderful."

"I wish you weren't doing this by yourself."

"I'm not by myself. I've got you, Em, and Danny."

"Have you thought any more about telling Cash?"

"I bumped into Rupe today," Tally said, ignoring his comment. "Right after the baby kicked."

"Did he notice?"

"I don't think so. I took off too quickly for him to get a good look."

Pete sighed. "Tally..."

"I know. I hear you, and I will. Just not yet."

"Okay, but don't leave it too long."

The front door slammed, and a smile spread across Tally's face. "Em's home. I'll see you tomorrow."

"Only if you're feeling better," she heard Pete say as she hung up.

"Em, in here," she said, almost bursting to share her news.

"You okay, Tal?" Em said as she appeared in the doorway. "I got a weird message from you on voicemail, but it cut off halfway through."

"Yeah, I saw Rupe, and it distracted me, but never mind that." She grabbed Em's hand. "Sit down."

Em frowned. "You saw Rupe? Are you okay?"

"The baby kicked."

Em squealed. "Oh my God. Is it kicking now?" She pressed the palm of her hand across Tally's belly, her beaming smile falling away when nothing happened. "Maybe it doesn't like me."

Tally removed her hand. "It doesn't work on command, you know."

Em chuckled. "Good point." Her head tilted to one side. "How come you saw Rupe?"

"I had a bit of upset at work and was getting some fresh air when I felt this weird flutter in my stomach. I was on the phone to you when Rupe saw me, and that's why I never finished the message."

"What was the upset at work?" Em said, homing straight in on the key point.

Tally pulled up the *Daily Mail* showbiz app, which had the photos of Cash, and passed her phone to Em. "Guess it was only a matter of time."

Em narrowed her eyes as she scanned the pictures. When she lifted her head, her face held a mixture of sorrow and outrage. "I'm sorry, babes."

Tally shrugged. "Yeah."

A moment of silence followed before Em threw her hands in the air. "I *knew* there was something I needed to talk to you about."

"What?"

"I need a favour."

Tally groaned. "Why do I get the feeling I am not going to like this?"

"Don't be like that. It'll be fun."

Tally rolled her eyes. "Now I'm definitely suspicious."

"David's brother is over from Canada."

"That's nice for him."

"Yeah," Em said. "David and Paul haven't seen each other for two years, so naturally, they want to spend as much time together as possible."

"Right. And...?" Tally already disliked the direction this conversation was taking.

Em grimaced. "I was hoping you'd come out to dinner with us. You know, so Paul doesn't feel like a spare part."

Tally blew out a breath. Even a fake date felt like a betrayal of her feelings for Cash "Do I have to?"

"No," Em said. "But you would be doing me a huge favour."

"I don't even know the guy. I barely know David."

"He's really nice. Honestly. And there's no worries about him coming on to you. He's got a girlfriend in Canada."

Tally glanced down at her ever-growing stomach. "I don't think I need distant girlfriends to fend off men. I have a built-in repellent."

Em snorted. "You could have a brood in there, and you'd still have to fight most guys off, but Paul's smitten, so you've no worries on that score. Come on, Tal, do it for me. I don't want Paul to have to play gooseberry, but equally, I don't want to give up seeing David for the next week."

Tally sighed and then grinned. "Look at you, Miss Infatuated. Who'd have thought?"

"Yeah, whatever," Em mumbled as her skin was tinged with pink.

"Okay. For you, I'll do it."

Em threw her arms around Tally. "I owe you."

"Yeah," Tally said. "And I'll be collecting."

17

"You look lovely, Tal. Positively blooming."

Tally glanced down at her bump and smoothed her hands over the dress Em had helped her choose. "You don't think it's too clingy?"

"No. All I see is a seriously hot momma," Em said with a giggle. "I've warned Paul he'll need to act as bodyguard."

Tally pulled a face. "Brilliant," she said in a sarcastic tone.

"Don't be like that. Paul's looking forward to meeting you."

"I'm not sure I can remember how to make polite conversation with strangers."

"Then make impolite conversation," Em said, shrugging one shoulder. "That'll be more fun anyway."

Tally steeled herself. She wanted to do this for Em, especially given how wonderfully supportive Em was being with Tally's pregnancy and all, but really, all she felt like doing was curling up on the sofa and falling asleep while watching trashy TV.

"Where are we going?"

"Trader Vic's."

Tally groaned. "Really?"

"What's wrong with Vic's?"

"Can't we just go down to the local?"

"No. David wants to show Paul the best London has to offer."

"But Mayfair? Do we have to?"

Em playfully bumped shoulders with Tally. "Oh, stop. You know the minute you get there, you'll be in your element. And I have it on good authority they do a fabulous No Tai Mai Tai."

Tally raised her eyes heavenward. "Lucky me."

Em laughed. "You're the queen of the mocktail these days."

"I miss alcohol," Tally said, sticking out her bottom lip in a half-wistful, half-playful mood.

"I've no idea how you do it, to be honest, babes."

"How do you know I don't keep a bottle of vodka under my pillow?"

Em laughed as a knock sounded at the front door. "Wouldn't put it past you," she said as she went to answer it.

Her greeting of David made Tally blush and turn away. It must have been exactly the same for Em whenever Tally and Cash locked lips. She winced at the memory. It didn't seem to matter how much time passed—the pain of losing Cash refused to abate.

Paul hovered in the doorway behind Em and David. His ears had turned red as he watched his brother and Em make out.

Taking pity on him, Tally waved him forwards with a warm smile. "Hi, Paul. Just shove her in the back."

Paul grinned, although he didn't do as Tally suggested, instead sidling past the still-snogging pair. He thrust out his hand. "You must be Tally." His handshake was as warm as his smile, and Tally's nervousness dissipated.

"Come on in. I'll get you a drink while these two... do whatever it is they're doing."

Paul snickered and followed her into the kitchen.

"We don't have much," Tally said with an apologetic smile as she held up a half-empty bottle of Bailey's. "Em's trying to be supportive by not keeping alcohol in the house, although she'll get smashed tonight, no doubt."

"I heard that." Em sauntered into the kitchen, towing David behind her.

"Are you denying it's true?"

"No." Em swiped the Bailey's out of Tally's hand and poured three healthy measures. She handed round the drinks. "But still..."

Em's attempt at putting on a hurt expression had Tally chuckling. "You don't fool me with that look."

"That's the problem," grumbled Em. "You know me too well."

As they arrived at Trader Vic's, Tally silently thanked Em for planning ahead. She'd booked them a table, which was just as well, considering the number of people waiting in line. With her swollen ankles, Tally wouldn't have enjoyed queuing up.

The hostess showed them to a booth at the rear of the bar. Em and David immediately got their heads together, giggling at nothing, like those in new relationships tended to do.

"Thanks for agreeing to come along," Paul said, handing her a drinks menu. "Three is definitely a crowd."

"No problem, although I can't promise I'll be much fun. This one has put paid to that." She pointed at her protruding belly.

"How far along are you?"

"A little over five months."

"It's very brave of you to have a child alone."

When Tally gave him a surprised look, his mouth twisted in a crooked smile. "David told me. I hope you don't mind."

"There was only one choice," she said with a shrug. "I'm hardly a pioneer."

"I still think you're being incredibly courageous."

Tally smiled. "Tell me about Canada," she said, anxious to divert the subject from one that made her heart clench. "I've never been. What made you move there?"

Paul's face lit up. "My girlfriend. Her company offered her a transfer to their head office in Vancouver. We both jumped at the chance of living abroad. That was five years ago now, and I can't imagine ever moving back to England."

"Five years, and she's still your girlfriend. You're a lucky man."

Paul laughed. "I know. She says the same thing. I'll propose one day, but for now, we're doing just fine as we are. Why rock the boat?"

"Indeed. As long as you're both happy, that's all that matters."

They ordered their drinks, Tally going with Em's suggestion of a No Tai Mai Tai. When the waitress brought them over, she took a sip.

"Hmm, not bad."

Despite her original reticence, Tally began to enjoy herself. Paul was great company and also madly in love with his girlfriend, which eliminated any awkwardness that might have been present. Even when the waitress asked him if he was looking forward to being a father, Paul was unfazed and played along beautifully. When the waitress moved away, the two of them burst into fits of laughter.

"Want to go?" Em said later that evening when Tally had yawned for the third time.

"Do you mind?" Tally said. "I don't want to spoil anyone's night, but I'm exhausted."

"I can take Tally home if you two would rather stay out," Paul said.

"Thanks for the offer," Em said. "But I'm kind of knackered myself. Let's go and have coffee at my place."

As the four of them left the bar and spilled out onto the busy Mayfair street, Tally stumbled over the step. Paul managed to catch her before she fell.

"If you're like this sober, I'd love to see you drunk." He slipped an arm around her waist to support her.

Tally glanced up at him. "Thanks for tonight. You've almost made me forget my troubles."

"I've had a great time. You're a top girl, Tally. Don't you forget that."

"I'll try not to," she said, reaching up to kiss his cheek.

"Hurry up, Tal, Paul," Em said. "David's managed to get a taxi."

"Coming," Tally said as she and Paul began to make their way to the taxi idling by the kerb. As she waited for Em to climb in, she sensed someone staring at her. With prickling skin, she scanned the opposite side of the street, and then she saw him.

Cash.

18

F rozen to the spot, Cash bit back the surge of anger that raced through his veins as he watched the stranger put his hands on Natalia. Who the fuck was this jerk anyway? The way she'd gazed up at him told Cash they knew each other, and the fierce burn of jealousy in his throat tasted bitter, becoming infinitely worse when she stood on tiptoes and kissed him.

When Emmalee shouted at her, Tally looked away from the bastard Cash was having serious thoughts about beating to a pulp. She made her way to the waiting cab, her eyes met his, and she blanched.

Well, wasn't that a fucking kick in the teeth.

He couldn't tear his gaze away. Five months without seeing her was a lifetime, especially as he'd found it difficult to go twenty-four hours without her in the past. His memory of her had not done her justice. She was more beautiful than he remembered—peaches-and-cream skin, those stunning blue eyes that were always able to see right through him, and the chestnut hair that used to fall in waves over the pillow when they made love.

He didn't know what made his gaze slip south. Maybe it was

the way she dragged her eyes away from his, or the fearful look she wore as she did so. It didn't really matter either way, because the minute he did, everything changed.

Shock coursed through him. Was he the father, or the guy she was with? He felt sick at the thought of her with another man, let alone falling pregnant by him. She hadn't said a word, which meant it wasn't his baby. Didn't it?

She turned away and began to get into the cab. He'd better act fast, or she'd be gone. He sprinted across the street and managed to get a hand on the door before it was slammed shut.

"Natalia, wait," he said, yanking the door back open.

Emmalee flashed him a look of surprise before her jaw clenched. "Go away, Cash," she said, leaning across Natalia to try to close the door.

Cash tightened his grip. "Please. We need to talk."

"You should have thought about that when you threw her out onto the street in the middle of winter," Emmalee said.

Cash turned his gaze on her, and he must have hit the right level of acrimony, because Emmalee shrank back in her seat.

"When will you learn to keep your fucking nose out of my business," he said.

"I don't think there's any need for that," one of the guys butted in. The one who hadn't touched his Natalia. The one who, up until that moment, might have kept his teeth.

Cash coiled his fists, having to draw on every single lesson Dr Bauer had painstakingly taught him over his long stay at the clinic. Natalia still hadn't said a word. Her hands protectively cradled her belly, and she stared straight ahead.

He took a punt. "Were you ever going to tell me?" he said softly.

That made her turn her head. Her eyes glistened as she looked up at him. "I don't know," she said, her honesty catching him off guard.

So it was his. A thrill of excitement made his pulse jump. He'd never thought about being a father, but this was Natalia, the love of his life. And the soon-to-be mother of his child.

Cash held out his hand. "Please, baby," he said in a placating tone, knowing he'd lost the right to call her that the minute he'd lied about not loving her. Then again, he didn't like following rules. "We have a lot to talk about. I know I've treated you terribly, but I can explain."

"Paul, close the door," Emmalee said to the one who'd laid his hands on Natalia. *His* Natalia. Paul leaned over and grabbed the handle, but as he tried to yank the door shut, Cash shoved him hard in the shoulder, and he fell back against the seat.

"Stay out of this," Cash growled. "It's none of your business,"

"Enough," Natalia said in a low tone. She stared straight ahead. "We'll talk. But not now. I'm tired, and I want to go home."

"Thank you," Cash said, the relief at her acquiescence making his head spin. He didn't know what he'd have done if she'd refused, but he was pretty sure hauling a pregnant woman out of a taxi was not acceptable, no matter how gently he would have gone about it.

She glanced up at him, her eyes brimming with unshed tears. "I'll call you."

She reached out and pulled the door closed. He lost sight of the cab as it was swallowed up by the busy London streets. Cash stared into the distance and tried to deal with what he'd seen. In a split second, his life had changed again. Why had she progressed this far into her pregnancy without letting him know he was going to be a father? Did she hate him that much? If she couldn't tell him something as important as this, he could only imagine how much he'd hurt her.

He had a lot of making up to do, but whatever it took, he'd do it. He still struggled to connect with the person he'd been before the accident, but this baby could be the catalyst that helped him reach the man inside. He missed that man more than he thought possible. But not as much as he missed her.

At least he'd passed another test that night. He'd managed not to break Paul's nose for daring to lay a finger on his girl.

Dr Bauer would definitely call that progress.

19

Tally twisted the phone over and over in her hand and then cleaned the screen by rubbing it on her jeans. She needed to stop procrastinating, but plucking up the courage to call Cash was proving difficult, despite the fact that this time he'd be expecting her call.

He'd want to know why she hadn't told him about the baby, and she didn't know what to tell him. Pete's warnings and Em's insistence that Cash had a right to know seemed obvious now. Why had she stubbornly dug her heels in and refused to share the news with him? Was it to punish him? Had she chosen to keep impending fatherhood a secret as a way to get her own back? If she had, that would make her a terrible mother.

She sighed, tossed the phone on the table, and allowed her head to flop back against the sofa. She stared at the ceiling. He'd looked so good the night before that it had taken every bit of her willpower not to leap from the cab straight into his arms. The five-month gap since she'd seen him hadn't dulled the intensity of her love for him one little bit. If anything, the enforced separation had honed it, sharpened the edges, causing her insides to churn with need. And all that despite how appallingly he'd treated her.

She gritted her teeth and picked up her phone once more. Her finger hovered over his name. Putting this off would not make it any easier in the long run. And knowing Cash, if she didn't call, he'd track her down to Em's new place, and she didn't want him to know where she was living yet.

She pressed Dial.

"Hello."

Her breath hitched, and her chest prickled. "Hi, it's Tally."

"Hi, sweetness."

Tally ground her teeth. "Don't call me that."

"Sorry." A pause. "Force of habit." More silence. "Can I come and see you?"

"No," she said firmly. "Why don't we meet at the same place you were the other night?"

"Which night?"

"The night you were photographed pawing that woman." A low blow, but she wanted him to hurt as much as she hurt. If she could wound him, maybe her pain would be a little easier to bear.

Cash hissed a breath. "Not every picture tells a story."

"Do you have a trope of lines you trot out whenever the situation fits? I seem to remember you using that one before."

"And I was proved innocent then too. Have you perhaps thought you may be a little too quick to believe everything you see or hear?"

Now it was Tally's turn to suck in a breath. "This was a terrible idea. Nothing's changed."

"Wait," Cash said as she pulled the phone from her ear, ready to hang up. "I'm sorry. Rail on me as much as you need to. I deserve it, and so much more. But give me one thing."

"What?"

"Meet with me. Surely you owe me that, especially after keeping something as important as a baby from me."

An ache started in her chest, rapidly growing outwards. She struggled to catch her breath. He was hitting back with his own low blows. "Fine," she eventually managed to say.

"If you don't want me to come to you, shall we meet at Rupe's place?"

"Is he there?"

"Yes, but I promise it will be you and me. Alone."

"I saw him," she said in a low voice, sorrow prevalent in her tone.

"Yes, he mentioned it."

"I was horrible to him. Will you apologise for me?"

Cash chuckled. "No need. He has a hide like a rhinoceros. You must at least remember that."

Tally's lips twitched. "Still, I treated him terribly."

"If it makes you feel better, I'll pass on your apologies."

"It would. Thank you."

The line went silent for a few seconds until Cash said, "So when are you coming?"

Tally let out a soft sigh. Delaying the inevitable would only make things worse. She glanced at her watch. "I can be there within the hour."

"I'll be waiting."

TALLY PAID the taxi driver and climbed out of the cab. She stood in front of Rupe's place, so familiar and yet so strange at the same time. She smoothed her skirt and pulled her ponytail tight. The strap on her handbag had fallen from her shoulder. She shoved it back into place and rang the bell.

As prepared as she had been to face Cash, nothing quite primed her for the way her heart raced, her stomach clenched, and heat spread through her core the minute he opened the door. He looked good. Better than good. Time seemed meaningless as they stared at each other before he broke the spell by stepping back.

"Come in. It's good to see you."

"Thank you." She sidled past, making sure she didn't touch him, even though all she wanted to do was climb up his body and kiss him until the hurt disappeared. But she needed to remain aloof. It was her only leverage to maintain control.

"Go through to the kitchen. I've made some coffee," he said, waving his hand to show her the way, even though she could find Rupe's kitchen with her eyes shut. She tried not to think about her first time there, when Cash had pinned her up against the kitchen cupboards and kissed her. He'd been angry that day, his kiss meant to punish rather than pleasure, but that hadn't stopped the thrill she'd felt as his mouth had touched hers for the first time.

"Good memories," Cash said, correctly reading her mind.

She lifted her eyes to his. "Yes."

He opened the fridge and took out some cream, poured a little into two mugs, and topped them up with freshly brewed coffee. The strong, chocolaty bitterness was pleasing to her nose as she sniffed deeply.

"You still love the smell, then?" Cash said, pushing a steaming mug towards her.

"Yes."

"Good. I wondered, you know, whether..." He nodded at her stomach. "Whether hormones may have changed that."

"Not that. But definitely some things." She smiled a little. "Believe it or not, I can't stand the taste of ice cream."

Cash waggled his eyebrows in mock horror. "Surely not."

Tally smiled at the warm laughter in his eyes. This was the Cash she loved, the man she knew. "See what you've done to me."

His face crumpled, and the momentary lightness between them evaporated. "Why didn't you tell me?"

The speed at which he cut to the chase caused a sickly feeling to grow in her gut. There was the question she'd been struggling to answer, both for herself and for Em and Pete when they'd pressed. And then, like an epiphany, it came to her.

She blinked slowly and then met his gaze. "You told me you didn't love me anymore. I didn't want you to feel trapped, like you had to be with me out of a sense of duty or pity." She shrugged. "So I kept it from you."

Cash sucked in a breath, making a hissing noise through his teeth. "God, I'm sorry."

"For what? Falling out of love with me? It happens all the time. There's not much you can do when the feeling has gone."

He raised his hands to his face and scrubbed hard. When he dropped them, his shoulders sagged, and his eyes held so much pain and sorrow that Tally's heart squeezed.

"I never stopped loving you."

Her knees trembled, and she gripped the kitchen countertop as her world folded in on itself. He'd been so convincing, and yet... he'd been lying? "But you said—"

"Never mind what I said. I was so angry, out of control, bitter at the unfairness of it all. Of how a random accident had taken from me the second most valuable thing in my life. When I threw that vase, I knew I had to make you go because if I didn't, I couldn't be sure the next thing I hit out with wouldn't have been my fist."

Tally gasped as Cash's words sank in. "You were going to hit me?"

"I don't know." He shook his head slowly. "I wasn't seeing straight. I've never felt fury like that in my life. Uncontrolled, scary as shit. But I knew you. I knew if I couldn't convince you I didn't love you anymore, you'd stick around to the bitter end. If I'd laid a finger on you, I wouldn't have been able to live with myself." He gave her an agonised expression. "So I did the only thing I could think of."

"Pushed me away," Tally whispered.

"Yes."

"Oh, Cash." Tally shook her head, regret making her stomach knot. She lifted her hands in the air and then let them fall.

"I did it for you, for us."

She closed her eyes briefly. "How's your hand? Can you play yet?"

"Not quite, but my physio says I'm making good progress. Maybe in a few months, I will be well enough to get back on court, although whether I'll ever reach the top again…" He let the words fade, as though speaking them aloud was too painful, too scary.

Tally narrowed her eyes. "Then what's changed?"

"I spent a few months in Germany at a mental health clinic near Hamburg. Me, seeing a shrink. Can you imagine?" He gave a small smile and a slight shake of his head. "They taught me how to control the anger through various coping techniques. They convinced me that the way I feel isn't my fault. It isn't the same as my father—more like a symptom of the accident. I'm not unique in that, but Dr Bauer, the psychiatrist I've been seeing, thinks I've made pretty incredible progress."

Tally rubbed her forehead. "So why didn't you come to see me when you got back? Why was it only a chance meeting that I'm here at all?"

Cash swept a hand down the back of his head. "The meeting last night may have been chance, but I was coming to see you anyway. Ask Rupe if you don't believe me. I carried out a little test, and once I was satisfied I'd passed, then I knew it was safe for you to be around me again."

Tally frowned. "Test?"

Cash sipped his coffee. "I reached out to a woman I used to see quite a bit of before I met you. She was a… regular companion whenever I was in London, but I never did like to spend much time with her. She always got on my nerves."

Tally winced as she figured out what "regular companion" actually meant. *His fuck buddy.*

"I knew if I wanted to make sure you were safe with me, I had to test my control on someone I was easily annoyed by. Suze was the best person I could think of. She's a nice woman, but dear God, she'd test the patience of a fucking saint. When I managed to survive a whole evening without feeling the urge to punch her, I knew I was cured—at least enough to control my anger. That meant I could see you again. If I hadn't bumped into you on the street last night, I would have come looking."

"Did you sleep with her?" The words were out of Tally's mouth before she could stop them. She dropped her head and steeled herself for an affirmative answer that would rip apart what was left of her ravaged heart.

"No."

Her head snapped up. "Oh."

"I haven't been interested in other women since I first kissed you right here in Rupe's kitchen. How could I? You ruined me for anyone else. After being with you, another woman would be like scoffing spam when you're used to dining on caviar."

A slow smile spread across Tally's face. "That must be killing you."

Cash raised an eyebrow, and then he grinned. "Never knew blue balls could be so painful. Especially as I lost you and my wanking hand at the same time."

Tally giggled. "Only you, Cash."

The smile drained from his eyes. "I've missed your laugh."

Her gaze locked onto his. "I haven't had much to laugh about lately."

Cash put his cup of coffee on the kitchen island and moved closer. Raising his hand tentatively, he tucked a stray lock of hair behind her ear. "Me either."

"So what happens now?"

"I don't know. One day at a time. I want to be there for you and the baby, but I'm not stupid. I know it's a long road back for us."

"What if we don't get there?"

Cash flinched, his grey eyes dark and troubled. "I can't think like that. I've said some terrible things that can't be unsaid. Treated you so very badly." His voice broke. "But if you let me, I will spend the rest of my life making it up to you."

Tears welled in Tally's eyes, but before they spilled over her lids, the baby gave an almighty kick. Her son or daughter certainly knew how to distract her at the most poignant of times. She put her hand over her belly, tears turning to smiles.

"The baby's kicking. Want to feel?"

With a rapt look on his face, Cash nodded. Tally took hold of his hand and placed it on her stomach. The minute she did, the baby kicked again.

"Feel that?"

"Yeah. Wow." His smile was broad, a delighted gleam in his eye. "Does it hurt?"

"No. It's sort of like butterflies. Looks a bit weird, though, like a scene out of *Alien*."

Cash laughed as he kept his hand in place, but the baby had stopped kicking.

"Show's over," Tally said. "At least for now."

He immediately dropped his hand, choosing instead to hold his arm close to his body and rub his palm up and down his forearm. She'd never seen him look so insecure, so uncertain of what his next move should be. She took a step towards him and closed her hand over his, stilling him. She brushed her thumb against skin that was softer than she remembered. His eyes briefly met hers before he dropped his head and stared at where their hands connected.

"I'm so sorry, baby."

A rush of love raced through her body, and the hairs on the

back of her neck stood up straight. Whatever had gone before, she needed him. Wanted him. He was the only man for her.

She wrapped her hands around his neck and tucked her head under his chin. His arms snaked around her waist, and he held her close.

"Let's look back only when it helps us move forward," she said.

He cradled her cheek. The familiar, tender touch left her breathless, and she tilted her head back so she could look at him.

"You're giving us a chance?" he asked.

"It's not a choice. Not for me. I need you. This baby needs you. I still love you."

He closed his eyes slowly, and when he opened them they were brimming with emotion. He began to cry, silent tears that mirrored the way she felt. Those salty tears were testament to the sadness and sorrow he must have carried around with him these past months while he fought a private battle—one he hadn't dared allow her to be a part of.

She wiped away his tears as her own began to fall. He touched his forehead to hers, and they silently cried together.

20

C ash waved away the overattentive waiter and held out a chair for Natalia. He sat opposite her and picked up a menu. "I'll order for us."

Natalia smiled. "Nothing changes."

"Oh, sorry. Do you want to choose?"

She rolled her eyes. "Cash, stop."

He frowned. "Stop what?"

"Treading on eggshells. I want the old Cash back. That's the one I fell in love with. I never thought I'd say this, but I miss the grumpy Irish git."

His lips twitched, even though he tried for a look of offence. "I was not grumpy."

"Yes, you were. Grumpy and fierce and in control. And pretty damned wonderful." She rested a hand on top of his. "Just be yourself, okay?"

"Careful what you wish for," he said, leaning back in his chair. "Fine, I'll order, but is there anything my son or daughter has taken a dislike to?"

As he spoke the words, a wave of pride and exhilaration rushed through him. He was going to have a child with a woman who'd changed everything for him, despite him putting her through hell. Christ, he was a lucky bastard.

"Ice cream as I mentioned, which I'm really pissed off about, and asparagus." She pulled a face. "Not so bothered about that."

Cash laughed. "Okay, no asparagus. At least you can still eat crème brulée."

"You remembered," she said softly.

"Some things are too important to forget. Like this." He reached around the back of his neck and unhooked the thin chain that held her engagement ring. "I know it's way too soon to be thinking about this, but I wanted you to know I still had it. When I was at my lowest in Hamburg, this ring kept me going. One day, when the time is right, I want to give it back to you."

"Oh, Cash." Her eyes glistened as he refastened the chain around his neck.

"So tell me, what have you been doing these past few months?"

She sipped some water. "I spent some time in Greece."

His eyebrows shot up. "Really? Whereabouts?"

"Safome." She chuckled when he gave her a confused look. "It's a small island not too far from Rhodes. I helped out in a café, feeding refugees."

His forehead creased. "Jesus. After all this time, you still have the ability to surprise me. What made you come back?"

She glanced at her hand cradling her stomach. "This one. When I found out I was pregnant, all I wanted to do was come home."

He nodded in understanding. "Why Greece?"

She chewed at the inside of her cheek, and he repressed a smile. Some habits never changed. "Because we'd never been there. I needed to be in a place that wouldn't remind me of us." She gave a glimmer of a smile. "Except it didn't matter. In the end, I discovered you can't escape yourself. I couldn't get you out of here." She tapped a finger against her chest. "Nor here," she said, touching her temple.

Cash was hit with a wave of regret so strong his breath caught in his throat. "I wish I could have dealt with this differently—"

Natalia held up her hand. "Remember, we agreed to stop looking back on bad memories."

Cash blinked slowly. He did not deserve this woman. She'd always been a better person than he was, and as a consequence, she made him a better man.

"Yes, we did," he said, lifting her hand to his mouth. As his lips touched her soft skin, a blast of desire made his stomach clench. He withdrew, and as his gaze met hers, he saw his feelings mirrored in her eyes.

"How's Rachael?" she said, breaking eye contact as she laid her napkin over her knees.

"Really good. She's missed you. She gave me such a hard time in the beginning, nagged me to contact you, but you know how stubborn I am."

Natalia raised her eyebrows. "You, stubborn? Surely not."

Cash laughed. "To be fair, she can't complain. I get it from her."

"Does she know about the baby?"

He rubbed his fingertips over his lips. "Not yet. I wanted to make sure you were okay with me telling her."

"Of course I am. She's going to be a grandma."

Cash paused as the waiter arrived with their food. "Not sure how she'll feel about the title, but she's going to be thrilled about the baby."

Natalia picked up her fork and attacked her food with enthusiasm. Cash repressed a smile.

"Let's call her soon."

Cash nodded. "How did Pete take the news?"

"He's been great," she said, her mouth half-full. "Very supportive. So has Em."

Cash blew out a breath. "I guess I'm persona non grata again."

Natalia shook her head. "Actually, no. Neither of them agreed with my decision not to tell you I was pregnant. They've both had periods of nagging me about it. Em has been particularly vocal."

"She looked pretty pissed off with me the other night in the taxi."

"She went into mother-hen mode, that's all. When we first split up, she was insistent I should go back to Ireland and talk to you, work it out."

Cash grimaced. "I'm glad you didn't. I had shit to work through, and the last thing I needed was to be even viler to you. I have enough guilt to deal with as it is."

She wagged her finger. "Uh, uh, uh. Happy thoughts."

He chuckled. "Yes, ma'am."

They finished their meal, and Cash slipped an arm around her waist as they strolled back to the car. He helped her inside and reached across to clip her seatbelt into place. She giggled at the familiarity. Cash walked around the car and climbed into the driver's seat.

"Let's get you home. You must be tired."

"I am, but before that, can you do me a favour?"

"Name it."

"I want to see Rupe."

∼

CASH PULLED up outside Rupe's house and twisted around in his seat.

"I'm trying not to be jealous about your excitement at seeing my best friend."

Tally gave a faint smile. "You know, one of the worst things about you and I splitting up was everyone else I lost at the same time as you. Your mum, Rupe, Anna. They're family. I felt like half of me was missing."

A flash of guilt crossed Cash's face. "I never thought of it like that."

She placed a hand on his arm. "I didn't tell you to make you feel bad, but when I bumped into Rupe on the street last week, I was so terrified he'd see I was pregnant that I forgot to be thrilled he was there. All I could think about was getting away from him as quickly as possible. Now that I don't have to hide anything, I'm eager to see him."

"Then let's go."

He tucked her hand inside his and pushed open the door to Rupe's place. Music blared from the living room, and Cash led her in that direction. Rupe was sitting in front of a roaring fire, a tumbler of whisky in his hand as he bobbed his head along to the music.

"Hey, stranger," Tally said.

Rupe jumped. Clearly he hadn't heard them come in. He set his drink down and leaped to his feet, his arms outstretched.

Tally threw herself into his embrace. "I'm so sorry about the other day," she whispered in his ear.

He pulled back and studied her face. "No apologies. Although I am considering getting glasses. Completely missed you had a passenger on board."

Tally laughed. "I hid it pretty well. One of the benefits of winter—big coats." She turned to Cash. "Would you mind making me a coffee?"

He raised an eyebrow. "Trying to get rid of me?"

"Yes," she said, waving her hand. "Now, scoot."

When Cash disappeared into the hallway, she took Rupe's hands and guided him to the sofa. "How have you been?"

"Terrible. I nearly swapped him for you."

Regret swarmed through her. "I'm sorry I didn't get in touch. I should have, but I was scared you'd tell Cash where I was, and I needed the clean break. It was the only way I could cope with losing him."

"You had Emmalee well trained. That girl would stand up well to torture."

Tally grinned. "She said exactly the same thing."

"Where were you?"

"Greece."

Rupe let out a low whistle. "Blimey. No wonder I didn't bump into you in Waitrose. When did you get back?"

"In January. I hadn't planned on coming home, but when I found out I was pregnant, I needed to be surrounded by familiar things."

"Makes sense."

She threw her head back. "Has he had it rough?"

Rupe nodded, concern etched in the line of his jaw. "Very. He hides it behind the usual Cash bluster, but he's been to hell and back. Don't underestimate the personal struggle he went through in Germany, Tal. The only thing that kept him going was the hope he'd one day be well enough to try to win you back, but at the same time, he was terrified you wouldn't want him."

She blew out a frustrated breath. "On the one hand, I know why he did it. On the other, I want to lamp him. We were getting married, and that means for better or worse, yet at the first sign of trouble, he pushed me away."

"For your safety."

Tally tilted her head to one side. "Do you think he would have been violent towards me?"

"No, I don't," Rupe said. "But it doesn't matter what I think. Cash was convinced you weren't safe around him, so he sacrificed his own happiness to protect you. That's how much he loves you."

She chewed the inside of her cheek. "How's he coping without tennis?"

"Have you asked him?"

She folded her arms. "I'm asking you."

Rupe picked up his whiskey, swirling the amber liquid around the heavy glass tumbler. "He's not."

"He said the physio is going well."

"It is. At first he had no grip. Couldn't hold a toothbrush, let alone a tennis racket, but he's definitely getting the strength back. It's a slow process, though, and you know Cash. Likes instant gratification."

"I don't want him hiding things from me."

"He's always been overprotective where you're concerned. You need to push him. Don't get me wrong—he's been working hard, but his entire focus has been on getting you back. And now he has..." Rupe paused. "Right?"

Tally smiled. "Right."

A look of relief swept across Rupe's face. "Now he can put more energy into his tennis, but he'll need lots of reassurance. His confidence is shot."

"I'll talk to him," Tally said as Cash walked back into the room, holding two cups of coffee.

"My ears are burning," he said, handing one over to her.

"You know what they say about eavesdroppers," Rupe said. "They never hear anything good."

21

"I'm nervous." Natalia worried her bottom lip with her teeth.

Cash pulled the car into a lay-by next to a woodland area. He reached over and gently tugged on her chin. "Stop chewing."

"I can't help it," she said, choosing instead to nibble on her fingernails. "I'm still not sure we should be dropping it on your mum like this. We should have called first."

"No, it's better this way," Cash said with a grin. "We'll be able to see her face."

"And what if she's horrified? Or disappointed?"

"Or thrilled and elated. Seriously, you think for one minute she's going to be anything other than excited about being a grandmother?"

"I don't know."

He unclipped his seat belt before doing the same to hers. "Let's go for a walk. This stress can't be good for the baby."

They headed into the woodland on a well-worn path until they reached the lake in the middle. They'd visited this place a few times when they'd returned from Paris after his accident.

Lilies floated on top of the water, and as they sat on a well-positioned bench that allowed them to take in the view, her shoulders relaxed, and she breathed out a soft sigh.

"Feeling better?" Cash said, weaving a lock of her hair through his fingers.

She nodded. "I love this place."

The weak spring sunshine lit up her face, making her look more beautiful than ever, and Cash caught his breath. Acting on instinct, he cupped her neck with both hands and leaned in. He paused, half expecting her to pull away, but when she parted her lips, he kissed her.

He'd been starved of her for so long. Desire swept through him, and a groan eased from his throat. He moved away from her mouth and trailed kisses across her jaw. She moaned softly, and he captured her mouth once more, his tongue darting inside. Her arms tightened around him, and her fingers burrowed into his hair.

"I've missed you so much," she whispered as his lips locked onto her neck. "But your timing is shit."

He pulled away and gave her a questioning look. "Why?"

She grinned. "Because all I want to do now is go back to your place and take you to bed."

He smiled wickedly. "Mum doesn't actually know we're coming."

She swept her tongue over her lips, making his pulse jump. "As tempting as that thought is, I need to get this over with. I'm not sure my blood pressure can take any further delays."

He stood and helped her to her feet. "You worry too much. Come on, then. Let's go. You'll feel better when it's done."

Five minutes later, Cash parked in the driveway of his mum's house, the same one she'd stayed in all those years she was in a coma after his father had beaten her half to death. After she regained consciousness, Cash had made several offers to move her somewhere else, but she'd refused. And she did seem genuinely happy there.

"Ready?" he said, threading his fingers through Natalia's.

"No," she replied, a glum expression on her face.

"Good," he said, planting a quick kiss on her lips.

He let himself in and headed to the back of the house. Undoubtedly, Mum would be in the garden. Unless it was snowing or pouring with rain, that was where she spent most of her time. He spotted her tending to one of her many borders.

"Shhh," he said to Natalia, raising a finger to his lips. "Stay out of sight."

Natalia played along, standing off to the side behind the curtains as he opened the patio doors.

"Hey, Mum."

Rachael spun around, her face lighting up. "What are you doing here? I thought you were in London." She tugged off her gardening gloves, tossed them aside, and gave him a warm hug.

"I was. But then I got all homesick."

She narrowed her eyes. "What's going on?"

Cash laughed. "Can't hide anything from you, Mother." He glanced over his shoulder and called, "Come on out."

Natalia appeared in the doorway, her footsteps tentative. Rachael froze, her eyes wide as her gaze swept from head to foot, lingering on Natalia's belly, and then a cry fell from her lips. She ran across the garden and swept Natalia into her arms.

"Oh, sweetheart," she said leaning back to give her the once-over. "How far along?"

"Twenty-three weeks."

Rachael hugged her again. "Please tell me you two are back together." When Natalia nodded, a tear slipped down her cheek.

Natalia met Cash's gaze, and he smirked. "Told you," he said.

"Told her what?" Rachael said, dabbing at her face with a tissue.

"She was worried you wouldn't be happy about the baby."

"Not happy? I'm absolutely thrilled."

Cash placed his arm around Natalia's shoulder and kissed her temple. "Can we stop stressing now?"

"I guess," she said with an embarrassed smile.

"Right, let me make some tea," Rachael said. "Tally, sit down. Cash can help me."

Cash followed his mother into the house. "Subtle," he said as soon as they were out of earshot.

Rachael switched the kettle on and turned to face him. "How did this happen?"

"Which bit?" Cash said, grinning. "Surely we don't need to have a birds-and-bees conversation, Mother."

Rachael rolled her eyes. "Very funny, Cash. You could have warned me."

"It was more entertaining this way."

"You are incorrigible," she said, giving him a playful shove. "But I can't tell you how happy I am for you both. Especially with what you've been through these last few months."

"Yeah, it's been rough."

Rachael glanced out of the window, and Cash followed her gaze. Natalia was sitting in a garden chair, head tilted back to catch the warmth from the sun, eyes closed, and a look of pure contentment on her face.

"Don't let her go again, Cash. I doubt you'll win her back a third time."

CASH SWITCHED off the engine and twisted in his seat. Even though his home was only ten minutes from his mother's, Natalia had fallen asleep on the journey back. Her cheeks were flushed, her wrist bent as she rested her head on her hand. Loath to wake her but left with little choice, he grazed her cheek with his fingertips. She muttered something unintelligible under her breath before her eyes fluttered open.

"Hi," he said.

She yawned, stretching her arms above her head. "I fell asleep."

"You did."

"I'm so exhausted these days."

"That's because you're busy growing a human being inside you." He unclipped her belt. "Come on, time for bed."

She smiled a slow, lazy smile as she looked at him through half-opened lids. "Now you're talking."

Cash laughed. "To sleep. For you at least."

"Spoilsport," she said, but she didn't complain when he gathered her in his arms and began walking upstairs.

He hovered outside one of the guest bedrooms on the first floor. Despite Natalia's comment, it didn't feel right to assume anything. He nudged the door open with his foot.

"What are you doing?" she said, cranking one eye open.

"Putting you to bed."

"Not in there, you're not."

"Are you sure?"

Natalia huffed. "Look, you can stand here talking about it, but I'm pretty heavy, and you don't want to put your back out."

He laughed. "You are not heavy."

"Cash, stop procrastinating. I don't want to sleep in there alone. I want to sleep in our bed with you beside me."

His breath hitched when she referred to *our bed*. He'd hated sleeping alone after they'd split last October. And now, once again, he'd be able to wake up next to her.

A soft sigh escaped her lips when he laid her down on their bed. Her eyes fell shut as he removed her shoes and socks. He dug his thumbs into the balls of her feet, the strength in his right thumb weaker than the left, but Natalia didn't seem to notice as she sighed again, louder this time.

"You always were a master at massaging feet," she murmured.

"Gotta be good at something."

She opened her eyes and fixed him with a stare. "Stop it."

He shrugged. "Get some rest. I'll go and grab your suitcase from the car."

He left before she could say anything else. He knew that look —the one that said she was about to go on a rant about his self-deprecating comment. The conversation about tennis was looming, and he was dreading it because he didn't know how he would react. Despite his successful test with Suze, he hadn't yet tested himself with Natalia.

By the time he returned with her case, she was fast asleep, still dressed in her jeans and T-shirt. She looked comfortable enough, so he simply unfastened the top button of her jeans, laid her pyjamas over the foot of the bed in case she woke, and quietly closed the door.

He lit the log burner, poured himself a glass of wine, and put on some music. Since the night he'd found out Natalia was pregnant with his child, he hadn't spent any time alone. Now that he had time to think about what it would mean and how his life was going to change, the most perfect feeling he had ever known swept over him.

Having a baby meant it was time to grow up, and that included putting things right with those who meant the world to Natalia—Pete and Emmalee. He hadn't had a chance to speak with them before he and Natalia had flown to Ireland, and he owed them a direct conversation.

He picked up his phone and called Pete first and then Emmalee. Humbled by their kindness and understanding after he fully explained himself, he acknowledged one more call he needed to make. He clenched and unclenched his right hand. His grip had improved, but he hadn't been working as hard as he could have these last couple of weeks. His desire to play again had always been phenomenal, but now he had the best reason of all: he wanted his son or daughter to be proud of the man he was and the things he'd achieved in life. He didn't want his career to end on a whimper, a result of fate dealing him a blow. He wanted to go out on a high, and on his terms.

He pulled up the right contact information and made the call.

CASH RUBBED sleep from his eyes and rolled over. He stretched out his legs, his eyes snapping open as he connected with someone. For a brief moment, he panicked. Was it Suze or some other faceless woman?

His vision cleared, and his heart began to race. Natalia was fast asleep, one arm thrown over her head. Sometime in the night, she'd swapped jeans and a T-shirt for her pyjamas, but the top had ridden up, revealing her smooth, round stomach. His hand crept forward tentatively, and he touched her belly. The skin was firm around the bump, and a thrill of excitement raced through him. As though sensing he was there, the baby kicked against his hand.

He pressed his lips against her stomach. "Hey," he whispered. "Take it easy in there. Mum's trying to sleep."

"What are you doing?"

A trace of a smile left his lips as he lifted his gaze. "You're awake."

She reached her arms behind her head and stretched. "Were you kissing my belly?"

He gave her a goofy grin. "What if I was?"

"That's weird."

"Not to me." He pushed himself upright. "You hungry?"

"Starving. I'm always starving."

"What do you fancy?"

"You," she said, reaching up for a kiss.

He groaned as her lips touched his, but then he pulled away. "You need to eat."

She narrowed her eyes. "Okay." She began to get up until he stopped her.

"Where do you think you're going? Get back in bed."

"I'm not an invalid," she said, hitting him with a scowl. "Plus, you're a terrible cook, and I want pancakes."

"I can get Anna over here within fifteen minutes."

"You'll do no such thing," she said as she stuffed her feet into slippers. "Besides, my back aches if I spend too much time in bed. I'm better moving around."

As she set off downstairs, Cash held back. He wanted to touch her so badly, but what if he hurt her in some way? But he hadn't missed the narrowed gaze she'd given him at his reluctance to become intimate, and he added that to the other difficult conversation they needed to have.

22

Tally had already mixed the pancake batter when Cash finally joined her in the kitchen. She glanced up as he slid onto a stool at the breakfast bar. Then she returned her attention to beating the mixture, when what she really wanted to do was beat some sense into him. Every time she tried to get close, he'd give in for a moment before pulling away, and she couldn't understand why. Their relationship had always been a physical one, and yet his reticence to become intimate was beginning to grate.

She added a ladleful to the pan, and the liquid sizzled. She turned down the heat a little and began chopping strawberries—well, *pulverising* them, but at least that helped with her irritation.

"Are you ignoring me?" Cash said with a wry grin.

"Yes."

He arched an eyebrow. "Why, what have I done?"

"Nothing."

He laughed. "Bit of a cliché."

She dropped the knife on the chopping board and planted her hands on her hips. "No. An accurate response. You've done precisely nothing."

"Ah," he said, an annoying smirk on his face. "This is because I haven't put out."

"Put out? What are you, sixteen?"

"Sometimes," he said, reaching for her.

She jerked away and turned her back on him. She dug two plates out of the cupboard, even though she thought about getting only one. She was being childish but couldn't seem to stop. It had to be her hormones.

Cash didn't speak as he watched her move about the kitchen, and they ate in silence, although his eyes rarely left her face. When she put her fork down, he stacked their plates and dumped them in the sink.

"Right, that's enough," he said. "I've let you have your little strop. Spit it out, Natalia."

Tally met Cash's gaze, her teeth grazing her bottom lip. She blew a deep breath out through her nose. "Are we only back together because of this baby?"

His eyes smouldered as he stared at her. "Well, I can't answer for you, but from my perspective, no, we're not."

"Okay," she said in a small voice as her shoulders drooped.

He moved around to her side of the table and pulled out the chair adjacent. He picked up her hand and pressed a kiss to her palm. "Talk to me."

"You haven't touched me since we got back together. Is it because I'm fat?"

An expression of horror crossed his face. "You are not fat. You're pregnant."

"Same thing," she said, gazing at the floor.

He put pressure under her chin until she had no alternative but to look at him. "I don't want to ever hear you talking like that again. For fuck's sake. I thought you'd got over the body issues you had when we first met. When will you learn, Natalia? The fact I'm physically attracted to you is only one part of the reason I love you so much."

She chewed the inside of her cheek. "I'm sorry."

He made an irritated noise. "I don't want you to be sorry. I want you to believe me. You're kind, funny, thoughtful, annoying, frustrating, and hot as hell."

She shook her head. "So what's wrong with me?"

He sighed and swept a hand over his beard. "Nothing."

"Then what's going on, Cash? We've been apart for five months. I expected to have to fight you off, and I was looking forward to doing just that."

His eyes slid away from hers. "I'm scared to touch you."

"Why?" When he didn't reply, her stomach clenched with fear. "Tell me."

He looked at her then. "What if I hurt you or the baby?"

She frowned. "How would you hurt us?"

The chair made a scraping sound on the tiled floor as Cash stood and crossed the kitchen. The muscles in his back were visible through his thin grey sweater, and they became taut when he placed his palms on the countertop.

Tally followed, her hand tentatively reaching out to rest on his shoulder. "Cash?" she said in a soft voice.

He turned around, a glimmer of fear flashing in his eyes. He cupped her face and pressed his lips to hers. Briefly—agonisingly briefly. But he didn't completely pull away. His lips were so close that if she leaned in an inch or so, they would touch again.

He shuddered as he breathed out. "I don't have the right words to explain how much I missed you these past months. Baby, I'm so scared that if I start something, I won't be able to stop."

"That's the thing, ace. I don't want you to stop."

He shook his head. "You don't know what you're asking."

She swept her thumb over his bottom lip. "Then show me."

His fisted hands were trembling, and the look he gave her made her knees shake and her skin burn. He was wrong. She knew exactly what she was doing. He needed to prove he had control and could pull back, adjust course when necessary, and she had every intention of pushing him into testing himself. When he remained frozen, she cupped both hands around the back of his neck.

"You're worth the risk," she said, standing on tiptoes until their lips were almost touching.

His breathing was ragged, and a low, tortured groan tumbled from his throat. His kiss, when it came, was far from gentle—and it was exactly what she craved.

His hands moved to her hips, and he gripped hard, pushing her backwards until she hit the wall. His tongue surged inside her mouth, probing, demanding, owning. Her lungs burned as she dragged her mouth from his and gasped for air. He manoeuvred her slightly, pinning her in place with his hips, which left his hands free to roam. He cupped her breasts and trailed soft kisses over her neck. She moaned softly.

"These are definitely bigger," he whispered in her ear. "I approve." He bent his knees and swept her up into his arms. "Promise you'll tell me if this gets to be too much."

A surge of desire took her breath away. "I promise," she said, the prospect of what was to come making her insides twist.

She wrapped her arms around his neck as he carried her upstairs. Even though she was heavier now that she was pregnant, Cash didn't seem to notice. He placed her back on her feet at the side of their bed. The sheets were still rumpled from the night of sleeping.

His eyes locked onto hers, and he trailed the tip of his index finger across her cheek and down her neck and allowed it to linger between her breasts. He deftly unfastened her pyjama top and slid it down her arms, tossing it aside.

"You're so beautiful," he said, his voice hitching.

He lowered to his knees and tugged down her pyjama bottoms. She rested her hands on his shoulders for support as she stepped out of them. Her heartbeat thrummed in her ears, and her breath came in short pants. After all his concern, she'd expected him to rip her clothes off and take her quickly. Instead, he was seducing her, taking his time, savouring every moment.

His mouth was level with her belly, and he pressed a kiss to it. "Hold on tight, buddy," he said, his eyes firmly on hers. "Your mum and I are about to have some fun."

Her skin prickled with anticipation as Cash slowly got to his feet. Crossing his arms, he gripped the bottom of his sweatshirt and pulled it over his head. He'd always been in great shape, and he clearly hadn't let his fitness slip over the last five months, despite not playing tennis professionally during that time. He shucked off his sweat pants and was already naked. Her gaze fell to his erection, and a swell of desire swept through her.

"Turn around," he ordered, his voice soft and gentle.

She complied, apprehension making her heart race even faster. Her shoulders tensed as she waited for him to touch her. Seconds passed, and still she didn't feel his hands on her skin.

"What are you doing?" she whispered.

His warm breath tickled her ear. "Admiring the view." He touched her then, cool hands tracking over burning skin as he rediscovered every inch of her body. His mouth followed the path his hands traced, and Tally's knees trembled as desire swept through her.

"Don't move." Cash gathered up their pillows and made a mountain out of them. "Lean on those," he said, his lips brushing her ear.

She bent over the pillows, using them for support. Cash swept a hand down her leg, coming to rest behind her right knee. His thumb brushed back and forth, and when his lips replaced his thumb, a spike of need hit hard.

"Cash, please," she said, her voice muffled in the pillows.

"Shush." He rubbed a hand over her backside and nudged her legs apart. His fingers began exploring, and when he slipped one inside her, she groaned loudly.

"God, I've missed this. I've missed you."

"Just the beginning, baby," he murmured. He slipped a second finger inside her, and her hips flexed involuntarily. "More?"

"Stop teasing me."

He chuckled. "Don't spoil my fun, sweetness."

He continued to torture her with his hands, his mouth, his tongue. She was close to climax, and it was coming fast. Five months without his touch, and yet her body remembered everything. Like a volcano about to erupt, a wave built inside her, and then she exploded. She squeezed her eyes closed. Stars flashed behind her lids.

"Shit," she muttered as her climax went on and on. Her arms gave out, and she collapsed onto the pillows.

Cash crawled up her body, keeping his weight completely off her, and yet, she was still cocooned by him, could feel the warmth of his body along her back. He brushed her hair away from the nape of her neck, and she trembled as he ran the tip of his tongue over her damp skin.

"I love how you taste," he murmured as he fastened his lips to the space between her neck and shoulder.

Her body cooled as he lifted himself away from her. He ran the palm of his hand from the top of her spine to her bottom, and she shuddered. His hands gripped her hips, and he eased her onto her knees, leaving her chest on top of the mountain of pillows and her backside in the air. She turned her face to the side, her breath coming in gasps.

Cash pushed himself inside, just an inch, gradually stretching, letting her body familiarise and adapt to him as he moved in deeper.

"Okay?"

The single word came out strangled, and she knew he was struggling to hold himself together.

"I won't break, Cash," she said, pushing herself backwards onto him, encouraging him to drive farther in.

He groaned, his fingers digging into her hips as he thrust once. "I don't want to hurt you or the baby."

"You won't. Go for it, ace. Lose yourself, and take me with you."

Her words broke the last of his resolve, and he let go, his thrusts coming faster and faster, their connected bodies slapping together.

He changed positions, leaning over her again, his palms flat on either side of her head, but he didn't relent on pace. She pushed back as he thrust in, and when she clenched her inner muscles, he groaned.

"Shit, you're killing me." He lifted her so she was virtually sitting on his lap, her thighs spread at either side of his. With his hands firmly on her hips, he lifted and lowered her, his timing perfect, and when his fingers teased the tight bundle of nerves at her core, she knew a second climax was mere seconds away.

"Holy fuck," he muttered, and as he came, he clasped a hand over her stomach. The protective move set her off once more, her body trembling with the physical effort of another momentous orgasm.

Neither moved as their breathing slowly returned to normal. Cash's body was slick with sweat that mingled with the dampness of her skin. His hand remained on her belly, and he rubbed in a circular motion. After a minute or so, he pulled out of her and tossed the pillows back in place.

She took hold of his arm and nestled it around her waist as a soft sigh fell from her lips. "Cash?"

"Yeah?"

"I knew you'd never hurt us. Time to start trusting your recovery, babe."

23

Cash paused. With his hand resting on her hip, he couldn't stop the involuntary squeeze. He'd struggled to keep himself in check, more than he wanted her to know. He'd had to constantly remind himself to think of her throughout their lovemaking. His desperate need to be inside her after such a long absence had almost brought back his previous selfishness. With his own needs and desires hard to ignore, he'd been terrified of simply fucking her. You didn't fuck the woman you loved. You cherished her, looked after her, put her needs before your own.

"Cash?" Her voice sounded tentative, even a little afraid. She twisted in his arms until their faces were inches apart. Her deep-blue eyes locked onto his. "Ace?"

"Are you okay?" he said, lifting his palm to her face. He caressed her cheek. Her skin was so soft beneath his hand.

"Of course I am. Why wouldn't I be?"

"I wasn't too rough?"

"Would I sound like a slut if I said not rough enough?" she said with a giggle.

He arched an eyebrow. "That sounds like a challenge."

"Maybe it is."

His stomach tightened, and his cock twitched. "Careful. Not only you to think about." He rested a hand on her stomach. "Did you hang on like I told you, buddy?"

Natalia laughed. "By her fingernails."

His eyebrows shot up. "Her?"

"Oh, I don't know what we're having. But it's better than *it*."

"Do you want to know?"

She shook her head. "Got to be something to look forward to after God knows how many hours of labour followed by all that pushing."

Cash flinched. He was apprehensive about the birth already. His knowledge about childbirth was zero, but he did know it was fucking painful.

"Hey," she said, gently nudging his chin upwards. "Don't worry. Millions of women do it every day, and they go back for more."

"Since when did you become an expert on reading me?"

She tilted her head to the side. "Oh, ace," she said with the special smile she kept only for him. "You can't hide anything from me."

He reached out and tucked a lock of hair behind her ear. "You'll let me be there? At the birth?"

"Who else's balls am I going to be able to squeeze when I'm in agony?"

He laughed then. It felt good. It had been a long time since he'd properly laughed, and a lightness spread through his chest. "Remind me to dig out my old rugby jock strap."

She nodded sagely. "I'll make sure it's packed."

He folded his arms around her, holding her close to his body. "When the fuck did I get so lucky?"

She rested her chin on his chest, her eyes searching his. "When are you going to play again?"

He ran a jerky hand through his hair at the abrupt change of subject. He'd known she'd start pressing the discussion soon, although he'd hoped to avoid talking about it for a little while. "I'm not sure."

She sat up, crossed her legs, and folded her arms. "We're having this conversation whether you like it or not."

He raised an eyebrow. "Is that so?"

"Yes."

He expelled a heavy breath. "I'm not ready." As she began to interrupt him, he placed his index finger against her lips. "But I am starting physio again."

"When?"

"I called. Last night when you were asleep. I'm booked in for this afternoon."

"Good." She gave him a warm smile. "I'm coming with you."

"I hoped you'd say that," he said, unable to stop his gaze sliding over her nakedness now that they'd got the awkward conversation out of the way. He expected her to cover up, especially with her earlier comment about being fat, but she didn't. Instead, she leaned back on her palms and uncrossed her legs. She parted her thighs, her eyes sparkling with mischief.

"Okay, ace, let's see what else you've got in the tank."

Cash grimaced as he completed his final exercise. His fingers were stiff, but from what he'd learned in Germany, that was a normal reaction to hard work. Natalia was sitting off to the side, an anxious expression on her face as she watched him push through the discomfort.

"How was that?" Liam, his physio, asked.

He flexed his right hand. "Difficult but nowhere near as bad as a few weeks ago."

"You're making great strides," Liam said. "Even in the couple of weeks we've been working together, I can see a huge improvement."

"Do you think he's ready to play again?" Natalia asked, earning a sharp glance from Cash. She waved away his annoyance with a flick of her wrist.

"I think that would be a good idea. A small tournament maybe. Nothing too strenuous. It will give us a good benchmark of where you are."

Natalia flashed a triumphant look in his direction. Cash withheld the urge to call her out. Regardless of whether he was ready physically, his reticence had more to do with his mental state. He was terrified of returning to competitive tennis—all those people watching, waiting, expecting him to fail. When he stepped back on court, he had to be certain that he was playing to win, not to simply make up the numbers.

"We'll see," he said.

"It's up to you," Liam said. "But you are physically ready. It depends on whether you're willing to take a risk."

Cash dug his fingernails into his palms as a flare of anger bubbled inside him. He'd decide when. Not Liam, who didn't have a fucking clue what it was like to live inside Cash's head. Liam could do his day of work and then go home and forget all about Cash and his problems.

"Can you give us a minute?" Natalia said.

Cash's head snapped up. He wasn't sure for a second whether Natalia was asking for time alone with Liam. But then he realised she was asking Liam to leave them alone.

"Of course," Liam said.

Cash marched over to the window as the door clicked shut. His chest rose and fell with the effort of keeping himself in check, and he called on Dr Bauer's mantra. *Controlling anger is a skill. The more you do it, the better you become.*

Cash instructed himself to relax, and he took a few deep

breaths. He counted to ten, and when he reached the end, he realised Natalia hadn't spoken a word.

He looked over his shoulder. She hadn't moved. Her legs were crossed, and she was fiddling with a paperclip, feeding it through her fingers, her attention utterly focused.

"What?" he said.

She ignored him. Instead, she tossed the paperclip back on the desk and stood, stretching out her back. Despite the churning in his abdomen, he began to smile.

"I know what you're doing."

She met his gaze, an innocent expression on her face. "What's that, ace?"

"I'm not ready."

"I know you're not."

Taken aback, he frowned. "Then what's this all about?"

She sauntered over, coming to a halt right in front of him. "You're not ready because you'll *never* be ready. If you wait for the moment when you feel prepared to take such a huge step, you'll be sixty and looking back with a head full of regrets. I won't let you be that person. If I have to forcibly drag you on court with a chain around your neck, I will."

He chuckled. "Kinky."

She moved into his body and wrapped her arms around his waist, her head resting on his chest.

"You have to do this, ace. I love you no matter what, but I *know* you. Not until you claw your way back to the top will you truly begin to put the anger behind you. Yes, you have coping mechanisms, and they're working—really well. But the catalyst is always the same. Your one true love. Tennis."

He stepped back a little so he could see her better. "You're my one true love."

A trace of a smile left her lips. "Okay, your other significant love."

He dragged a hand through his hair. "I don't know, babe."

She gripped his upper arms. "I do. What about Houston on the fourth of April? A two-fifty. You like playing in the States."

"No. I don't want you flying long haul, and I can't do this without you."

She scrunched her nose up. "Then it'll have to be Estoril on the twenty-fifth. I don't fancy Bucharest the week before."

He laughed. "You always did have the tour dates memorised."

She tapped her temple. "That's right, ace. All up here. So?"

His mouth creased as he thought about it. "That might work. It'll give me time on the practice court too. Are you going to be okay to fly?"

"I think I'm fine up to thirty-odd weeks. I'll check with the doctor."

His stomach somersaulted. "Then I guess the decision is made. I'd better get myself a coach."

24

Tally stuck her head down the toilet and heaved. With nothing left in her stomach, all she did was bring up foul-tasting bile. This wasn't morning sickness—she was well past that. No, her nausea was caused by nerves. Since she'd persuaded Cash to return to tennis after nine months out, she was terrified of what it would do to his re-emerging confidence if things didn't go well.

She'd been so happy to see him on court again. Even watching him practice had given her the tingles, and his improvement over the last four weeks had been nothing short of miraculous. When he completed his final practice session the previous night, she almost forgot he'd been out of the game for so long. His ranking might have been low, but that was only because he hadn't played competitively for so long. It didn't mean his talent was gone.

His talent was very much present.

Tally flushed the toilet and wiped her mouth with some tissue. She dug around in her bag and found a packet of mints. She slipped one in her mouth, fixed her hair, and headed outside.

She found Brad pacing and rubbing the back of his neck so hard he'd probably taken the skin off. He spun around when the door clicked shut, and gave her a worried smile.

"Are you okay?" He held out a bottle of water. "You look terribly green. Shall I get Cash?"

Tally patted his arm. "I'm fine. No need to bother Cash with this, right, Brad?" She twisted the cap off the water and took a sip.

His eyebrows pinched together. "I don't know. He'll bloody kill me if anything happens to you or the baby."

"Nothing is going to happen to either of us." She sighed and rubbed her forehead. "I'm nervous for him, that's all. I puked because I'm shit scared."

Brad put his arms around her. His solid frame felt so good, and she leaned on him, absorbing his emotional as much as physical support.

"He's going to be fine. I'm so glad I could spare the time to help him back on his feet. He's playing great, Tally, especially considering how long he's been out. One step at a time. Agreed?"

She nodded. "Agreed."

"Right, I gotta go get our boy. You okay finding your way courtside?"

"No problem. I'll see you shortly."

As Brad walked in the direction of the locker room, Tally headed outside and slid into her seat. She dropped her sunglasses in place and glanced around the court. Day one of a two-fifty tournament would usually see the stadium a third full, especially for the early game.

But not that day. The stadium was packed, the crowd buzzing —an energy driven, no doubt, by Cash's first appearance at a tournament in almost ten months.

The crowd began cheering. Tally fixed her eyes on Cash as he walked onto court. She fidgeted in her seat, and nervous tension bit at her insides, but as she watched him go through his familiar set-up routine, a crumb of hope bubbled up inside.

He *had* to do well.

"You okay?" Brad slipped into the seat next to her. "You're still a bit green."

"I'm so glad you're here," she said, squeezing his hand.

"Me too. He's got this."

Tally nodded in direct contradiction to how she felt inside. She didn't know whether to chew the inside of her cheek or nibble on her fingernails. The baby was doing cartwheels in her belly, no doubt picking up on her anxiety. She rubbed her bump in an attempt to calm both the baby and herself.

Cash removed a racket from his bag and glanced up at the players' box. The wink he gave her was brief, but she caught it all the same. It was his way of telling her he was okay. She blew out a heavy breath and steeled herself for what was to come.

In the first set, Cash made too many unforced errors, and it went to a tiebreak, which he lost seven points to two. Tally's nervousness increased. She jiggled her knees until Brad laid a hand on them, stilling her.

"Relax. This isn't good for you or the baby."

"He has to win. He has to win," she muttered under her breath as Cash got ready for set two. He tossed his racket into his left hand and flexed the fingers on his right.

"He's struggling with his hand," she whispered to Brad. "Maybe this was too soon."

"It's bound to be a bit sore. He's been on court a lot these past few weeks, and playing a match will be more intense than any practice session. Stop worrying. He's tough."

Cash stepped it up in the second set, and when he won it six-four, Tally leaped to her feet. Their eyes met, and she smiled tentatively. He winked again, more obviously this time. It was exactly what she needed, and a calm settled over her as she retook her seat.

Cash made no mistakes in the third set, and his confidence grew with every hit of the ball. He trounced his opponent six games to one. He'd won. The crowd went crazy, Cash clearly the favourite. As Tally watched him sign balls and toss them into the crowd, he might never have been away. Relief wasn't a strong enough word to describe her feelings as Brad led her off court.

CASH WAS in a playful mood when they arrived back at the hotel. It appeared she wasn't the only one relieved at getting that first match out of the way.

"I thought you were going to be sick when I lost that first set." He flopped onto the bed.

Tally hung her bag over the back of a chair. "I did puke before the match. Brad nearly had a heart attack."

Cash sat upright, a deep frown pulling his eyebrows together. "He never said anything. Are you okay?" He held out his arms, beckoning her over.

"I'm fine. I asked Brad not to say anything. You didn't exactly need the worry before the match."

Cash tugged her down beside him. "It's my job to worry about you and this little one." He laid his hand across her stomach.

Tally rolled her eyes. "Come on, ace. Don't go all caveman on me."

Cash moved so quickly Tally barely had time to think before she found herself beneath him, his legs and arms caging her.

"Are you taunting me, McKenzie?"

Tally grinned. "You make it so easy."

Cash arched an eyebrow. "Payback time." He began to tickle her, and she giggled and writhed beneath him, but as quickly as he'd started, he stopped. He drew back and studied her face, his expression sombre.

"What's the matter?"

"I can't lose you again," he said, his voice tinged with fear and sorrow.

Tally reached up and cradled his face, lightly scraping her fingertips through his beard. "You're not going to lose me. We've had our share of bad luck, ace. We have so much to look forward to." She dropped one hand and placed it over her stomach.

Cash settled his hand over hers. "You're right. We do."

25

"Here," Cash said, tossing a room service menu at Natalia. "You pick."

As Natalia rang room service to order their breakfast, Cash drifted over to the window. He flexed his right hand. His joints were stiff. Liam had warned him this might happen. Hours on the practice court followed by four matches on the bounce—it wasn't too surprising his hand felt sore. At least he'd made the final, albeit at a small tournament. But it was a start.

"You can't hide it from me."

Cash glanced down when Natalia laid a hand on his back. His face twisted in a grimace, and he shrugged. "It's fine."

"Come with me," she said, leading him over to the sofa. She urged him to sit. Reaching behind her, she picked up a brown bottle and unscrewed the lid before pouring what looked like olive oil into her hands.

"What's that?"

"Massage oil. Give," she said, holding her hand out, palm up.

"You don't have to do this," he said, placing his right hand in hers.

"I know." She began to rub his joints, one at a time, and gradually, the stiffness receded. "I've always loved your hands," she said with a shy smile as she removed the excess oil with a damp cloth.

"I love them when they're exploring your body," he said, drawing a laugh from her.

"You have a one-track mind."

He tugged on her arm, and she fell into his lap. He drew her mouth towards his, her lips warm, soft, and achingly familiar. Cash groaned when a knock at the door interrupted his intentions.

"I'll get it," she said, clambering off his lap.

"Perfect fucking timing," he muttered, glowering at the waiter as he placed their breakfast on the dining table. He'd never stayed at this hotel before, and if they were going to be that fucking efficient with room service, he wouldn't be staying again.

Natalia saw the waiter out and sat at the table. She dug her fork into a pile of scrambled eggs and made a contented sound.

"Have you decided whether you're playing Madrid or Rome yet?" she said, reaching for the salt.

Cash cut into his omelette. "I'm not playing either."

Her mouth twisted in a wry grimace. "Why?"

"It's too soon."

"Mentally, or physically?"

Cash met her gaze. "Both. I need a couple more two-fifties under my belt and maybe one or two five hundreds before I tackle the masters."

"So Geneva, then, in a fortnight? Or would you prefer Lyon?"

He shrugged. "I don't suppose it matters."

She frowned. "What do you mean?"

He captured her hand, the feel of her skin comforting him. "You'll be back at work by then. You've only got another week off, and I hate the thought of doing this without you."

Natalia sighed as realisation dimmed the earlier sparkle in

her eyes. She dropped her fork with a clang. "This isn't going to work, is it?"

Panic swarmed his insides. Oh God, she'd changed her mind about them getting back together. "What do you mean?"

"I'm going to have to resign from work."

Even as relief coursed through him, Cash shook his head. "But you love your job."

She rose from her chair and nestled into his lap, her hands curving around the back of his head. "I love you more."

His heart squeezed as he brushed his lips over hers. "I don't want you to feel you have no other choice."

She shrugged. "I'll be starting maternity leave soon. All I'm doing is bringing that forward by a few weeks. And after the baby's born, I want to take some time off anyway."

Hope blossomed in his chest. "And you won't be leaving Pete in a hole?"

She gave him a tight smile. "I hope not. I've messed him about so much already that I can't help feeling bad. In a way, this will be better because at least he'll know where he stands and can get a permanent replacement."

"When will you tell him?"

Her mouth twisted in thought. "Well, if you're not playing anywhere next week, I'll fly back and tell him then."

He kissed her. "We'll do it together."

As they crossed the hotel reception, Cash stopped to sign a couple of autographs and pose for selfies with some fans. Natalia melted into the background. She was so good at giving him the space to play the part he needed to play. There was a lot of interest in him since his return to the tour, but both his fans and even the press had been considerate of his privacy.

He signed the final autograph on the peak of a baseball cap

and looked around for Natalia. He spotted her sitting in one of the many chairs dotting the lobby. She was leaning forward, elbows on her knees, and seemed to be in conversation with the woman sitting opposite. The woman had her back to Cash, but there was something vaguely familiar about her posture.

Cash set off towards them, but as he got closer, Natalia leaped to her feet. Her face flushed, and she said something to her companion, who immediately stood and began walking away. Natalia crossed over to him and linked her arm through his.

"Ready, ace?" she said, not quite meeting his gaze.

"Who were you talking to?"

"No one of consequence." Her face turned even more red. "Come on, you don't want to be late."

Skin prickling at a possibility he didn't want to acknowledge, he shook her off and began following the woman.

"Cash, don't." Natalia's pleading voice behind him added weight to his theory.

He broke into a jog as the woman stepped into the lift. The doors began to close, but he managed to stick an arm through the gap, and they sprang back open. Cash's hands clenched into fists, his spine rigid with fury.

"What the *fuck* are you doing here?"

26

"Shit, shit, shit," he heard Natalia say as she appeared beside him, her hand clutching her belly. She tentatively touched his arm. He wrenched his shoulder upwards, shaking her off.

"I asked you a fucking question," he said to his former agent, Kinga, who was cowering at the back of the lift.

"Cash, leave it. You're going to be late for the tournament."

He glowered down at Natalia, his fisted hands by his side. "I don't give a flying *fuck* about the tournament."

He turned his furious gaze back to Kinga. The last time he'd seen her was after it all came out about her being the one who'd taken the photographs of him with Gracie, his mother's carer—a vicious and cruel act that had caused Natalia to think he'd cheated on her. And if memory served him correctly, he'd been very clear that he never wanted to see Kinga again.

As the lift doors began to close once more, he grabbed her by the elbow and yanked her out.

"You had better start talking, Kinga, and do it quick."

"Cash, let her go," Natalia said. "You're making a scene."

"It's fine, Tally," Kinga said. "I knew what I was doing coming here."

"So you admit it, then?" Cash said, his jaw clenched tight. "You're here because I'm here?"

"Yes."

He glared at Kinga, the muscles in his arms quivering with the effort of holding them by his side. Natalia flinched, but Cash had to give Kinga her due—she stood tall and met his gaze.

"I nearly came to see you many times after I heard about the accident, but it didn't seem appropriate, considering how we parted company."

"Appropriate?" Cash's tone was glacial. "If you'd come to see me, I'd have stayed in the fucking coma."

Natalia laughed in an obvious attempt to lighten the mood, but her smile fell when Cash shot her a ferocious glare. "This is not even remotely funny."

"No, it isn't," Natalia said. "And nor is missing the final. Let's do this later, shall we?"

"There is no later," Cash said. "Leave, Kinga. I have no interest in anything you have to say."

Cash gripped Natalia by the elbow and moved her towards the front of the hotel. Their car was waiting outside, and Cash opened the door for her, only then releasing her elbow. After he'd climbed in his side, he started the engine. His fingers whitened due to his ferocious grip on the steering wheel, but he didn't move the car. He sat frozen in place, his gaze forward, his jaw clamped shut. When he felt calmer, he turned to look at Natalia.

"What did she want?" he said.

"I don't know. I didn't get a chance to ask her."

"So what did you speak about? Because I saw you talking."

"I thought I saw her yesterday. Yes, I know," she said holding up her hand as Cash opened his mouth to interrupt. "I should have told you. But I wasn't sure. When you were signing autographs, I spotted her. We'd been sitting together about thirty seconds when you saw us."

He released his grip on the steering wheel and flexed his hands. "I can't go there again with her, Natalia. I can't forgive her for trying to split us up."

Natalia grimaced. "After all you've suffered, do you really want to go through your entire life holding onto that grudge?"

"Maybe," he said with a shrug.

"That's a lot of bitterness to carry round, ace."

He sighed. "I know."

Natalia covered his hand with hers and squeezed. "There has to be a reason she's turned up now. She's had lots of other opportunities to get back in touch. Aren't you even a little bit curious?"

"Not really."

Natalia chuckled. "Remind me never to piss you off, ace."

His anger drained away, and he smiled. He wrapped his hand around the back of her neck and leaned in for a kiss. "You couldn't, sweetness."

She caressed his cheek with her knuckles, the loving touch more than he deserved. "So are we going?"

"Yep," Cash said. "And based on how angry I am, I pity my opponent."

TALLY'S EYES FLEW OPEN, and she held her breath as she tried to figure out if she'd been dreaming. No, there it was again, a soft tapping noise. She turned her head. Cash was fast asleep, his hair tousled, his chest slowly rising and falling. She drew back the covers and climbed out of bed, being careful not to rock the mattress too much. She shrugged into her dressing gown and padded across the bedroom. As she opened the door to the living room of their suite, a shaft of light shone across the bed, and she hesitated, waiting for Cash to stir. When he didn't, she closed the door behind her and stood in the centre of the living room, waiting.

The tapping sound came again, and she approached the door and drew to a halt. Someone was outside, but the knocking was tentative and almost too quiet to hear. She peered through the peephole and then opened the door.

"What are you doing here?" she whispered to Kinga. "It's one in the morning."

"I know. I'm sorry, Tally. I didn't know what else to do."

"Are you staying in this hotel?"

Kinga nodded.

"Okay, let's go." Tally picked up a key card and clicked the door shut behind her.

She followed Kinga down the hallway and into the lift. Kinga's room was two floors down, and only when she was inside did Tally breathe properly.

"How did you know which room we were in?"

Kinga had the grace to look embarrassed. "I followed you when you got back from the tournament. He did you proud."

Tally nodded. "He was pissed off, which is why he hammered the poor bugger. His opponent's first final too."

Kinga laughed. "Cash never gave an inch, no matter who was on the other side of the net. Friend, enemy, experienced or naïve —they all get the same treatment."

"True," Tally said.

"When are you due?" Kinga pointed her chin at Tally's stomach.

"July sixteenth."

"I'm so happy for you both. It'll be the making of him."

Tally smiled. "He'll have to grow up, that's for sure."

Kinga sank onto the couch. "I'm sorry, Tally."

"What for?"

"I should have come when I heard about Cash's accident. I should have been there to support you."

"You heard him earlier today. He wouldn't have thanked you."

"Would you?"

She shrugged. "I guess."

"Then I let you down, and for that, I apologise."

Tally sat beside Kinga and patted her hand. "I wish you could work things out. I know how much he means to you."

Kinga gave her a small smile. "I never did deserve you as my friend. You're a good person, Tally."

"How's William?"

For the first time, Kinga's face lit up. "He's amazing. I don't know what I'd do without him."

"Say hi to him for me."

"I will."

The two women fell into silence. "So what's going on?" Tally finally asked. "Why are you here?"

Kinga pinched her nose between her thumb and index finger. "I need to speak to you both. Together."

"I'm not sure I can make that happen."

"Will you try? For me."

Tally chewed on her lip. "I'll see what I can do," she said, getting to her feet.

Kinga saw her out, and Tally crept back to her suite. The lock beeped as she inserted the key card. She opened the door as quietly as she could and slipped inside. The room was still in darkness, and all was quiet. She let out the breath she'd been holding. She'd be able to sneak back into bed without Cash suspecting a thing. At least that would give her some time to figure out how to broach the Kinga subject before they were due to fly back to the UK.

She tiptoed across the living room and pushed open the door to their bedroom. Her side of the bed was still rumpled, the sheets scrunched where she'd tossed them aside.

And unfortunately for her, the bed was empty.

She jumped when a lamp in the living room came on. She

slowly turned around. Cash was sitting in an armchair, one ankle crossed over the opposing knee.

"Where have you been?" he said softly.

"Busted," Tally said with a smile, hoping to defuse the approaching situation. "I thought you'd still be asleep."

He shrugged. "I must have sensed you weren't next to me."

She walked over to him and knocked his foot off his knee, allowing her space to climb into his lap. She curved her hands around his face and leaned in for a kiss. Relief hit her when he relented, and his mouth moved softly over hers. His hands curved underneath her backside, and he stood, allowing her to wrap her legs around his waist. He carried her into the bedroom and laid her gently on the bed. After crawling in beside her, he drew her close, his front to her back, his hand protectively resting on her belly.

"So has Kinga told you what she wants yet?"

She stiffened in his arm. "How did you know?"

"I didn't until you just confirmed it."

She twisted her head and looked over her shoulder. "Sorry for sneaking out."

"No, I'm sorry for making you feel you had to."

Tally held back her surprise. Cash seemed calmer about Kinga than he'd been earlier that day. "She wants to talk to us both together."

Cash sighed. "Of course she does. Nothing like a bit of drama to make Kinga happy."

"Then you will?"

He pulled a face. "Best get it over with."

27

"Thank you for coming."

Cash ignored Kinga's waved hand inviting him to sit. Instead, he paced, his hands resting low on his hips. Natalia tried to catch his eye, no doubt as a way of telling him to sit the fuck down, so he purposely avoided meeting her gaze. Since reconciling, he found it difficult to refuse her anything, and he knew if he glanced across, her pleading look would be impossible to ignore.

"What's this about, Kinga?" Cash said, his tone clipped and cold. "I thought the last time we spoke I made myself perfectly clear that it was, in fact, the last fucking time."

Kinga's trembling hands were clasped in her lap, the knuckles white as she was clenching so tightly. "You did. And I had every intention of respecting your wishes."

"But then, as usual, you decided to do what's best for you."

Kinga flinched. "That's not fair."

Cash made a big deal of looking at his watch. "Can we get this over with, please? I'm on a clock here."

"Cash, enough," Natalia snapped. "Sit down, be quiet, and

hear her out. There was no point agreeing to come if all you are going to do is act like an idiot."

Outwardly, he kept his face impassive, but a chuckle almost spilled from his lips. Natalia was the only woman he'd ever allowed to challenge him so openly, and he loved the way she called him out when he was being a dick, loved how she grounded him, how she made him a better man.

He did as she asked and sat beside her. She casually rested her hand on the inside of his thigh, and her thumb began skimming back and forth. The gesture was meant both to calm and warn him. Out of the corner of his eye, he saw she was wearing a small, satisfied smile. His lips twitched in response.

"Fair enough," he said, his gaze falling on Kinga. "What's up?"

She leaned towards them, forearms on her knees, her hands dangling between her parted thighs.

"I'm dying, Cash."

The sound of Natalia's gasp competed with his thumping heartbeat, and he sagged against the back of the couch. "What?" he managed to croak.

"A few months ago, William and I were on holiday when I began to feel unwell," Kinga said as he and Natalia gaped at her. "Nothing major, just lacking in energy, a little depressed, off my food. But when it didn't get better once we returned home, I went to see the doctor."

"What is it?" Cash said, finding his voice. "What's wrong with you?"

Kinga forced a smile. "Breast cancer. At least that's where it started. I've got a secondary tumour in my stomach."

Horror congealed in his chest, and he scraped a hand through his hair. "Jesus Christ."

"What can we do?" Natalia's face had drained of colour, and her hands twisted in her lap. "There must be something. A second opinion. We'll pay for private care, won't we, Cash? We'll sort it."

Kinga rose from her chair and came to sit beside Natalia. She picked up her hand. "I've had second opinions and third ones. There's no point, Tally."

Natalia began quietly sobbing, and her shoulders shook as Kinga pulled her into a hug and whispered comforting words in her ear. There was something definitely wrong with that picture. It should have been the other way around. Cash launched out of his seat, his hands clenched by his side. This wasn't fucking happening. This *couldn't* be happening.

"Cash."

He twisted his head to find Kinga beside him. She rested her hand on his shoulder.

"Fuck, Kinga." His hatred of her had dissipated, washed away by the awfulness of the situation. He wrapped his arms around her, only then realising how thin she was beneath her clothes. "I've got you. We're both here for you."

She broke down then, huge sobs wracking her tiny frame. Cash met Natalia's gaze over the top of Kinga's head, and she nodded in understanding and silently left the room.

28

Tally wandered around in a daze, eventually finding herself at the beach. She shucked off her shoes and dangled them between her index and middle fingers as she paddled in the water's edge, ignoring the biting cold of the Mediterranean Sea. Her knees trembled, and she stepped out of the water and sank to the ground. Her dad had been forty-four when he'd lost his battle. Kinga was thirty-one. It was so unfair, so wrong on multiple levels.

And so terribly sad that it took a tragedy to bring people back together.

She glanced at her watch and realised a couple of hours had passed since she'd left Cash with Kinga. After slowly getting to her feet, she set off towards the hotel. When she opened the door to their suite, Cash wasn't there, but her mobile phone showed that he had tried to call her twenty minutes earlier. The voicemail message asked her to head back to Kinga's room.

Tally knocked quietly on Kinga's door. Cash opened it, his face bruised with exhaustion and sadness, and when she held out her arms, he fell into them.

"Where's Kinga?" she said when they broke apart.

Cash jerked his head in the direction of the bedroom. "Asleep."

"What are we going to do, Cash? This is awful. Just awful."

"Whatever I imagined she wanted, I never expected this."

"Where's William?"

"On his way. Apparently, she insisted on speaking to us alone. He'll be here in the next couple of hours."

Tally pressed her palms to her face. "Poor Kinga."

"They're getting married. That's why she came to see me. She's desperate for us both to be there."

A tear slid down Tally's face. "Marriage without a future. Oh, Cash, what can we do? What do you do in a situation like this?"

Cash folded an arm around her shoulders and kissed her temple. "You love them, I guess," he said simply. "Do whatever it is they need. This can't be easy for you either. Must bring back memories of your dad."

She closed her eyes and took a deep breath, trying to push aside terrible visions of her dad towards the end, a keen and alert mind atop a ravaged body that insisted on keeping him alive long past when it should have given up. She remembered the intense pain of those final days, when even heavy doses of morphine didn't give him any respite.

"Yeah, it does bring back memories," she said. "Look, Cash, this is going to get rough. If you don't have it in you to commit to what's necessary, you owe it to her to tell her now before she begins to rely on you."

He shook his head. "I'm going nowhere."

Tally kissed his cheek and leaned against his shoulder. "Neither am I."

"Let's leave her to sleep."

He was quiet on the walk back to their room, and Tally didn't feel much like talking either. Her back was killing her, and as soon as she shrugged off her jacket and tossed her bag, she dug her fingers into the tight muscles and stretched.

"Why didn't you tell me your back was hurting?"

"Because we'd be talking about nothing else. It's always sore. I blame you."

Cash chuckled. "You do that, sweetness. Stay there. I'll run you a bath."

As Cash headed off to the bathroom, Tally stared out of the window. She clasped a hand over her mouth, gulping down breaths of fear for what Kinga was about to face. Cancer—a fight she would ultimately lose, no matter how much money was thrown at her or how much love was bestowed.

Only one good thing had come out of that day. Cash had finally learned his lesson—one he should have learned long before now, especially with his history. Life was far too short to hold stupid grudges about things that ultimately didn't matter. Yes, Kinga had tried to break them up, but that had happened a lifetime ago.

Tally didn't hear Cash come up behind her, and she jumped when he wrapped his arms around her waist. He rested his chin on her shoulder and spread his palms wide across her stomach. "You okay, babe?"

"Not really," she said, turning in his arms.

His hand cupped the back of her neck, and he brushed his lips over hers. "Your bath's ready."

She knitted their fingers together. "I'm so scared, Cash. I need you."

Cash nodded in understanding. "I need you too, baby. Now more than ever."

~

WILLIAM SHOOK CASH'S HAND, and the two men briefly clapped each other on the back. They'd never been close, but tragedy often brought people together.

"Thanks for changing your plans. I know it's important to get your career back on track." William turned to Tally and hugged her warmly.

Cash shook his head. "There's nothing more important I need to do right now other than be here for her. For you."

"And I believe we have a wedding to plan," Tally said, desperately trying to sound bright in the most awful of circumstances.

William grinned. "Yes, and quick, before she changes her mind."

"As if." Kinga appeared from the bedroom. She was dressed for dinner yet looked so very tired, dark circles framing eyes that brightened considerably as they met William's loving gaze.

He strode quickly across the suite, his arms gentle as he held her close. He kissed her temple and tucked a lock of hair, which had escaped her chignon, behind her ear. "How'd you sleep, angel?"

The heavy emotion in his voice brought tears to Tally's eyes. She stole a look at Cash. The despair on his face mirrored her own feelings.

"Good," she said. "I'm ready to eat if you three are."

"We can order in if you're too tired," Tally said.

"Nonsense," Kinga said. "Anyway, Cash is paying, so I'm going to order the most expensive thing on the menu."

Cash laughed. "Big Mac and large fries it is, then."

"Cheapskate." Kinga dug him in the ribs, and he faux groaned.

He slung his arm around her shoulders. "As if I could take a snob like you to McDonalds."

Tally hung back, watching Cash tease Kinga. Her heart ached for him, for Kinga, for them all. She dashed her tears away with the back of her hand before Kinga could see how upset she was. Kinga needed her to be strong, not some weak emotional wreck.

"I know it's hard." William brushed a comforting hand down her arm.

"How long has she got?"

He shrugged. "A few months at best. She's refused treatment. Says she doesn't want to spend her last few months with her head down the toilet, and the thought of losing her hair when there's no real hope... well, you know Kinga and her crowning glory."

"Yeah."

"Do me a favour, Tally."

"Anything."

"Help me give her the best wedding day possible."

29

"Hold still." Em repinned a stray lock of hair that refused to stay put. She added an extra clip. "There, that should do it."

"Can I look yet?" Kinga said.

Em covered Kinga's eyes with her hand and spritzed hair spray all over her up-do. "Tal, get the mirror."

Tally pushed the floor-length mirror into place. Good job it was on wheels. She had no chance of carrying it, not in her condition. She caught a glimpse of herself sideways. Jesus, she was huge—and she still had seven weeks to go. At this rate, she'd probably give birth to a two-year-old. She winced. That would be bloody painful.

"Okay, Kinga. Stand up and turn around."

Tally's hand shot to cover her mouth as she got her first proper look. "Oh, Kinga. You look so beautiful."

Kinga wore an expression of awe. Tally remembered having that same feeling when Em weaved her magic the night she met Cash. That event had forever changed the course of her life. Sadly, Kinga's course was set, but at least she would carry the memories of this day with her until the very end.

Kinga clasped her throat, her lips parting as she drank in her reflected image. "Is that me?" she whispered.

"Yep." Em rested her hands on Kinga's shoulders. "Go on. You can say it. I'm a fucking genius."

Kinga turned around and planted a kiss on Em's lips. "You are a fucking genius."

"Whoa there," Em said, giving Kinga a playful swat. "Kiss me like that again, and I might have to tell William you've swapped sides."

Kinga laughed, her girlish giggle making Tally's stomach tighten. This should be a happy occasion. Kinga deserved a future. Marriage, kids, grandkids. Not this. Not the path chosen for her.

"Won't be a minute," Tally said as a sob bubbled up in her throat. She dashed out of the room and staggered outside, where she sucked in huge gulps of air. Her lungs burned. She couldn't do this. She couldn't stick around and watch someone else she cared about fade away before her very eyes.

"Hey." Em gripped Tally's shoulder and gave it a little shake. "Pull yourself together, Tally. This isn't about you. It's about her."

"I know. I know." Tears streamed down her face. She was losing it. "I can see Dad. I'd forgotten what he looked like. But now, I can see him so clearly, Em. It's coming. It's coming for her. What happened to Dad is going to happen to Kinga. I can't do this. I can't."

Em's sharp slap brought Tally's hand to her face.

"What the hell, Em?" she said, clutching her cheek.

"Sorry, babes, but you're going to have to hang onto the hysterics. By all means, lose your shit, but do it later in the privacy of your hotel room. I get how hard this is for you, Tal. I was there, remember? I know the memories of how fucking awful it was for your dad at the end are all resurfacing when you thought they were long buried. But you can't do this. I'm not the biggest Kinga fan, but right now, I'm standing shoulder to shoulder with that woman. *You* need to do the same."

Tally buried her face in her hands. Em was right. She had to find a way to push the bad memories aside and focus on making Kinga's day a happy one. She took a deep breath and blew it out slowly through her mouth.

She met Em's gaze. "You're right, and I'm ready."

"I'm always right, but you're definitely not ready. Go to the bathroom in the lobby. I'll sort Kinga's final touches and meet you in there in a few minutes to fix your make-up."

Em disappeared, and Tally made her way to the bathroom. She chuckled when she faced herself in the mirror. No wonder Em had said she wasn't ready. Mascara streaks lay in tracks down her cheeks, and she'd smudged her lipstick.

After Em touched up her make-up, they took their places next to Rupe in the conference room of the hotel, which was doubling as a wedding venue. Kinga had point-blank refused to get married in a church, making it clear that just because she was dying, that didn't mean she was about to turn to a God she didn't believe in.

William looked so smart in a black tuxedo, his wild curls tamed for once. He was standing at the front of the room with his best man beside him. He caught Tally's eye and smiled as the wedding march began to play. Tally twisted in her seat as the double doors at the back of the room opened and Kinga appeared, her hand tucked into Cash's arm.

Tally met Cash's gaze as he matched Kinga's footsteps and they made their way up the aisle. The outpouring of love in his eyes made her stomach clench. When they reached the end, he placed Kinga's hand on top of William's and came to join Tally.

"Is she okay?" Tally asked, receiving a nod of confirmation from Cash. He grasped her hand, knitting their fingers together.

"Love you," he whispered.

Tally swallowed past a huge lump in her throat, blinking furiously as her tears, once more, threatened to fall. She was an emotional wreck these days. The slightest thing set her off.

As Kinga and William began to read the vows they'd written for each other, the baby chose that exact moment to perform acrobatics in her stomach. She cradled her bump, top and bottom, and rubbed her hands back and forth. Cash's hand covered hers, and he tracked her movements as they both tried to comfort their baby. More tears fell. The contradictory experiences were messing with her head. When her baby made its entrance into the world, Kinga's time would be ending.

"I've got you, babe," Cash murmured, but instead of stemming her tears, his words made her sob harder. At least she had an excuse. People were supposed to cry at weddings.

Kinga and William headed back down the aisle as husband and wife. Kinga was flushed, a bright smile gracing her face. She was gazing up at William, her hand tucked into the crook of his arm. As the guests filed out behind the happy couple, Cash stopped Tally from following.

When the room was empty, she turned to him. "What's going on, ace?"

Cash held both her hands in his. He skimmed his thumb over her knuckles, his eyes cast downwards. He dropped her left hand, reached into his tux jacket, and pulled out her engagement ring.

"I promised myself I'd do this when the time felt right, and I don't know about you, but I can't think of a better time."

He got down on one knee, her left hand still cradled in his, and when he raised his eyes, they were glistening with emotion.

"When I said these words to you in Paris, I never thought anything could separate us. We've been dealt a shitty hand since then, and although there are still difficult times ahead, I see so much hope in our future. You, me, and our baby.

"Natalia McKenzie, I love you more than I ever thought possible. You're my light, my life, my heart and soul. My everything. Will you marry me?"

Tally thrust out her left hand. "Don't you ever try to leave me again, Cash Gallagher," she said in a choked voice.

He slipped the ring onto her finger. "Never, baby."

30

Cash refused to let go of Natalia's hand as they found their way into the adjacent room where the wedding breakfast was being held. He kept rubbing the pad of his thumb over the diamond ring he'd slipped onto her finger—a place it never should have left.

Rupe waved to let them know where they were sitting. Cash acknowledged him then glanced around for Kinga. He spotted her showing anyone within touching distance her wedding ring. It made him smile to watch her. A lot of people in the room didn't know how ill she was, and she wanted to keep it that way.

An uncomfortable feeling stirred in his chest, the same one that emerged whenever he thought about the weeks and months ahead. He'd put a brave face on, but Natalia's warning about how tough it was going to get had started to hit home. He'd never been around sick people. When his mum had been comatose, she'd only ever looked like she was asleep. What Kinga was about to face was horrific.

"You okay, ace?"

He glanced down at Natalia's beautiful upturned face and

bent his head to kiss her warm, soft lips. "As good as you are, sweetness."

Her eyes glazed over as though her memories had taken her far away. When she refocused, her expression was resolute. "You know the best thing about all of this?"

"What?"

"It brought you and Kinga back together."

He grimaced. "I'd rather she wasn't sick and I still hated her guts."

"You never hated her guts."

"Yes, I did. You know my history with Kinga. All the years I spent fending off her unwanted advances. But it was almost sport for me. Something to liven up my dull personal life. It didn't really matter, you see, because the women in my life didn't matter. If Kinga's power play scared them off, I didn't give a shit. And then you came along."

He slipped his hands around her waist. He couldn't get as near to her these days. Her pregnant belly kept him at a distance, but he nestled as close as he could.

"I knew that first day you were different. Special. And I think that's why I was never able to forgive her for what she did. She knew, deep down, there was no chance for me and her. And she also knew how important you were to me and that, after years of fucking around, I'd finally found the one. You made me so happy, yet still she tried to split us up, knowing it would break me." He shrugged. "It made me question how much she really thought of me if she could stand by and watch me in pain."

"God, Cash." Natalia brushed his lips with hers. "We need to be completely honest with each other from now on. If we'd been truthful from the start, no one would have been able to split us up. I can stand anything, except being apart from you."

Cash touched his forehead to hers. "I hear you, baby."

"Come on, ace. Let's go and join Rupe and Em. I don't know about you, but I'm starving."

Cash laughed. "You're always hungry."

"I know," she groaned. "I'm going to have to be on a diet for a hundred years after I've had this baby."

"That looked deep," Rupe said as Cash slipped into the seat next to his.

"You're a nosy bastard."

"I prefer to say that I'm interested in the well-being of my best friends."

"Bullshit," Cash said. "If you must know, I've put the ring back on her finger."

Rupe punched his arm. "About fucking time. Hey, darling," he said to Natalia, holding his hand out. "Let's see it."

Natalia frowned and then realised what Rupe was going on about. She held out her left hand, drawing a loud gasp from Emmalee.

"Are you sure, babes?" Emmalee said.

Cash clenched his jaw and took hold of Natalia's hand. "She's sure," he said with a glare in Emmalee's direction.

"I am," Natalia said, backing him up. "It's what I want."

Cash flashed a triumphant look at Emmalee.

She met his gaze with a stern face, and then she smiled. "Then I'm happy for you both."

Cash tried to hide his amazement, but Emmalee's wry smile in his direction said he'd failed. He and Emmalee had always had a tricky relationship, moving along the spectrum from almost friends to definitely enemies. She only had Natalia's best interests at heart, but it grated that she sometimes thought he didn't.

"Can we keep this between us for now though?" Natalia said. "This is Kinga's special day. I don't want anything to detract from her being the centre of attention."

"Good call," Cash said. "Today should be about Kinga."

The wedding reception went off without a hitch, and as soon as the tables were cleared away, revealing a dance floor, Cash tugged on Natalia's arm. "Come and dance with me," he said, rising from his chair.

She immediately stood and allowed him to lead her onto the dance floor. He pulled her into his arms and stared into her eyes. She giggled as he whirled her around. "I never did thank Rachael for teaching you to dance."

"And I never thanked her either. Having that first dance with you is the reason we are together now."

"Even if you were furious at the time."

Cash chuckled. "Never has anyone been able to make me as furious as you. Nor as happy," he added as he bent to kiss her.

"Can I cut in?"

Rupe appeared from his right, and although Cash almost told him to sod off, Natalia's enthusiastic nod changed his mind.

"If you must," Cash said with a grin that looked more like a grimace.

He wandered back to their table, where Emmalee was knocking back copious amounts of wine. Her eyes were glazed, a sign she was well on her way to being pissed. But in his experience, pissed Emmalee had a less vicious tongue than sober Emmalee.

"How're you doing?" he said, slipping into the seat next to her. "Are we friends yet?"

She gave him a tight smile. "Do we have a choice?"

He looked over at Natalia in the arms of his best friend. "I guess not."

Emmalee hesitated as if considering her next move, and then she scraped her chair back, rose from her seat, and held out her hand. "Come on, then, stud. Show me some of those dance moves."

Cash laughed as he took her hand. It felt strange having his arms around Emmalee, but at least they were putting the past behind them. Emmalee was Natalia's best friend, and she wasn't going anywhere. He wasn't either, which meant they had to find a way to get along—for Natalia's sake.

"Cash!"

Natalia's panicked voice reached him. He let go of Emmalee and spun around. Rupe was on the other side of the dance floor holding Natalia's hand, his face aghast. Natalia was clutching her stomach. She was wildly looking around, and when she spotted him heading over, her face crumpled.

"What's the matter?" he said, catching her as she half fell into his arms.

"My waters broke. Oh God, Cash, the baby's coming."

31

"Isaac," Cash barked into his phone. "Get the fucking car around the front, now."

"What's happening?" Kinga dashed over with William in tow.

"Natalia's in labour," Cash said, trying desperately to keep panic out of his voice. "The baby's coming."

"Now? But it's too early."

He glared at Kinga. "Fucking genius," he said through gritted teeth as fear flashed across Natalia's face. "Come on, baby. Isaac will be waiting outside. Everything's going to be okay."

Her whole body shook as he put his arm around her. He glanced over his shoulder and began snapping out orders. "Emmalee, Rupe, follow us there, yeah? Em, call the hospital and tell them we're on our way. And call Pete."

She nodded. "Leave it with me. We're right behind you, babes."

Natalia barely acknowledged Emmalee. Her face was pale, far too pale. "I'm scared, Cash."

He pulled her closer. "I know, baby. I'm scared too. Let's get you to the hospital. I'm right here."

Isaac had the back door open, and as soon as Cash had helped Natalia inside and climbed in after her, Isaac floored the accelerator. As he turned a corner a little too fast and they were jostled, Cash tapped him on the shoulder.

"Fast, but in one piece, okay, Isaac?" Cash said.

"Yes, sir."

Natalia groped for his hand, her fingers curving around his.

"Any pain? Or contractions?" he said.

She looked up at him, her eyes wide and fearful. "I haven't felt the baby move."

Cash swallowed hard. He could not let her see how terrified he was for both her and their child. He couldn't allow anything to happen to Natalia, and his mind was running useless scenarios about what he'd do if he were asked to choose. It wasn't a choice. He'd pick Natalia every time, but if that happened, would she ever forgive him?

"We'll be there soon."

Isaac worked miracles, getting them to the hospital in twenty minutes when thirty had been much more likely. Her contractions had started on the way, and she'd spent most of the journey gripping his hand and trying to control her breathing.

He helped Natalia from the car. He wanted to run ahead, to shout for someone to come and help them, but he forced himself to stay calm and walked at her pace into the hospital.

"Sit down," he said, pointing to a row of chairs. "I'll get someone."

He strode over to the reception desk. "We need help," he said to the nurse with a glance over his shoulder. "My fiancée's waters have broken. She's almost thirty-three weeks pregnant. We were booked in for July."

"Okay, sir," the nurse said, moving at a fucking snail's pace. She handed him some forms. "Can you fill these in?"

"Did you hear what I said?" he snapped. "She's in labour. Can you fucking get someone?"

The nurse peered over the top of her glasses. "There is no need for profanities. I *am* getting someone. Now, I suggest you calm down, fill in the forms and allow me to do my job."

Cash snatched the clipboard off the counter. "Make it quick." He sat beside Natalia and began to fill in the bloody form.

She placed a hand on his arm. "I need you to keep calm, ace. I'm panicking enough for both of us."

He scrubbed a hand over his face, his smile weak as he looked at her. "Sorry, sweetness."

His writing was barely legible as he wrote answers on the form. He had to ask Natalia one or two questions, and by the time he'd scrawled his signature at the bottom, a wheelchair had appeared.

"Thank you." The nurse took the clipboard from him and gave it a cursory glance. "Okay, Natalia, pop yourself in here, my darling. Let's go and take a look at you."

"It's Tally," Natalia managed to gasp out as another contraction hit her. She doubled over, taking short, sharp breaths. Once it had passed, Cash helped her into the wheelchair.

"Tally it is, then." The nurse scribbled something on the clipboard then tucked it into a slot at the back of the wheelchair. She began pushing Natalia down the corridor and then glanced over her shoulder. "Are you coming, Daddy?"

Cash bolted after them, feeling like a complete dick. This was so far out of his comfort zone, and the reality of having a baby was hitting home. He'd never thought about how dangerous it might be for Natalia. He'd assumed everything would be fine, never thinking for a second there might be complications.

He wasn't prepared.

The nurse ushered them into a private room and settled Natalia into bed. A few minutes later, a doctor appeared. He was at least forty years old, which weirdly gave Cash some comfort. Surely a medical professional of his age would have the right level of experience to give Natalia the best care.

The doctor took the clipboard from the nurse and glanced at it. Satisfied, he attached it to the bottom of the bed and peered over the top of his glasses.

"Tally, I'm Dr Saunders. I'm going to be looking after you." He turned to Cash. "Are you the father?"

Mute, Cash nodded.

He turned back to Natalia. "Try not to worry. I know it's scary, especially as you're early. I'm going to examine you, okay?"

Natalia nodded and waved her hand. "Cash."

"I'm here, baby," he said, finding his voice. He clung tightly to her hand as the doctor examined his girl. He'd never felt so fucking inadequate in his entire life.

"Right, Tally. I don't want you to worry, but you're definitely in labour. You're already four centimetres dilated."

"Oh God," she muttered as the remaining blood in her face drained away, leaving her pale and gaunt. "Can you stop it?"

Dr Saunders shook his head. "Your waters broke. That means we have to let the labour play out." He made some notes on the clipboard and handed it to the nurse. "This is Louise. She's going to be with you the whole time. We'll get a foetal monitor on you so we can monitor the baby's heartbeat, and I'll be back to check on you shortly."

"Wait, you're leaving?" Cash thrust his arm out, making Dr Saunders draw to a halt.

"She's in good hands. Louise is a very experienced midwife."

"But she's not a fucking doctor, is she?"

Dr Saunders frowned. "Mr Gallagher, please stay calm. I'm aware you're concerned, but let us do our job. Neither the baby nor Tally are in any immediate danger. I'll be back soon. I do have other patients."

Cash's hands curled into fists. "Is this a joke?"

"Cash," Natalia snapped. "Stop it. Just stop, okay? I don't need you going postal on me. I need you here. Man up, for fuck's sake."

"Shit." He dragged a hand through his hair. "Sorry," he

muttered to the doctor, stepping out of his way. He pulled up a chair next to Natalia's bed and ignored the disapproving glance from Louise.

"Don't lose it, okay? I need you."

He pressed the back of her hand to his forehead. "I'm not going to lose it." He met her gaze. "I'm here, baby."

"Good. Because I can't do this alone."

"You're not alone."

Louise attached the monitor to Natalia's stomach. A thudding sound, like horses galloping, flooded the room. His heart leaped with relief.

"A nice strong heartbeat, Tally," Louise said with a warm smile. "No signs of baby being in distress."

"Thank God," she whispered, her hand flexing inside his.

He squeezed back then released her hand when his phone vibrated in his pocket. He glanced at the screen.

"Emmalee and Rupe are here, and Pete's on his way. Do you want me to get them?"

Natalia shook her head. "I only want you."

He stroked her cheek with the back of his hand. "Okay, baby. Shall I go and tell them you're all right?"

She nodded. "But come straight back."

He closed the hospital door behind him and strode back to reception. He didn't want to be away from Natalia a moment more than necessary. Emmalee jumped to her feet the minute she saw him.

"Is she okay? What's happening?"

"She's definitely in labour, so one way or another, the baby's coming. I'll let you know more as soon as I know anything."

"I want to see her." Emmalee took a step towards the door, but Cash gripped her arm.

"No. She doesn't need crowding."

"But—"

"For fuck's sake, Emmalee. She doesn't want anyone in the

room apart from me, okay? Now, sit down and wait it out. Or better still, go home. It's going to be a while."

Emmalee jutted out her chin. "I'm not leaving."

"Up to you." He signalled to Rupe and then pointed at Emmalee. "Stay with her."

Rupe nodded. "Sure thing. Give Tally our love."

When he returned, Natalia was sitting up in bed, sipping a cup of tea. A little more colour had flooded her cheeks, and she definitely appeared calmer.

"That's better," he said, tucking a lock of hair behind her ear.

"Did you tell them?"

"Yes. Emmalee is an annoying bitch at times."

Natalia gave a small smile. "She can be." As her face twisted in pain, the smile fell, and she thrust the cup of tea at him. Her hands curled around the bedcovers. "Ow, ow, ow," she said, doubling over.

"What can I do?" Cash put the tea down and started wringing his hands. God, he felt fucking useless, surplus to requirements.

Louise bustled over and clutched Natalia's hand. "Okay, sweetie, breathe. In, out. Come on now, deep breaths."

Cash began to pace. He didn't like this. Not one bit. He hated seeing Natalia in pain when there wasn't a fucking thing he could do about it.

HOURS PASSED, and as each one did, his girl became more and more exhausted.

"I can't do this anymore," she said when she'd been in labour for seven hours. "I'm tired."

Cash leaned forward in his chair and held her hand. "You can, baby. You're the strongest person I know."

"I can't." She began to cry.

A fist closed around his heart and squeezed. He nestled next to her on the bed and pressed a cool cloth to her damp forehead.

"How much longer?" he asked Louise.

"It could be minutes, or it could be hours." When Cash gave her a horrified stare, she smiled and patted his shoulder. "Everything is going well. The baby is doing great, and Mum is doing great. It'll happen."

Late evening became night, and night became dawn. Natalia's contractions grew longer and more painful, and he was about to insist on a caesarean when Louise, during yet another fucking examination, looked at them both and smiled.

"Ten centimetres. Are you ready to meet your baby?"

The news had an immediate impact on Natalia. She perked up, a steely determination appearing on her face as she reached for his hand. "Let's do this."

The staff wheeled her down the corridor to the delivery suite that had the equipment they'd need when the baby was born. That fact alone made him feel sick. Everyone was behaving as though this was completely normal, but it wasn't. The baby shouldn't have been there for another seven weeks. He was no expert, but he knew that wasn't good. How would he cope if things went wrong?

Whatever happened in the future, he would never forget what Natalia went through in that room. He stood by, helpless, as her face turned redder and redder and she pushed and heaved and screamed. Whoever said childbirth was a miracle was a fucking idiot.

After she'd been pushing for two hours, two goddamn awful fucking hours, she turned to him, sweat pouring down her face even though he'd been mopping it every ten seconds.

"I can't. I can't," she sobbed. "No more."

Agony scored a fucking big cut in Cash's heart. "You're amazing," he said, kissing her hand. "You're doing amazing."

Dr Saunders smiled encouragingly. "Almost there, Tally. Next contraction, big push, okay?"

She clung to Cash's hand as another contraction tore into her. "Oh God, no," she yelled, pushing with every ounce of energy she had left. At that moment, he hated the baby, hated what it was doing to her. She wasn't ever doing this again.

"Okay, the head's out," the doctor said with a bright smile. "Stop pushing for me, Tally, just a second."

"Is it okay?" Cash said with an anxious glance at Louise.

She ignored him, instead passing the doctor a couple of horrific-looking medieval silver things. Natalia seemed out of it, as though whatever he was doing with those instruments didn't matter.

When Saunders finished messing about, he looked up. "Ready? Big push."

Natalia grimaced and gritted her teeth. With Cash lifting her up, she pushed once more, and out came the baby with a whoosh.

"Congratulations, you two," Dr Saunders said as Natalia collapsed against the pillows. "You have a daughter."

"Can I see her?" She raised her head. Cash put his arm around her shoulders to help her see better.

The doctor held up this tiny little thing, her face red and angry as she whimpered.

The first thought that hit him was, *I know you.*

Different emotions scattered throughout his body, taking his breath away with their intensity. Nothing in either of their lives would ever be the same again.

"Oh, Cash," Natalia said as tears began streaming down her face. "She's amazing. She's the image of you."

"Poor thing," Cash said with a grin. He leaned over and kissed Natalia, and when he gazed into her eyes, the pain that had necessitated their daughter's arrival into this world seemed to disappear, the night of tension and terror vanishing, memories already being wired differently so the two of them could inaccurately look back on this experience as a true miracle.

"You are something else," he said. "I couldn't love you more."

"Four pounds one ounce," Louise said, making a note on Natalia's chart. She wrapped up the baby and placed her into a glass incubator.

"We need to take her to NICU," the doctor said.

"Why? What's wrong?" Natalia said, panic leaching into her tone.

"She's fine," Dr Saunders said in a reassuring voice. "But she's small. It's routine, Tally. She'll be able to get the extra help she needs."

"I want to go with her."

"We need to take care of you first, and then you can be with her."

"Cash, go with her," Natalia said as their daughter was wheeled towards the door. "I don't want her to be alone."

"Baby, she's not alone. Let's go up together after you've been seen to."

"I didn't even get to hold her." Smiles gave way to tears as Natalia began to sob. He wrapped his arms around her and let her cry into his chest.

"You will," he whispered, brushing her face softly. He kissed the top of her head. "We both will."

She nodded and sniffed loudly as she wiped her nose with the back of her hand. Cash chuckled and reached into his pocket for a tissue. He passed it to her.

She blew her nose. "I'm such a classy girl," she said with the hint of a smile.

"I know. I'm the luckiest guy in the world," Cash said.

"Do you think Em's still here?"

He gave a wry smile. "Knowing Emmalee, I'd say it's a safe bet."

"Can you go and tell her and Pete? I don't want them worrying."

Cash shook his head. "I'm not happy about leaving you alone."

Natalia rolled her eyes. "I'll be fine. There's not a lot you can do," she said, tilting her head towards the doctor, who was doing things to her that Cash didn't want to have to think about. "Go on. And tell Kinga I'm sorry for ruining her day."

Under duress, Cash set off for the reception area, but about halfway there, his legs buckled, and he leaned against the wall. He closed his eyes and let the joy of what had happened over the last few hours seep into his bones. He wanted to remember this moment for the rest of his life. He had a daughter. A precious baby girl. And as clichéd as it sounded, his life had changed forever. But what surprised him more was how much of a positive change he knew it was going to be.

After composing himself, he opened the door to the reception area. Emmalee was asleep, her head resting on Rupe's shoulder. Cash glanced around and chuckled. Everyone had turned up. Pete, Brad, Jamie, Kinga—still in her wedding dress—and William. The only person missing was Mum, but he hadn't exactly had time to call her. She'd be disappointed when she found out she'd missed the birth.

"Hey," Cash said, his voice sounding exhausted even to his own ears.

Like a choreographed move, everyone jumped up at virtually the same time.

"Tally?" Emmalee said. "The baby?"

A broad grin spread across his face. "A girl. Four pounds something I can't remember. She's perfect. They've taken her to intensive care, but it's routine apparently. Natalia's fine. Exhausted but fine."

Cash found himself surrounded as they all hugged him and

then hugged each other. He managed to extricate himself and caught Pete's eye.

"My girl okay?" Pete said, his eyes glistening with emotion.

Cash nodded. "She's better than okay. They're... looking after her, and then we're going to see the baby, but after that, I'm sure she'll be dying to see you."

Pete shook Cash's hand and clapped him on the back. "Well done," he said gruffly as though Cash was the one who had performed the impossible.

"I'll come and get you as soon as she's rested."

He wandered over to Kinga. Her small hand was clutching William's much larger one. "Natalia wants me to apologise, even though I know you'll be fine. She didn't want anything to detract from your day, and yet, in her mind, she's managed to do that rather spectacularly."

"Tell her not to be so ridiculous," Kinga said. "We had a wonderful day, made even more wonderful by this amazing ending to it."

Cash nodded. "I knew you'd see it that way, but you know Natalia."

"I do," she said with a smile. "Tell her we love her, and we can't wait to see the baby."

When Cash pushed open the door to the delivery suite, Natalia was alone. She was sipping on a cup of tea, and her normal pale complexion had returned.

"I could murder one of those," he said, nodding at her cup.

She pointed at a tall cabinet behind him. "Good job Louise brought you one, then. She's gone to fetch a wheelchair, and then we can go to see the baby."

He lowered himself onto the bed and tilted her chin up to his. Her eyes seemed to hold a newfound knowledge and wisdom.

"I will never forget what you did today. What you went through."

She put her cup down on the cabinet beside her then

removed his from him and placed it next to hers. Her arms curved around his neck, and she kissed him. When they broke apart, her eyes were brimming with tears.

"I love you," she whispered.

He was about to kiss her again when Louise arrived with a wheelchair.

"Okay, kids. Want to go and see your baby?"

Excitement crossed Natalia's face, and she gripped Cash's hand. "Try to stop us."

32

Tubes. So many tubes everywhere. But it didn't matter because those tubes were helping her little girl. Her daughter. Saying the words to herself brought a thrill of excitement. She could barely believe what had happened since the previous day. Kinga's wedding and Cash's proposal were like memories seen through a veil, but the memories of how this precious gift had arrived were crystal clear.

She clutched Cash's hand. She wanted to look at him but couldn't tear her eyes away from the tiny person inside the incubator. The nurse showed them both how they could touch her, and as soon as Tally caressed her baby's soft skin, tears trailed down her face.

"Look what we did, ace."

"What *you* did," he said with an unmistakeable tone of pride in his voice. His arm was comforting around her shoulders, and an innate peace settled over her.

"She's perfect," Tally said turning towards him. "A tiny replica of you."

"But she has your eyes, sweetness," he said, his gaze locked on his daughter. "I never could take my eyes off you, and now I can't take them off her either. I'm in love with two girls. You and her."

"Do we have a name yet?" Shelley, the NICU nurse who was looking after their baby, asked.

Tally glanced at Cash. "I haven't even thought about it."

"I have," he said.

"Really? What were you thinking?"

"Darcey."

Tally cocked her head to the side. "Darcey Gallagher. I like it." She stroked the baby's cheek with her finger. "What do you think, little one?"

"It means descended from the dark one in Irish."

Tally's finger stilled. Her eyes locked onto his. "How long have you been thinking of that?" she said, feeling a tinge of sadness.

He held his hand up. "Hear me out. I was in such a dark place before I met you. From the outside, I had everything, but in reality, I had nothing that mattered. When I had the accident, I almost went back there and lost everything. Yet now look at us."

He held out his index finger. The baby instantly curled her tiny hand around it, and a rarely seen peace settled over his face.

"She *is* descended from the dark one. But you and her, you help me choose the light."

A wave of emotion washed through Tally as she rested her head on his shoulder. "Then Darcey it is."

"So what do you think?" Tally pressed her nose against the glass, behind which her daughter was fast asleep, oblivious to the three pairs of eyes staring at her.

Em squeezed her arm. "She's totally awesome."

Pete looked as though he might burst with pride. "She's beautiful, Tal. Just like her mum. How are you doing?"

Tally grinned. "I'm sore as hell." She turned back to face her daughter again. "But I'd do that every day if it meant she was my reward."

"I'll call in to Toys R Us later and buy you a rubber ring to sit on," Emmalee said with a giggle.

Tally dug her in the ribs. "Supportive."

"Have you thought of a name?"

She nodded. "Darcey. Cash chose it."

Em squinted through the glass. "It suits her. Where is Cash anyway?"

"Gone to call Rachael. She'll be gutted she wasn't here. We should have asked you to call her, but it was all a bit fraught."

Em hugged her. "I was so worried about you."

"We hadn't noticed," drawled Pete. "Your constant pacing, chewing of nails, and jumping every time the door opened hid your feelings pretty well."

"You can let some of them go, Dozer," Em said.

Pete laughed. "And where's the fun in that?"

Tally watched two of the most important people in her world banter, and let happiness soak into her bones. She closed her eyes, savouring the moment. She couldn't remember the last time she'd felt so euphoric, so ecstatic with life. Tears pricked the back of her eyes, and when she opened them, they spilled over. A sob broke from her throat, causing both Em and Pete to jerk their heads in her direction.

"Babes, what's the matter?" Em was by her side in an instant.

"I'm so happy." Tally licked the salty tears from her lips and brushed her hand across her face to wipe away the rest. "I never thought I could feel like this."

Two sets of arms wrapped around her, and the three of them huddled together. They were all crying and laughing so hard, they didn't hear Cash come back until he spoke.

"Room for a fourth?" he said, his warm hands wrapping around Tally's waist.

Em and Pete stepped away, allowing Tally to fall into Cash's arms. "Hey, now," he said, drying her eyes with a torn tissue. "I hope to fuck they're happy tears."

"They are," she said, sniffling. "Is Rachael coming?"

Cash nodded. "I've sent Isaac to fetch her. I could barely get a word in with all the questions she hit me with as soon as I told her you'd had the baby. She'll be here first thing tomorrow."

Tally laughed. "I can't wait to see her."

Cash glanced over his shoulder at Em and Pete. "Do you mind giving us a bit of space?"

"Oh, sure." Em and Pete left the NICU, and as soon as they'd disappeared through the door at the end of the corridor, Tally looked up at Cash and frowned.

"Something wrong?"

"No," he said, taking hold of her hand. He pushed open the door to the intensive care unit. "I just want us to be alone with our daughter."

33

The bright springtime sun woke Tally earlier than she would have liked. She rolled over. Dust motes floated in the air, catching the sunlight through a crack in the curtains. They resembled a thousand stars twinkling in the sky.

Her body was sore, as though she'd had a seriously heavy session at the gym, and every muscle ached. But none of that mattered because she had a daughter.

Love she never thought she'd be capable of filled her heart as it expanded to make room for the new addition in her life. When she'd fallen in love with Cash, she'd assumed nothing would ever top that. How wrong she'd been. And yet with the arrival of their baby, her love for him had grown too.

She pushed herself upright. It felt strange to be alone after spending forty-eight hours surrounded by people. Cash had reluctantly gone back home the night before to get some sleep but only after she'd bullied him by saying he'd be no bloody use to her if he didn't rest up.

She swung her feet over the side of the bed and thrust them into her slippers. She shrugged into her dressing gown and padded out of her room, the need to see her daughter pressing her forward even as her body asked for more rest. She'd have to express some milk soon. Despite the fact Darcey was being fed through a tube, Tally still had a job to do.

The NICU was quiet with only Shelley inside, tending to the four babies who needed extra care. Tally paused outside the door, her eyes fixed on her daughter. She was so beautiful, perfect in every way, and even though she was a preemie, the doctors said she was doing fantastically well and they expected to be able to remove her breathing tube sometime that day.

"Precious, aren't they?"

Tally jumped. She'd been joined by a woman in her fifties with dark hair pinned up in a neat bun.

"Sorry," Tally said. "I didn't hear you come in."

"Which one is yours?"

Tally pointed. "The one at the front, on the right-hand side."

"Ah, a girl. She's beautiful."

"Yes," Tally said. "She is."

"And you, are you doing okay?"

"I'm fine." She laughed. "A little stiff and sore, but that's to be expected." Tally tilted her head to one side. "Are you here visiting someone?"

The woman nodded. "My granddaughter."

Tally glanced at the babies. Two boys and two girls. Tally's gaze fell on the cot opposite Darcey's. "She's a little cutie."

"I'm Meredith, by the way," the woman said, holding out her hand.

"Tally."

"Have they said when your little one will be able to go home?"

"Not yet. I'm expecting a few weeks, though." Tally made a move towards the door. "Are you coming in?"

Meredith shook her head. "No, I have to be somewhere. I'll pop back later."

"Well, it was nice to meet you. Maybe we'll bump into each other again."

"That would be lovely." Meredith turned around to leave and then spoke over her shoulder. "Take care of yourself, Tally."

"You too." Tally pushed open the door to NICU. She was anxious to touch Darcey. Without the feel of the baby's soft skin beneath her fingers, she no longer felt whole.

"Morning," Shelley said as she grabbed a chair and placed it in front of Darcey's cot. "How are you feeling?"

Tally sank into the chair and opened the round door that separated her from her daughter. She relaxed the minute her hand touched Darcey's skin. "Knackered. Euphoric."

Shelley laughed. "Pretty normal, then. You okay to get some feed ready?"

Tally grinned. "Sure am. Can I do it?"

"Absolutely."

Shelley helped her connect the pump. If anyone had told her she'd be doing this a week ago, she'd have laughed in their face. But it felt completely normal. A means to an end to give her daughter the best nutrition possible.

Shelley showed her how to add the milk to the feeding tube, and although she was desperate to feed her baby via natural means, at the moment this was the best she had. As she injected her milk into the feeding tube, protective instinct flooded through her. God, she loved this kid. More than anyone else alive, including Cash. She would do anything to protect her baby. She'd kill for her. Die for her.

"You started without me?"

She glanced around in time to see Cash walk in. "I woke early and couldn't wait to see her. You look much better."

He grinned, the smile she loved, and bent down to kiss her cheek. "Amazing what eight hours of sleep will do for a man."

"I missed you," she said, resting her head on his shoulder when he pulled up a seat.

"Did you sleep okay?"

"Too good. I want to be able to say I was awake all night

because I couldn't sleep without you beside me, but I'd be lying. Dead to the world until I woke this morning."

"We'd better make the most of that. When this little one comes home, times are going to change."

"Can't wait," she said.

Cash curled his fingers around hers. "I wanted to talk to you about that."

Tally frowned. "What, her coming home?"

"Yeah. I don't want you exhausted all the time. What do you think about getting a nanny?"

Tally stiffened. "I'm not sure about that."

Cash casually rested his hand on her inner thigh. "Think about it. No need to make a decision right now."

A nanny... she'd never even considered it. Darcey was her baby. She didn't want some stranger doing all the things she should be doing. Feeding, changing, getting up in the middle of the night, looking after her when she was sick. That was what she'd signed up for. What she wanted.

"Stop stressing," Cash said, correctly reading her inner turmoil. "I don't mean full-time. Just someone to take the load when you need a break, and give us some alone time."

"What about asking Anna to come across for a little while?"

"I did think about that, but she looks after her grandkids on Tuesdays and Thursdays."

Tally wrinkled her nose. "Of course. I'd forgotten."

"Don't worry about it for now. It'll be a while before she's ready to come home. We can see how it goes."

Tally handed the empty vial to Shelley and opened the incubator, touching Darcey's warm little body with the back of her hand.

"I never did thank you for agreeing to move to London. I know how much you miss home."

Cash shook his head. "No, you were right. Our place in Ireland is great, but it's too remote. We can always go back for weekends, and when she's older, maybe then we can think about moving back permanently."

His phone buzzed with an incoming call, earning him a sharp glance from Shelley. "It's Mum," he said, standing up. "I'll take it outside."

He closed the door with a quiet click, and Tally watched as he sauntered down the corridor. He still had the best arse she'd ever seen.

"Looking forward to her coming off the ventilator later?" Shelley said.

Tally dragged her attention back into the room. "Can't wait. Does that mean I'll be able to hold her?"

"It does."

A thrill of excitement ran through her, and goose bumps sprang up on her arms, making the hairs stand on end. "I can't believe she's well enough to come off it today."

"Yeah. She's a tough one."

"Takes after her dad," Tally said. "He's made of strong stuff."

"He's passed it on to his daughter, then."

"How long do you think she'll have to stay?"

Shelley shrugged. "Difficult to say. But if she carries on doing as well as she has the last twenty-four hours, I would say she'll be ready to go home in a few weeks once she's put some weight on."

"Mum's here," Cash said, sticking his head around the door. "I'll go and get her."

"Great," Tally said, smiling broadly. She couldn't wait to show off her daughter.

"Do you get on well with your mother-in-law then?" Shelley asked.

"Extremely," Tally said, even though the title of *mother-in-law* wasn't quite accurate yet. "She's like the mother I never had."

Shelley gave her a sympathetic look. "Oh, I'm sorry, sweetie."

Tally shook her head. "Don't be. My mum walked out on me and my dad when I was four. And now I've got Darcey, I understand that decision even less. I can't imagine ever being able to leave her."

"Yes, I'm sure," Shelley murmured.

A tap on the window alerted her, and she turned her head. Rachael couldn't have been smiling any wider. Her smile was so wide that her cheeks had to be aching. Tally waved while Cash ushered his mother into the room.

"Oh my goodness." Rachael squeezed some hand gel into her palms and rubbed them together. "She's so beautiful."

"Here," Cash said, pulling up a chair so his mother could sit.

Rachael hugged Tally warmly. "I'm so sorry I wasn't here, darling. Are you okay?"

"Don't worry. It didn't exactly go according to plan."

"But look at her," Rachael said. "May I?"

"Go ahead," Tally said, unfastening one of the two round plastic coverings that allowed access inside the incubator.

Rachael touched Darcey's foot. "She looks so much like you, Cash."

"So everyone keeps saying. Poor kid."

Rachael gave him an admonishing look. "You were a beautiful baby, and you're beautiful now."

"You got that right." Tally looked up at him.

Cash kissed the top of her head. "How about we leave Grandma with Darcey and I take you for some breakfast."

She felt a momentary stab of panic. Surely it was too soon to leave her?

"Please," Rachael said eagerly. "It would give me time to get to know my granddaughter."

Cash folded his fingers around Tally's hand and tugged her to her feet. "Come on, babe."

"A coffee would be good," Tally admitted, and as if the universe was plotting against her, her stomach rumbled. "And a bacon sandwich," she added with a grin.

She must have glanced over her shoulder five times between

leaving the NICU and disappearing through the door at the end of the corridor. She didn't miss Cash rolling his eyes. Maybe it was different for guys, but her anxiety levels increased every time she was away from her daughter.

"Relax." Cash squeezed her hand. "I know it's difficult. It is for me too."

"Is it?" she said, a note of hysteria leaking into her tone.

"Yes," he said reassuringly. "But you have to calm down."

"Oh God," she groaned. "I'm going to be one of *those* mothers, aren't I? I'll be acting all weird and neurotic every time my precious offspring is out of sight."

Cash laughed. "Give yourself a break. She's only a day old, and we weren't exactly expecting her yet." He put his arm around her shoulder and kissed her temple. "I get it."

She leaned into him, hoping his strength would bolster her. "I don't know what I would do without you."

"You'll never have to find out."

By the time Cash had put a steaming cup of coffee and a bacon sandwich in front of her, Tally realised how right he'd been to make her take a break. With some food inside her stomach and a good slug of caffeine, her earlier panic subsided.

"I hate it when you're right," she said, tearing off another chunk of sandwich. "This is really good."

"Life would be easier if you did exactly what I said, without argument," Cash teased.

"Dream on," she said.

He grinned. "Gotta have goals."

"Speaking of which," Tally said, giving him a firm, no-nonsense stare, "when are you getting back on tour?" A dart of sadness swept through her as she realised they'd had this conversation several times over the course of their relationship.

Cash teased his beard with his fingertips. "I don't know. A while. With Darcey coming early, and Kinga... my head's not in it."

Tally groaned. "I feel awful."

"Why?"

"Because yet again, I'm keeping you from doing what you love."

Cash clasped her hand, a mischievous expression on his face. "Yes, you are. Six weeks, the doctor said when I asked him."

Tally frowned, and then she clapped a hand over her mouth. "You didn't."

"Oh yes, I did," he said, looking rather pleased with himself. "Still, I'm sure there's other stuff we can try." He winked.

"I can't believe you spoke to the doctor about when we could have sex." She giggled. "You have no shame."

"Sweetness, I don't think it's a secret we have sex. Otherwise, we wouldn't have Darcey, and besides, it's going to be fucking difficult keeping my hands off you, so I wanted to know the boundaries."

"Even with my jiggly bits." She wobbled her flabby post-pregnancy belly, which still looked as if she had a baby inside.

Cash scowled, his light mood dissipating like a puff of air. "Don't, Natalia. Just fucking don't, or I am seriously going to lose my temper."

"Oh, come on, Cash. Not exactly attractive, is it?"

His scowl deepened. "I am not having this fucking conversation," he hissed. "But it's good to know you think I'm so shallow that my absolute idolisation of you is purely skin-deep."

He launched himself to his feet, causing the chair he'd been sitting in to scrape loudly against the floor. Several heads turned their way as Cash stormed out of the hospital canteen, his back rigid, fists clenched by his side.

Tally sighed. They'd been having such fun. Why did she have to go and ruin it with her hang-ups? She recalled a conversation she'd had with her dad when she was thirteen. She was way more developed than most of her friends at school, and she'd taken to wearing huge jumpers to cover her breasts, which had become a fascination for boys and girls alike. When her dad tackled her about her radical change in clothing, she told him she was saving up to have them cut off. He'd laughed and ruffled her hair and told her not to worry about it, that her friends were jealous because she was growing up faster than they were. She'd always struggled with her desire to be stick thin. Unfortunately, she had a body frame that would never bend to that shape. She knew how much Cash hated it when she was hard on herself, but she couldn't seem to stop picking the thread.

She rose from the chair and followed him outside. He hadn't gone far. He was resting his palms against a floor-to-ceiling window, his shoulders hunched as he stared down into the hospital gardens. He flinched when her hand landed on his back, and she did her best not to follow suit.

"Sorry, ace."

He hesitated and then turned his gaze on hers. "I hate it when you do that."

"I know."

"Then why?"

She chewed her lip. Simple question. Difficult to answer. "I don't know. I've always been the same. I saw a photo of my mother once, in a shoebox in my dad's wardrobe." She grinned at the memory. "I was snooping for Christmas presents. She had exactly the body shape I would have loved. Tall, thin, great legs. I've always thought one of the reasons she left is that I must have been such a disappointment to her."

Cash's eyes softened, and he held out his arms. She went to him willingly, tucking her head under his chin. He kissed the top of her head.

"Baby, you were four when your mother left. Whatever the reason, I doubt it was because she looked into the future and saw you might not quite fit into size-eight jeans. If I can say anything to reassure you, it's this: I *love* your curves. I adore every single thing about your body." He withdrew slightly, allowing their eyes to meet. "And your 'jiggly bits,' as you so eloquently put it, are what allowed our daughter to be born. Are you saying you'd change that?"

Tally shook her head vigorously. "Absolutely not."

"Then stop, okay? If you seriously want to get fitter, when your body has had time to recover, we'll do it together. But know this. I. Don't. Care."

She tilted her face up, and he took her cue, his mouth covering hers for too brief a moment. When he pulled back, she mourned the loss of contact.

"I could kiss you all day," Cash said. "But I figure it might be time to feed the baby."

"What makes you say that?" Tally said with a frown.

Cash glanced down, a cheeky grin gracing his face. "Because, sweetness, you're leaking on me."

34

Cash watched through the window as Natalia lifted Darcey from her cot. His daughter was bawling, her little face screwed up as she railed at whatever outrage had irked her. Natalia cradled the baby over her shoulder, her mouth moving as she talked to Shelley. He tried to lip read but couldn't make out what she was saying.

How had he got so lucky? He was so in love, so obsessed, he could barely remember life before his daughter came along five weeks ago.

As though sensing his adoring gaze through the window, Natalia turned. She smiled and waved him inside. As soon as he walked through the door, she held Darcey out in front. "Someone wants her daddy, I think. Maybe you'll have better luck calming her."

He took Darcey from Natalia and settled her in the crook of his left arm. "It's because she knows she's leaving hospital today, and it's probably scary going somewhere new," he said, rocking her. "After all, this is all she knows."

Within a minute, he'd appeased her. She curled her hand tightly around his outstretched finger and gurgled.

Natalia shook her head. "How do you do it?"

Cash grinned. "Luck of the Irish, baby," he said, kissing Darcey's forehead before laying her gently back in her cot. He tucked her in, and she made a contented snuffling noise and promptly fell asleep.

"Clearly," Natalia said as she folded Darcey's blanket. She added it to the suitcase full of things their daughter had collected since her birth and extended stay in hospital. "Jeez, babies need a lot of stuff."

"I can't wait to get out of here." Cash moved behind Natalia and curved his arms around her waist. "It's been a long five weeks."

She leaned into him. "Are the press outside?"

"Yes, but don't worry—Isaac's waiting for us. He'll have the car ready to go. Just ignore them."

Natalia made a soft sigh. "You'd think, given the length of time you've been out of the public eye, they wouldn't be interested."

"We'll soon be home. A quick run of the gauntlet, and we're free," Cash said, turning her in his arms. He pressed a soft kiss to her lips.

"Knowing my luck, I'll trip over the hem of my skirt and go splat on the pavement. Think what an amazing photo opportunity that will be."

Cash grinned. "I won't let you fall, baby."

"Is Rachael at home?"

"Yep. And Emmalee, and Rupe. And Pete."

"Is anyone else coming?"

He stroked his beard thoughtfully. "William said if Kinga's feeling up to it, they may pop over."

"No Brad or Jamie?"

"Oh yeah, them too."

Natalia chuckled. "So we're having a massive welcome home party?"

"You weren't supposed to guess."

She narrowed her eyes. "Tell me you're joking."

He painted on the most innocent face he could muster. "Sweetness, would I?"

A soft sigh escaped her lips. "Okay, I'll play ball on one condition."

"Name it."

"They get one hour to fawn over the baby, and then that's it. I want them gone." She rested her forehead on his shoulder. "I want it to be us. You and me and Darcey, relaxing in our own home, sharing a glass of wine and a bit of peace."

"Okay. One hour. Might need to make that wine nonalcoholic, though, baby."

Natalia twisted out of his arms and returned to Darcey's suitcase. She reopened it, pulling out several bottles of expressed milk. She held them aloft while wearing a triumphant look. "I've thought of everything."

Cash laughed. "I'm so glad being a mother hasn't dampened your spirit."

Natalia grinned. "I haven't had a drink in over eight months. Eight very long months. Tonight, I want nothing more than to sit on the sofa with my seriously hot fiancé beside me and a very cold glass of Chablis nestling right here." She held her hand up in a semicircle and tapped her palm. "With any luck, Darcey will be exhausted from being passed around and fall fast asleep."

"Hot fiancé?" Cash said with a raised eyebrow. He caught her hips and tugged her closer, whispering in her ear, "That makes me think of all sorts of possibilities."

Natalia pulled back a little and met his gaze. Laughter lines crinkled the edges of her stunning blue eyes, drawing him in as they always had. "Well, seeing as we have around a week to go, let's see how creative you can be, ace."

"Oh, baby," he said in a teasing tone. "That sounds awfully like a challenge."

Natalia picked up one of the bags and thrust it at him. "You always did love a challenge."

As they got set to leave, Shelley appeared and gave them both a hug.

"You've been amazing," Natalia said. "We couldn't have got through this without you."

"It's been my absolute pleasure, sweetie. Don't take this the wrong way, but I'm delighted you're going home."

Cash kissed her cheek. "So are we. Thanks for everything."

Shelley ducked her head to hide the flush that swept across her face. "Good luck, you guys. Not that you'll need it."

Cash picked up the bags while Natalia cradled Darcey. As he ushered her out of the NICU, she glanced up at him, her eyes sparkling with laughter. "Still got it, ace," she said, jerking her head back.

Cash rolled his eyes. "She's older than my mother."

A few of the staff had gathered in the reception area to say goodbye, but a throng of photographers who were camped on the pavement outside the hospital caught Cash's attention. The sliding doors at the entrance were tinted, making it difficult for the photographers to see inside, but Cash counted at least twenty. Isaac had the back door to the car open, his large frame dwarfing the people around him. As Cash's eyes met Natalia's, panic flitted across her face.

"It's okay," he said. "Here, give Darcey to me."

He nestled the baby into his arms and pulled up her blanket so her face couldn't be seen. The hospital security guard kindly picked up their bags and ventured outside. The minute the automatic doors opened, multiple flashes went off, almost blinding him.

He cursed, tucked Natalia's hand inside his, and made a beeline for the car. As soon as Isaac spotted them, he muscled a few overly keen paps out of the way, leaving the pathway clear.

The noise was intense with photographers and reporters shouting demands and instructions.

He urged Natalia into the car and climbed in beside her. Isaac slammed the door. Cash strapped Darcey into the car seat.

"Go, Isaac," he said as the camera flashes continued to intrude into the car.

They moved away from the hospital, leaving the paparazzi behind, and Cash took a breath. As he blew it out, he released the enormous tension that had been riding him hard for the last five weeks.

"You okay, babe?" he said, tucking a lock of hair behind Natalia's ear.

"I am now. I've been dreading that."

"I'd love to know where they get their information from."

Natalia wrapped her fingers around his. "Don't sweat it, ace."

Cash almost growled, the noise rumbling low in his chest. "It was bad enough before, but now..." He pressed his finger to his daughter's hand, and Darcey automatically grabbed on. A flush of intense love swept through him, taking his breath away.

"I know," Natalia said softly, correctly reading the rapt expression on his face. "Makes you look at things in a whole new way."

As the car turned into the narrow driveway that led up to the Victorian detached property he and Natalia now called home, their family and friends were camped outside. Cash began to regret agreeing to the welcoming committee, especially when a soft sigh escaped Natalia's lips.

"I'm sorry, baby. I shouldn't have caved to pressure. I can still tell them the party's off."

She gave him a quick smile. "I want to say yes, but remember... one hour. Then they're gone."

He unclipped his seatbelt and shuffled towards her then cradled her jaw with his hand, relishing the soft skin beneath his fingers. Her breathing kicked up a notch as he leaned in. "Love you so much." His mouth closed over hers in an all-too-brief kiss.

"Hold that thought, ace," she muttered against his lips before he reluctantly pulled away.

As Cash got out of the car, Rachael reached them. She hugged him tightly as though she hadn't seen him in weeks. "I'm so glad you're both home."

"Us too," he said, extricating himself from his mother's arms so he could unhook Darcey's car seat. He lifted his daughter out of the car and held a hand out for Natalia. "Mum, do us a favour. After an hour, call a halt to things, okay? Natalia's tired, and I don't want everyone outstaying their welcome."

"Leave it with me." She linked her arm through Natalia's and seized the car seat from Cash. "Get the cases, darling," she said, drawing a giggle from Natalia. Rachael was one of a few people able to get away with ordering Cash about.

For the next hour, everyone fought over who would get to cuddle Darcey next. Natalia sat back, allowing them all to have a piece of her precious child, but Cash could see her hands itching, wanting to snatch Darcey away from them.

"Soon be over," he said, nuzzling her ear.

"I'm trying so hard." She rested her head on his shoulder.

"You're doing great, baby. We're the first out of all of us to have one, apart from Mum. It's a novelty, that's all."

True to her promise, after an hour Rachael began to corral the group into leaving. Their friends extended the hour with goodbyes and promises that they'd be there if either Cash or Natalia needed them, and then he was finally able to close the door. He sagged against it and closed his eyes, relishing the silence.

When he walked back into the living room, Natalia was settling Darcey into her Moses basket. He waited for her to finish, and then he snaked his arms around her waist, his chin resting on her shoulder. "Alone at last," he murmured, his teeth nipping her earlobe.

Natalia covered his hands with her own and tilted her head to the side, giving him access to her neck. "Ace?" she said as he kissed from jaw to shoulder.

"Yeah?"

"You know what I really want?"

"Me." He smiled against her neck.

"Before that."

"Name it."

"A bath."

Cash straightened. "You got it, sweetness. Stay here, and I'll go and run it."

TALLY TUCKED the covers around Darcey, her heart bursting with love. Ever since she'd gone into labour, she'd suffered so much stress and worry, but all that was behind them. They were home with their perfectly healthy daughter. Darcey's arrival seemed to have grounded Cash. He was centred and calm, as though having Darcey had finally chased away his demons. Sometimes, when Cash didn't think she was watching, she caught him gazing at their daughter with a mixture of wonderment, adoration, and love.

She leaned over the Moses basket and kissed her sweet baby, breathing in that special smell only babies had. She was desperate to hold her, to feel her safe and warm in her arms, but Darcey had been passed around too much already and was fast asleep, arms angled next to her head. Her plump cheeks were flushed and her mouth parted. She looked so much like Cash it was uncanny. There was certainly no denying she was his child. If Darcey hadn't had Tally's eyes, Tally wouldn't have believed she and her daughter were related.

She stretched out her back. A bath, bed, and falling asleep in Cash's arms sounded like her version of heaven. She placed the baby monitor on the table next to the Moses basket and grabbed the other one to take upstairs with her. She'd almost reached the bathroom when a knock at the door halted her progress.

"Great," she groaned. "Who's forgotten something?"

She trudged back downstairs, eyelids heavy with exhaustion. She unbolted the door and opened it a crack. Her eyes widened.

"Meredith," she said, immediately recognising the woman she'd had a brief conversation with outside the NICU the day after Darcey was born. "What are you doing here?"

Meredith was wringing her hands, her face full of angst. "Can I come in, Tally? I'm afraid I haven't been completely honest with you."

Tally frowned. "It's not a great time. I've only just got home from the hospital."

"I know. I followed you. I've been waiting for everyone to leave."

"You followed us?" Hairs stood up on the back of her neck. A stranger had managed to follow them home, to find out where they lived. She'd hoped they wouldn't have to live surrounded by walls and gates and cameras, but it looked like she'd been wrong. "Why?"

"Let's do this inside."

Meredith began to move forward, but Tally put her arm out, blocking her entrance. "Actually, I think I'd rather do it right here. What's going on?"

Meredith looked her straight in the eye. "It has taken me a long time to pluck up the courage to do this. Tally, I'm your mother."

35

Tally stared as her jaw dropped open. Her stomach tied itself in knots, and a horrible sickly feeling spread through her gut. Her mouth dried up as she gave a slow, disbelieving shake of her head.

"Impossible. My mother left when I was four, and I haven't seen her since. And her name was Martine, not Meredith. I'm not sure what game you're playing here, but at least get your facts straight."

"I changed my name some years back. Meredith is nothing like Martine. Please, if you let me in, I'll explain everything."

Meredith tried to capture Tally's hand in hers, but Tally snatched her hand away. "Don't touch me."

"I know what you must be thinking."

"No you don't," Tally said. "You don't know anything about me. Anything at all."

"Please. I'd like an opportunity to explain."

"I'm not interested!" She was yelling now, her stomach tightening painfully. This could not be happening. It had to be a lie. A cruel, vicious lie.

"What the hell is going on?" Cash appeared behind her, his

hands warm and comforting as he placed them on her shoulders. "Who are you?"

"I'm—"

"This is my mother, apparently," Tally cut in, bitter and hurt. "At least according to her."

Meredith pressed her hands together and gave Tally a beseeching look. "Please, Tally, let me come in."

Cash stepped in front of Tally, partially blocking her view of Meredith. "I think Natalia has made it clear she doesn't want to speak to you. Now, you can leave under your own steam, or I can call my security to have you escorted. Your choice."

"Cash, surely you know how wonderful it is to have your mother back in your life after a long absence. I'm only trying to give my daughter the same opportunity."

Tally gasped at the blatant cheek of the woman. Cash's whole body stiffened. She placed a warning hand on his back, even though it wouldn't make a difference.

"How fucking dare you," he bit out. "My mother had no choice. She was in a fucking coma. You, on the other hand, pissed off and left your daughter without a backward glance." He leaned in, his face inches from Meredith's. "I don't know what your game is, but know this. We're not interested. Now, fuck off."

He slammed the door. His body trembled as he pulled Tally into his arms. "You okay, baby?"

She nuzzled against his chest. "No, I'm not. What could she possibly want after all these years?"

"No idea. But I don't want you worrying about it right now. Your bath's ready."

He pointed her towards the stairs, but Tally veered off, heading for the living room instead.

"Babe, where are you going?" Cash called after her.

Ignoring him, she headed straight for Darcey's basket. As she lifted her in the air, her daughter immediately began to cry, incensed at being woken. Tally cradled her, kissed her warm, plump cheek, and whispered loving words into her ear. How could her own mother have left her? Nothing could ever tear her away from her daughter.

Her tears began to mingle with Darcey's, and she startled when Cash wrapped his arms around them both.

"I'm so sorry, baby."

She leaned into him, absorbing his strength because she had none left. An aching hollowness that had started in her stomach spread to her heart. She'd thought her mother couldn't hurt her any more. Turned out she was wrong.

"How could she do it, Cash? How did she walk away, leaving her child behind? I don't understand. She must be evil."

Cash kissed her temple. "I wish I had the answers for you, but I don't." He lifted Darcey out of her arms, rubbing soothing circles on his daughter's back. "Go and get in the bath. You're exhausted. I can't promise you'll feel better after some rest, but it couldn't hurt."

She nodded in agreement. No doubt her overtiredness was making this fubar situation appear worse. With a firm grip on the handrail to support herself, she trudged upstairs.

Steam rose from the bath, along with the scent of salts and bubbles Cash had added. She stripped off and sank down into the hot water. Closing her eyes, she steadied her breathing and tried to push her mother from her mind. She'd been there about five minutes when Cash appeared.

"Want me to scrub your back?" he said, wiggling his eyebrows.

She grinned. "Thank God for you. Is Darcey okay?"

"She's fine. Fast asleep again. I'm starting to feel hopeful we have one of those babies who sleep sixteen hours a day."

Tally tapped her head. "Touch wood."

Cash sat on the edge of the bath and tugged a stray hair from the corner of her mouth. "I found this on the floor in the hall." He held up a piece of paper.

"What is it?"

"Your mother's phone number with a plea for you to call her. What do you want me to do with it?"

Tally's first instinct was to tell him to tear it up into a million pieces and throw it away, but then a sliver of curiosity crept in. Why had her mother chosen now to come back into her life? Was it anything to do with Darcey or Cash, or a complete coincidence?

"Nothing for now," she said. "I'm going to talk to Pete. He's always been very unwilling to share what happened between my mother and father, but now he's got no choice. I'll call him tomorrow."

"Okay. I'll leave it on the hall table downstairs."

As Cash stood to leave, she wrapped her hand around his forearm. "I don't know what I'd do without you, ace," she said, trying to paint on a bright smile but knowing she'd fallen way short.

Cash leaned over, kissing her briefly on the lips. "I'm here, sweetness."

DARCEY WOKE TWICE in the night, disproving Cash's theory that she was going to be one of those rare children who slept through from birth. At least Tally had some milk expressed, so Cash took one shift, and she took the other.

When she finally woke the next morning, the utter exhaustion of the previous day had receded, and she felt more able to cope with the shock of her mother turning up after a twenty-two-year absence. Cash's side of the bed was cold, meaning he'd been up for a while, and when she looked across at Darcey's cot, it was empty.

A slow smile crept across her lips. God, she was lucky. Her time without Cash during the early part of her pregnancy seemed like another lifetime, almost as though it hadn't happened to her. She shook off any regrets that she hadn't told him sooner. They were no use to her now.

She rose out of bed and pulled on her dressing gown. As she headed downstairs, the smell of freshly brewed coffee tickled her nostrils. At the entrance to the kitchen, she paused and drank in the scene before her. Cash was holding Darcey over his shoulder, one hand curved under her bottom while he poured coffee into two mugs with the other. He was humming a lullaby under his breath.

"If all those female fans could see you now," Tally said with a grin.

Cash glanced around, a look of contentment plastered on his face. "Dream stuff. That's me, sweetness."

"You got that right," she said, holding her arms out.

Cash passed Darcey over. "We didn't wake you, did we?"

"Nope. Dead to the world. Hi, baby girl," she said, kissing her plump cheek. "Has she been fed?"

"Yep. And winded. And changed. I told you, dream stuff."

Tally laughed. Holding Darcey in exactly the same position as Cash had, she swept her free hand over his arse. "More like hot stuff," she said, tilting her face up for a kiss. Cash obliged, his lips warm, his kiss all too brief.

"Not in front of the B.A.B.Y.," he said, wagging his finger at her.

"That is never going to work."

"You're probably right. Never have been able to keep my hands off you." He passed her a cup of coffee, and she took a sip.

"Just what I needed."

"Are you calling Pete this morning?"

Tally sighed. "Yeah. I'll see if he can come around after work."

"How do you feel about it today?"

She shrugged. "I don't know. I'm overwhelmed by so many emotions—anger, confusion, frustration—and I can't help being suspicious as to why she's chosen now to turn up. Pete's going to have no choice but to tell me what happened now."

"You never asked him about her?" Cash said, with more than a hint of incredulity to his tone. "Or your dad?"

Tally shook her head. "I was too young when she left, and by the time I reached my teenage years, I was so pissed off that she'd abandoned me I wouldn't have wanted to talk about her even if they did want that discussion—which they didn't."

"Should make for an interesting conversation later, then."

Darcey wriggled in Tally's arms, her legs surprisingly strong as she kicked out. She screwed her face up, intense concentration making her eyes disappear behind scrunched lids, before she let out a loud wail.

"Here, give her to me," Cash said. "Call Pete."

Tally clicked the living room door shut and picked up her phone. She sat on the window seat, her knees curled into her chest. The sky was a deep aqua—very unusual for England, where soft blue was the norm. She pushed open the window, and a light breeze blew hair across her face.

"Hey, Tal," Pete said when he picked up her call. "Hope we didn't outstay our welcome yesterday."

"Of course not," she lied. "We loved having you."

"How's Darcey settling in?"

"Great," Tally said. "She woke a couple of times last night, but she seems to like her new home."

"And Cash. Is he pulling his weight?"

"Enough to make me think I'm surplus to requirements, apart from providing a food-on-demand service. The two of them are inseparable."

Pete's sigh of relief was unmistakeable. "That's good."

"You had doubts?"

"Honestly, yes, I did. The two of you have had more than your fair share of ups and downs, and I wasn't sure whether he was cut out for fatherhood."

"He'd say the same thing, but honestly, Pete, he's the most natural parent I've ever seen. When I woke up this morning, he'd already fed and changed her and was making me a coffee with one hand and holding Darcey with the other."

Pete chuckled. "I'm happy for you, Tally. You deserve the best of everything. About time the rollercoaster pulled into the station so you could get off, right?"

Tally bit her lip. If only that was the reality. "I was wondering if you wanted to come for dinner tonight."

Pete's pause was brief, but it was there. "Is everything okay?"

He's always been able to read me.

"Yes," she answered a little too quickly. "I'm making pasta."

"Well, in that case, I wouldn't miss it. What time do you want me?"

"Seven? You can see Darcey before I put her down."

"Seven it is."

She tossed her phone to one side and stared out of the window, hoping for some inspiration or at least an idea of where to start the conversation with Pete.

Trouble was, it didn't matter where she began, because even though she knew nothing of the reason her mother left, the fact neither her father nor Pete had ever spoken to her about it meant only one thing—she wasn't going to like what she heard.

36

"She's adorable," Pete said as Tally tucked the bedclothes tightly around Darcey and nestled Gary the Gorilla next to her, a gift from Kinga that Cash detested. He thought it wasn't feminine enough for his special girl, but Darcey loved it, and Tally had discovered her daughter slept better when Gary was in close proximity.

"She wasn't adorable at three this morning," Tally grumbled. "Screamed the house down. Good job we don't have close neighbours. They'd be reporting us for noise pollution." She leaned over the cot and kissed her daughter's forehead. "Wouldn't change a second, though."

Pete draped an arm casually over her shoulder. "Let's go and eat, and then you can tell me what's bugging you."

Tally gave him a weak smile. "Am I that transparent?"

"Nah," Pete said. "But I've known you your whole life, kid."

Cash had already put the water on to boil, so they were ready to eat five minutes later. Pete did his usual trick of wearing more sauce than he ate, and the familiarity of it comforted Tally when she needed it the most. This wonderful man had been her saviour after her dad died, taking her in, letting her disrupt his perfect bachelor lifestyle with teenage hormones and temper tantrums.

As he dropped his fork, a goofy grin appeared on his face, and he pointed to his red-splattered shirt. Tally jumped from her chair and flung her arms around him.

"I don't tell you this often enough, Uncle Pete, but I love you to death. I'll never forget what you did for me when Dad died."

"Hey, hey," he said, absentmindedly patting her arm. As she pulled away, she caught the puzzled look he gave Cash, who simply shrugged.

Pete tapped the rim of his wine glass. "Why don't you fill that up and then tell me what's going on."

Cash did the honours, and when he searched for Tally's hand beneath the table, his long fingers easily wrapping around hers, a tidal wave of emotions hit her. Blinking back imminent tears, she squeezed his hand, hoping he understood the silent message.

"Not long after you left yesterday, there was a knock at the door. I assumed one of you had forgotten something. When I opened it, a woman I had a brief conversation with at the hospital the day after Darcey's birth was outside. At the time, she told me her name was Meredith and she was visiting her granddaughter. She seemed lovely. Warm."

Tally paused to take a sip of water.

"I was confused about what she was doing at my house, until she blurted out she was my mother."

Pete gasped, a strangled, shocked, quick intake of breath. "No. That can't be right. Your mum's name was Martine."

"I know. That's what I said. She told me she changed her name years back. That Martine was nothing like Meredith."

Pete scrambled to his feet and began pacing. He was blinking rapidly as though he couldn't quite believe what was unfolding in front of him, and he kept tugging on the tails of his shirt as he flashed the occasional sideways glance at her.

"What else did she say?"

225

"I didn't give her much chance to say anything. She told me she wanted to explain. I refused, and then Cash turned up and asked her to leave."

"I actually told her to fuck off," Cash said.

His interjection was a welcome relief, and even Pete's lips curved upward with the hint of a smile. "Right answer."

"She left a contact number," Tally said. "Wants me to call her."

Pete stopped pacing and sat back down. He picked up Tally's free hand, leaving her other one still firmly in Cash's grasp. "She's bad news, Tal. I know your dad and I weren't exactly forthcoming in telling you what went on, but believe me when I say it was for your own good. We only ever had your best interests at heart."

"I understand." Tally's heart began to pound. "But now that she has turned up, I need to know what happened. I need to know everything."

He nodded, but the maelstrom of emotions shifting across his face told a different story.

"Everything," she reiterated. "I don't want it sugar-coated, and I don't want anything left out. I'm a big girl now with a child of my own."

He sighed as his eyes fell shut for a second or two, no doubt allowing him time to gather his thoughts. "I hoped this day would never come. When your dad died, I expected you to ask about your mum, but you never did. Almost as though you thought it was disrespectful to John. As the years passed, I began to hope we'd never hear from her again and you'd forget all about her."

"And if she hadn't turned up, you'd have been right."

"Still fucking everything up," Pete muttered, almost to himself. He took a sip of wine—well, more like a gulp—and when he placed the glass back down, his face had taken on a resigned, if not quite receptive, expression.

"From the moment your dad met Martine, he idolised her.

There was nothing he wouldn't do for that woman, and although it kills me, I have to admit she did seem to feel the same way about him, at least at first. Thirty years ago, she was a real stunner, and your dad was convinced he was punching above his weight. But for whatever reason, Martine chose him.

"I remember on their wedding day John pulled me to one side and told me how happy he was, that all his dreams had come true. And when you were born, his life was complete. A stunning wife and a beautiful daughter. Who could hope for more?"

"Not me," Cash murmured.

Tally turned to him and smiled. He was looking at her with such reverence, almost in awe. She'd seen that same look on his face several times since Darcey had been born, as if he couldn't quite believe he was living this life. The irony was that she, too, thought she was punching above her weight.

"For the first year or so after you were born, everything seemed fine, but Martine wasn't the sort of woman who relished being cooped up all day, especially with a baby. She began to crave excitement, something to contrast what she saw as a dull and boring existence. John tried his best, taking her to concerts, the theatre, nightclubs, even though he'd rather have stayed at home and cuddled up on the sofa with you and her. Over time, their innate differences began to show.

"And then, without warning, Martine seemed to accept her new life. She stopped pestering your dad to take her out. John was thrilled, obviously. The late nights while he was trying to build a career were beginning to take their toll, so her change of heart couldn't have come at a better time."

"How old was I then?" Tally said.

Pete's nose crinkled. "About eighteen months."

"So what went wrong?"

"John was desperate for you to have a sibling, and he pushed your mum pretty hard, but Martine wasn't the maternal type. I don't doubt she loved you then, but the thought of going through all that again... well, let's just say she didn't hide her horror. After a while, John gave up on the idea of another child and poured all his love into you.

"It took a while for him to realise something wasn't quite right. It started with little things. Money would go missing from his wallet. An antique clock that had been left to him by your grandfather disappeared, supposedly broken. She lost her engagement ring. She'd always been slight, but she began to lose weight, enough that you could see her bones sticking through her clothes."

"Didn't get my arse from her, then," Tally said, earning a sharp look from Cash.

Pete might as well have been in a trance for all the notice he took of the interruption. "When you were about two and a half, John came home from work early because he felt unwell. As soon as he opened the door, he knew something was wrong. You were clawing at the sides of your playpen, screaming for Martine at the top of your lungs. There was no sign of her. John picked you up and began shouting for her as he searched room to room. He found her passed out in the bathroom with a needle sticking out of her arm."

"Drugs?" Tally whispered as Cash pressed closer.

Pete nodded. "Heroin. John called an ambulance, and she was rushed to hospital with a suspected overdose. When she recovered, she told John she'd tried it a few months earlier because she was bored." Pete's incredulous tone verbalised exactly how Tally was feeling inside.

"She took heroin as a way to mitigate *boredom*?"

"Believe me, your dad was just as horrified as I was. Because she'd OD'd with you in the house, social services got involved and threatened to take you into care. Your dad was almost insane with worry he'd lose you, and after several meetings, social services agreed to leave you in his care, but only if your mother went into rehab."

"And did she?"

"Yes. The first time was fairly successful, and John thought that was it. She'd won her battle with heroin."

"But she hadn't?"

"Over the next eighteen months, your mum relapsed seven times."

Cash hissed. "Holy shit."

"And that's why he threw her out?" Tally said.

Pete shook his head. "No. John supported her the whole way through. He was insistent she'd recover. He fully believed his love would be enough to get through to her. He never stopped loving her even after everything she'd done. The lying and stealing, selling things of sentimental value. Even with her neglect of you, he refused to give up on her, but it didn't make a difference. By then, Martine had only one love in her life—heroin—and she'd do anything to get her next fix."

"So what did happen?" Even as Tally asked the question, she almost wanted to slam her hands over her ears, to beg Pete to stop talking. She didn't want to know. She didn't *need* to know what the catalyst had been to her mum finally leaving. If her dad had forgiven everything that came before, the inciting event must have been truly awful.

"She'd been out of the last bout of rehab about six weeks. For the first two, John told me she was clean, but he knew the minute she relapsed. All the sneaking around and the lies began again, but this time, he made sure she couldn't get her hands on any money, and they didn't have much left in terms of possessions to sell. She'd already sold anything of value. He was insistent that if she couldn't pay for the drugs, the pusher wouldn't supply them. But he'd forgotten she did have one thing of value. At least to a certain type of person."

As an unbelievable realisation swept over Tally, she wanted to turn back the clock, to forget she'd asked Pete to come over. She wanted to run upstairs and cuddle her daughter, to be connected to something innocent. Surely that would make this horror go away. Her mouth seemed to move without her brain giving permission.

"Go on," she said, her voice scratching, as if the sound were being forced through wire wool.

"Your dad found out she was turning tricks in return for her daily fix."

Even though she'd guessed, hearing the actual words was the worst thing that had ever happened in her life. Her mother had been a prostitute, selling her body to God knows who in return for heroin. She half expected a panic attack, but instead of the clammy sweats, escalated breathing, and constricted heart, she felt cold. Ice cold.

"How did he find out?" Cash asked.

Pete grimaced. "She gave him an STI."

"They were still sleeping together?" Cash's voice sounded strange, although that could have been because a fog had covered Tally, making it difficult to hear, like the way she felt when her ears kept popping during a plane's descent.

"He always believed she'd win the battle in the end. And still, he forgave her, until he found out she was taking Tally along when she met her... clients."

"What?" Tally managed to force the word through a mouth devoid of saliva. Her top lip was stuck to her teeth, and a cold sweat drenched her. Cash's arm shot out to steady her, and she realised she'd started to waver.

"I got you, baby."

"She took me with her?"

Pete nodded. "John went crazy when he found out. I happened to be visiting when she staggered through the door with you in tow, reeking of booze and fags and sex."

"Fuck," Cash bit out.

"She was high. And belligerent. She told John it was no fucking big deal. Said it was part of your sex education. I swear,

Tal, when she said that, I thought he was going to kill her. He screamed at me to grab you, which I did. He had her by the hair. He dragged her upstairs, made her pack a bag. He chucked some money at her when he pushed her through the front door and told her if she ever came near you again, he'd kill her. She believed him. *I believed him.*"

"Didn't she fight back? Didn't she fight for me at all?" Tears dripped down Tally's cheeks and over her chin, but she didn't bother to wipe them. As terrible as her mother had been, something deep within her still craved a mother's love.

"I'm so sorry, Tally, but in the end, she loved heroin more than she loved you. I hope you understand now why your dad and I never spoke about that time."

She rose from her chair and cocked her head at the bottle of wine.

"I'm going to express some milk," she said to Cash. "Then you're going to pour me a very large glass of wine."

As she headed for the stairs, Cash must have started to come after her because she heard Pete say, "Let her be," before their voices faded.

Her legs might as well have been made of lead as she hauled herself upstairs. She couldn't believe it. Her mother was a junkie and a prostitute who'd taken her own daughter to watch while she was fucked by God knows how many men at a time. And all to chase her next fix. She'd had it all—a healthy and happy child and an adoring husband who worked hard to forge a career that meant he'd be able to take care of them both. Yet she'd chosen to shoot her veins full of crap instead. Heroin had been preferable to life with her daughter.

No wonder Tally had confidence issues. Hatred rushed through her, making her light-headed with the strength of it. Martine, Meredith—whatever the hell her name was—had turned up the previous day wanting to explain. How could she explain what she'd done? How could anyone *excuse* that?

Tally bent over Darcey's Moses basket, and as she looked at her sleeping daughter, the anger drained away. Darcey had her arms up by her head in a pose of surrender, blissfully unaware of the terrible truths her mother had heard that evening. Tally couldn't imagine anything tearing her away from her daughter. She could never envisage a time when she'd choose drugs over her precious baby girl.

She sat in the rocking chair and attached the breast pump. Closing her eyes, she gave herself over to the odd suckling sensation. By the time she'd finished, she had enough feed to last Darcey through that night and half of the next day—and she'd made her decision.

Her legs were lighter on the way down. Taking control had removed the heavy weight from her shoulders, the weight she'd borne since her mother had turned up unannounced the previous day.

Cash clambered to his feet as soon as she appeared. She swapped the bottled breast milk for a large glass of wine. She took a sip. And then another, larger one.

"I needed that."

"Are you okay?" Cash asked, concern lacing his voice.

She nodded. "I am." She faced Pete. "I'm going to agree to her request to see me. And I want you here when she comes."

37

Cash waited for Natalia to climb into bed before he flicked off the bedside lamp, which plunged the room into darkness except for a trickle of light that bled through the curtains. With only the sound of Darcey's soft breathing, Cash could trick himself into thinking they didn't have a care in the world.

Except that Pete's revelations—and Natalia's response—meant anything but.

She curled into his side, needing contact with him as much as he did with her. He draped an arm around her waist, his thumb gently brushing her hip, and he waited. After a couple of soft sighs, Natalia lifted her head off the pillow.

"You think I'm making a mistake, don't you?"

He hesitated, wanting to take a second or two to make sure his response was the right one.

"I'm torn between wanting to support you and being worried that meeting your mother will bring you further heartache. We've both had our fair share of that, and I hoped that now it was our turn to live the happily ever after."

She kissed his shoulder, the closest part of his body to her mouth, and then left her lips there. Her breath was hot against his skin, and he tightened his hold on her hip at the resultant rush of pleasure.

"I'm strong enough to deal with this, ace. Trust me."

"I do trust you, but I'm aware of how much your mother leaving impacted your entire life. I know she's the reason you're so down on yourself about who you are and the way you look, and it pisses me off."

"I know." She giggled. "Couldn't miss the death stare when I mentioned not getting my arse from her."

"You saw that, then?"

She waved her hand in front of her face. "Yep. Got the burns to prove it."

He chuckled, despite the seriousness of the situation. "I don't want her to hurt you any more than she already has."

Natalia set her jaw. "She won't."

"Hell of a shock though, baby. Even you can't have imagined the real reason she left."

"No."

Her voice broke slightly on the painful admission, and Cash rolled over and held her gently against his chest. He stroked her hair while trying to come up with some fantastically brilliant sentence that would make her feel better. He sensed her pain keenly, as sharp as if it were his own.

"Will you stay with me when she comes?"

"If that's what you want," he said.

"It is—but try to hold that Irish tongue of yours."

"I have no idea what you're trying to insinuate," he teased.

They fell into silence. Exhausted, Cash drifted into near sleep. As he was on the brink of unconscious bliss, Natalia spoke.

"Cash?"

He forced his eyes half-open, even though he could have sworn someone had glued tiny weights to the lids in the short time he'd had them shut. "Yeah, baby."

"I know we can't have sex yet. But I need to forget everything. I need you to make me forget."

Natalia's plea dragged him from sleep. Cash leaned up on his elbow. Her face was half in shadow, but he could see well enough to read she was telling the truth rather than saying what she thought he might want to hear.

He cradled her cheek, and then his hand shifted to cup the back of her neck. He moved his face closer until he could taste her sweet breath. Her lips parted in anticipation.

"I love you," he whispered before softly covering her mouth with his.

~

EM WIDENED HER EYES, like a cat with a thermometer suddenly stuck up its arse. Her mouth opened and closed in a fishlike movement. When she finally spoke, it was in true Em style.

"Holy fucking shit."

"You do know when Darcey gets bigger, you're going to have to temper that language. Otherwise I'm going to have the most foul-mouthed toddler this side of Chelsea."

Tally's teasing made Em's lips twitch. "Better tell that soon-to-be-husband of yours to shape up as well, then. He makes my foul mouth look like a honey pot."

"He's been told," Tally said, switching Darcey to her right side before her arm went dead. Darcey pulled a face, making her feelings clear about being moved around while sleeping. Fortunately, she didn't wake.

"I can't get my head around it," Em said. "I mean, it's like something out of a movie rather than real life."

"Try being inside my head."

"And Dozer kept this to himself the whole time."

"Yep."

"So when are you seeing her?"

Tally let out a soft sigh. "Tonight."

"How do you feel?"

She grimaced. "Confused, angry. I can't understand how she could have done it. I mean, why would she take something like heroin in the first place, especially when she had everything she could possibly wish for?"

"I can't answer the why, babes, but heroin is a tough nut to crack. Remember Harry Roberts who was in sixth form with us? He came from a good family and had the brains to rival Stephen Hawking. And yet he went through shit for years before his parents finally got through to him."

"I know, but Harry was a kid wanting to experiment. My mother was in her thirties. And she started taking drugs because she was *bored*. What kind of excuse is that?"

"It's not an excuse, babes." Em leaned over Darcey's pram and fixed the covers, which the baby had kicked off. "Do you look like her?"

Tally shook her head. "She's very different to me. Taller, thinner—much thinner," she added with a wry smile. "Dark hair, brown eyes. She wears the years of drug abuse on her face. You can tell she's been to hell, although beneath that, she's still pretty."

"Your brain must be spinning with it all."

"I'm overwhelmed." Tally swept a tired hand over her face as Em stood and slung her bag over her shoulder.

"Let's go for a walk. You look like you need the fresh air."

Em grabbed Darcey's buggy and, rather annoyingly, managed to set the damn thing up with no trouble—something Tally still hadn't mastered.

"A walk sounds good." Tally carefully tucked Darcey into her buggy, relieved when she managed it without waking her. She grabbed a light jacket and her keys and waved her hand. "You're on godmother duty."

"I was hoping you'd say that," Em said, her wide grin growing even wider. She clutched the handle of the buggy and wheeled it outside.

They weren't too far from Holland Park, which was one of the main reasons Cash and Tally had chosen the house they were living in. While she missed the countryside surrounding their home in Northern Ireland, in London she had the best of both worlds—amenities close by and lots of lovely green open spaces on the doorstep.

They wandered around for a while with Emmalee constantly cooing over Darcey. Tally noticed a few odd glances from people who were probably trying to figure out why her face seemed familiar, but apart from that, they were left alone, although she remained conscious of a paparazzo with a long lens taking snaps that would go viral in hours.

"I need to get back," Tally said when Darcey began to stir. "She'll need a feed soon."

"Do it here," Em said, pointing to a bench beside the children's play area.

Tally rolled her eyes. "Oh yeah. Lovely. My tits on display in the newspapers."

Em laughed. "I'll shield you with my jacket."

"Not gonna happen," Tally said. "Believe me, since being with Cash I've had my eyes well and truly opened about how crafty the press can be. I'm a journalist, and I love my profession, but there are some people out there whose job it is to follow around celebrities and wait for an opportunity to get a snap that will earn them big bucks."

Em raised an eyebrow. "Celebrity, huh?"

"Not me, idiot," Tally said, getting in a good dig with her elbow, which made Em groan. "But can you imagine how embarrassing that would be for Cash?"

Darcey's grizzling had now progressed to full-on wailing.

"We'd better go, then," Em said. "Before your delightful daughter's crying punctures my eardrums."

They hadn't been back long when Cash arrived home, which Em took as her cue to leave. She and Cash shared an awkward half hug. Tally chuckled to herself. Those two vacillated between best buddies and worst enemies.

By the time Tally had seen Em out with a promise to call as soon as her mother had left, Cash already had Darcey in his arms. He was standing by the window, quietly humming to her. She was wide awake, her large blue eyes fixed on his face. Tally couldn't blame her. She'd found herself doing that hundreds of times, both before she'd ever met him and many times since.

She rested her shoulder against the doorframe and watched the two of them, her heart swelling with love and pride. So many women out there were stuck with useless fathers for their children, or blokes who scarpered the minute they heard the patter of tiny feet. Yet there she was, lucky enough to have snared a guy who was not only seriously hot and talented but could also win a prize for dad of the year.

"Spoiling her again?"

Cash glanced over his shoulder. "Yep." He cocked his head, signalling for her to go to him. She wandered over, slid her arm around his waist, and leaned her head on his shoulder.

"Nervous?" he said.

"A little." Tally sighed. "But she wanted to see me, so I'm going to let her do the talking."

"Good idea." Cash moved away to settle Darcey in her Moses basket. Once satisfied she was comfortable, he turned around. "Come here, baby," he said, holding his arms out.

She didn't need a second invitation. He wrapped his arms around her, his embrace warm and solid—he was her rock in the middle of a stormy sea. As he rubbed her back and stroked her hair, she gradually began to relax, her shoulders retreating from underneath her ears to rest in a more normal position.

She caught sight of the clock on the wall. Two hours until she would come face-to-face with the woman who had abandoned her twenty-two years ago, choosing drugs over her own daughter.

Nerves swarmed her stomach. What if Meredith sucked her in, gave her hope she could have a mother who cared, and then broke her heart all over again?

38

N atalia leaped several inches in the air when the knock at the door finally came. Cash briefly touched her arm, and his quick squeeze seemed to settle her.

"I'll get it," he said, sharing a quick glance with Pete. Cash had managed to catch up with Pete earlier without Natalia overhearing. To say Pete hated Meredith—whom he insisted on calling Martine—was an understatement. The look on his face when he spoke about her reminded Cash of his own expression when he was on tour and had to face a reporter he particularly abhorred.

He arranged an impassive expression on his face as he opened the door. Natalia's need to give this woman a chance to explain didn't negate the fact that Martine had walked out on her own child. If she was hoping to make an ally of him, she was going to be sorely disappointed.

"Come in," he said.

Martine thrust a Hamley's bag towards him. "I bought this. For the baby."

The phrase *shove it* was on the cusp of his lips, but he accepted the gift. "Thanks," he said in a tone that was anything but grateful. "This way."

He waved her ahead of him. Her footsteps seemed incredibly light for someone who was going to have to try to explain to her daughter why she'd abandoned her, but when her gaze fell on Pete, she froze.

"I thought it was going to be just us," she said, her eyes darting between Natalia and Cash.

Cash brushed past her, leaving Meredith standing in the doorway. He sat on Natalia's left and clasped her hand, noticing how stiff her fingers were and the rigidity of her spine. He gently brushed his thumb over her knuckles, something that usually soothed and relaxed her, but not today.

"Natalia wanted him here, so he's here. Problem?"

"I don't suppose so," she said, her steps wooden as she crossed the threshold. "Peter."

Pete nodded curtly. "Martine."

"It's Meredith now."

Pete gave a smile, but it didn't reach his eyes. "You can try to pass a lion off as a cat, Martine, but it'll still rip your throat out at the first opportunity."

She blanched, and her hand fluttered to her neck. She closed her fist around a pendant on a thin silver chain.

"I know what you think of me," she said, directing the comment at Pete. "But a lot of time has passed since we last saw each other. I left Martine behind a long time ago."

"Habit of yours, is it—leaving people behind?" Pete said.

"I was glad to leave you behind," Meredith hit back.

"Stop it," Natalia said softly. She turned her gaze on her mother. "Sit down, Meredith."

Relief flooded Meredith's face, and she did as Natalia asked. "Thank you for agreeing to see me."

"Let's get some ground rules agreed on, shall we?" Natalia said, her voice much stronger than Cash had expected, given her tense body language.

She pointed at Pete. "This wonderful man here took me in

after Dad died. Clothed me. Educated me. Let me cry on his shoulder. Supported me financially and emotionally through university. Even gave me my first job when I graduated. He's done nothing but be there for me, so whatever goes on here today, the first time you badmouth him, you're gone. I won't hear one word said against him. Is that clear?"

"Yes." Meredith's voice was barely audible.

"And you," she continued, locking her gaze onto Pete. "Quit the needling. And stop calling her Martine. If she wants to be known as Meredith, then respect that."

Pride surged within Cash. Whenever he thought Natalia might need propping up, she always proved him wrong. What a woman. Both he and Darcey were the luckiest people in the world. He vowed, right then, to make sure his daughter grew up knowing what an amazing mother she had.

"I'll try," Pete said.

Natalia flashed him a sharp look. "You'll do better than try," she said as she reached for Cash's hand and settled back on the sofa. Her fingers were much less stiff this time. Taking control seemed to have steadied her. "Why did you come here the other day?" she said to Meredith.

"I wanted to see you."

"Why now?" Natalia shot back. "Why after all these years?"

"How much has he told you?" Meredith said, cocking her head towards Pete.

"Everything," Natalia said.

"Then you'll know your father threatened to kill me if I ever came near you again. I believed him, and I wouldn't have blamed him. I deserved it for the way I behaved."

"My father has been dead for ten years." Natalia winced as the words spilled from her lips.

"I didn't know that. I only found out a year ago that he'd died."

"So why not come then?"

Meredith's shoulders fell. "I was scared. It took me that long to pluck up the courage to decide to find you. This isn't easy for me."

Cash bristled. *Isn't fucking easy for Natalia either.* He was on the verge of speaking his mind when Natalia's grip on his hand tightened—a warning to shut the fuck up.

"I understand that." Natalia paused. He could almost see her brain ticking. "Why didn't you tell me who you were when we spoke at the hospital?"

Meredith gave a tight smile. "I don't know. I almost did, when I said I was visiting my granddaughter. But then I lost my nerve." Meredith glanced around. "Is she here? Can I see her?"

"She's with my mother," Cash said, suddenly thankful Natalia had agreed with his suggestion, even though she hated being separated from Darcey.

"Yeah. Her *actual* grandmother," Pete muttered.

Cash's lips twitched. His relationship with Pete had always been a difficult one, but at that moment, they were on the same side: Natalia's.

Meredith appeared to ignore Pete's jibe, but the faint tinge of red that bled into her cheeks told Cash she'd heard.

"Maybe another time," she said.

"How long have you been clean?" Natalia asked.

"Seven years."

"No relapses?"

"None. I've really kicked it this time. And I'm not going back." She shuddered. "Never."

"How can you be sure?" Natalia said.

Leaning forward, Meredith rested her forearms on her knees. "If you've never been addicted to drugs, it's impossible to understand how they *consume* you. Nothing else matters. The only thing you think about is how and when you'll get your next fix and how incredible it will feel when you do. I'm not excusing what I did. Nothing can excuse the way I behaved, how badly I treated you and John, but there's no way I'm ever going back to that life."

A tear slid down Meredith's cheek. Cash caught Pete rolling his eyes, clearly unimpressed with the show of emotion.

"I did love him, you know," Meredith said. "In the beginning, he was my whole world, and when you came along, I thought my life was complete."

"But you soon got bored, right?" Natalia said, a hint of bitterness leaking into her voice. "I mean, it's so dull being a wife and mother, isn't it?"

Meredith winced as Natalia's intended barb hit its target. She reached into her bag for a tissue and dabbed at the corner of her eye.

"I was young and stupid. Always looking for excitement, something to make me happier. If only I'd realised I already had everything I needed to do that."

Natalia snorted. "I'll give you stupid, but I'm not accepting youth as an excuse. You weren't a teenager. You were a grown woman in her late twenties with a husband and a child. Older than I am. If you're going to try to explain, at least be honest."

Meredith seemed to crumple, her body curving in on itself. "You are so like your father. Even though John and I were the same age, he was light-years ahead of me when it came to maturity."

Natalia's expression softened at the comparison to her father, but Pete was unmoved, his face stoic. "You always were a commanding manipulator, *Meredith,*" he said, his voice heavy with sarcasm.

"Stop it, Pete," Natalia said in a firm tone.

Pete's head snapped around. "Don't tell me you're buying this crap. You're a better judge of character than that."

"I didn't say I was buying anything," she said. "But I invited Meredith so I could hear her side. Please, I need to do this."

A slew of emotions flashed across Pete's face, and then he

sighed. "I'm sorry," he said to Meredith, although Cash could have sworn he was grinding his teeth through the apology.

Meredith responded with a glimmer of a smile. "I can't thank you enough for taking care of my daughter when I didn't. I never said that. I should have."

"Well, you have now," Pete said gruffly. "And she was never any trouble."

Natalia laughed, a genuine hearty laugh that thawed the room. "You liar. I brought plenty of trouble, but you dealt with it beautifully."

"You told me you were an angel as a teenager," Cash said, diving on the opportunity to keep the mood light for a few moments more.

Natalia gave him a grateful look. "We all have our secrets, ace," she said, briefly touching her head to his.

"I'm not here to ask for forgiveness, Tally," Meredith said. "I don't have the right to ask you to forgive me. I have to earn that right. All I want is the opportunity to do that, but I don't want to cause trouble between you and Peter."

Natalia locked eyes with Pete, and a silent conversation seemed to pass between them. Eventually, Pete blew out a heavy breath and inclined his head.

"Would you like to come for dinner on Friday night?" Natalia said to Meredith. "Cash's mum will be here. It would be good for you two to meet."

Meredith's eyes widened, and she clasped her palms to her face. "I'd love to."

"This doesn't mean everything's okay. We've got a very long way to go, and who knows if we'll ever get there. But like you said, you want a chance, and I'm willing to give you that."

Meredith sagged back in the chair and began to cry. "I don't deserve it," she said through her tears. "But thank you. Thank you so much."

Once more, Cash's chest swelled with pride. Natalia's capacity for forgiveness astounded and humbled him. He'd been on the receiving end of her generous spirit, so he could at least empathise with Meredith.

"Let's leave it there for tonight," Natalia said. "Although I'm sure I'll have more questions."

"Of course. Anything you want to know, just ask." Meredith stood and picked up her bag.

"I'll see you out."

As soon as Natalia left the room with Meredith in tow, Cash looked over at Pete. "Thoughts?"

Pete scrubbed a hand over his face. "I don't know. She seems different. Like she said, she's going to have to prove herself, but I'll tell you one thing—I'll be watching her every fucking move."

39

Tally opened the front door and burst out laughing. Rupe was standing outside, wearing a foppish grin and holding a teddy bear almost as big as he was.

"Thought I should bring a date," he said.

"You lunatic," she said, tugging him inside.

It had been a good idea to invite Rupe and Em as well as Rachael that night. Although she'd had a couple of conversations over the phone with Meredith, they'd been understandably strained, and sometimes she ran out of things to say. Her mother was still a stranger, after all, and would be for some time to come. Rupe would add much-needed lightness to the evening, and Em would use her keen radar for judging people.

"Where's my girl?" Rupe said, kissing her cheek.

"I take it you don't mean me." Tally cocked her head. "Your goddaughter is in there."

Dragging the enormous stuffed bear by the arm, Rupe headed for the living room. Tally giggled at the ridiculous scene as she followed him down the hallway.

Cash's eyes widened when he saw what Rupe was holding.

"What the fuck, Witters? Where the hell are we supposed to put that?"

"Duh," Rupe said. "Darcey's nursery, of course." He shoved the bear in Cash's face. "Here, hold this. I need to see my girl."

Cash tossed the bear to one side, where it rather unfortunately landed with its arse in the air. He looked over at Tally with an amazed expression. "At least it's better than Gary the fucking hideous Gorilla. Although we're going to need a bigger nursery."

"Am I the first?" Rupe said, swinging Darcey in the air. She gurgled happily, and he pulled her close, covering her face in sloppy kisses.

"You are," Tally said. "Drink?"

"Please. God, she's changing so fast."

"Tell us about it," Cash said. "Every day, something else is different. And I used to think all babies did was sleep, cry, and shit."

"She does plenty of that too," Tally said, passing Rupe a gin and tonic.

"Thanks, darling. No, you sit," Rupe said when there was a knock at the door. He laid Darcey in her Moses basket, where she groused at the loss of contact. "I'll get it."

"It's probably Em or Rachael. I asked Meredith to come half an hour after I invited the rest of you."

"It's both of them," Rupe shouted.

"Jesus," Em said as she walked into the living room and spotted the huge bear. "Who bought that?"

"Me," Rupe said proudly. "Isn't he amazing?"

"Are you trying to make up for something else lacking, Rupe?" Em said, earning a dig from Rupe's elbow.

"Not that you'll ever find out, Fallon, but I definitely don't have an issue in that department."

"Bullshit," Cash coughed out. Rupe stuck up his middle finger.

"Now, now," Rachael scolded, giving Tally a hug and then leaning over Darcey's cot. "Can I hold her?"

Tally nodded. Rachael was the only one who ever asked. Everyone else seemed to think Tally's daughter was their property, and while she loved the people in this room to bits, it sometimes irked her when they assumed it was okay to maul Darcey.

Rachael settled her granddaughter into the crook of her arm. She hummed softly to Darcey, her eyes full of love. Occasionally, she'd glance at Tally and Cash and nod as if to say *Bloody well done.* Tally couldn't have agreed more. All mothers had to feel the same about their own children, but Darcey was utterly gorgeous. From birth, she'd looked so much like Cash, and as she grew, her features became even more like his but with a femininity that took the masculine edge off. She was going to be a heartbreaker.

"There's nothing quite like holding your baby's baby," Rachael said, her expression a mix of love and awe. "You're going to have a queue of boys at your door when this one gets older."

"No, we won't," Cash said firmly. "Because I'm locking her up until she's at least thirty."

"Have you spoken to Meredith this week, babes?" Em said.

"Yeah, a couple of times." Tally pulled a face. "It's a bit weird, like trying to make small talk during your first week at a new job. That's why I'm glad all of you could make it this evening."

"What's she like?" Rupe asked.

"The complete opposite to me," Tally said. "She wears the ravages of years of drug abuse, but she's quite attractive beneath all that."

"She seems genuine," Cash said. "Which is another reason we wanted you all here."

"To suss if she is as genuine as she's trying to make out?" Em said.

"Precisely," Cash said. "Because if she isn't, we need to know."

"Good job you invited me," Em said. "Nose like a bloodhound. If she's taking the piss, I'll know."

"Why else do you think you're here?" Cash drawled.

Em narrowed her eyes until she saw that Cash's were sparkling with laughter. "Your son is a little shit, Rachael," she said, poking her toe at Cash's shin.

The doorbell rang, saving Rachael from responding. Tally stiffened, but Cash rested a soothing hand on her arm. "It'll be fine, baby."

As he went to let Meredith in, Rachael, Rupe and Em were focused on the door that led to the hallway, their faces full of curiosity and suspicion in equal measure. Tally laughed nervously. It was as though they were expecting a circus freak to walk in.

Meredith seemed a little taken aback by the welcoming committee. As her gaze sought Tally's, one eyebrow twitched upwards, but her expression was soft and warm, and she didn't appear to be offended. "It's good to see you again, Tally."

Tally stood to greet her, and the two women awkwardly shared a brief air kiss.

"Let me introduce you. This is Emmalee Fallon, my best friend since, like, forever. Rupe Fox-Whittingham, who is Cash's lifelong friend, and Rachael, Cash's mother."

Everyone shook hands and murmured greetings. Tally caught Em's eye. Her friend mouthed, "Relax," while nodding encouragingly.

"And this is Darcey," Tally said, taking the baby from Rachael.

"Oh my goodness, she's stunning," Meredith said, twisting her head to glance over her shoulder at Cash. "No denying you're the father."

Cash laughed. "So everyone says." He draped his arm around Tally's shoulder and gazed down at Darcey. "But she has Natalia's eyes. And her temperament, thank God."

Tally grinned and squeezed his waist. "Yeah, let's just say, I'm the calmer out of the two of us."

"That's Tally-speak for 'Cash is a bit fiery,'" Em said.

"Okay, let's eat," Cash said. "Before everyone jumps on the bash-me bandwagon."

The dinner went off without a hitch. Everyone did their best to make Meredith feel at home, and Tally began to relax. When Darcey's cry echoed over the intercom, Cash started to ease out of his chair until Tally stopped him. "I'll go," she said.

"Can I come?" Meredith asked, her eyes pleading for Tally to agree.

"Sure," Tally ground out, her voice raw and her throat tight as a nervous knot formed in her stomach. She wasn't sure how she felt being alone with Meredith. But it was too late to say no. She'd agreed.

They walked to Darcey's nursery in silence. Tally lifted her daughter out of the cot and settled in the rocking chair that overlooked the small garden at the back of their house. Midsummer's day had passed, but the sun was still high in the sky. It would be a couple of hours yet before it disappeared behind the houses.

She lifted her shirt and unfastened her nursing bra. In seconds, Darcey had found what she was looking for and began noisily suckling. Tally met Meredith's gaze. Her mother's expression was a mixture of regret and wonderment.

"I can see already you're a wonderful mother," she said, her lips turning upwards in the beginnings of a smile.

"Not sure about that," Tally replied. "I'm doing my best, like most mothers out there."

Meredith's eyes drained of the smile. "I'm so sorry, Tally. I can apologise to you every day for ten years, and yet I know it won't make up for what I did."

Tilting her head back, Tally studied Meredith's face. Then she softly sighed. "Can I ask you something?"

"Anything."

"Were you thinking of Dad and me at all when you allowed those men to fuck you in search of a fix?"

Meredith's head flinched as though she'd been slapped across the face. She sucked in a breath, making a whistling noise through her clenched teeth. "Wow, you don't pull punches, do you?"

"You said I could ask you anything."

Meredith's lips twitched. "Yeah, I did say that. Probably wasn't prepared for a question like that, though."

"You don't have to answer."

Meredith glanced around the room. Realising the only chair was the one Tally occupied, she perched on the windowsill instead.

"It was so long ago it's hard to remember what I was thinking at the time. But what I do know is the draw of heroin chased all other thoughts from my head. The rush was all I thought about, all I *craved*." She shook her head. "If I could have my time again, I would never have tried it. Heroin ruined my life—and it ruined yours."

"No, it didn't." Tally glanced down at her daughter, happily feeding and oblivious to the tension in the room. "I think I've done okay." She laughed then. "Managed to snare the hottest guy this side of the Atlantic, although if you ask me how I did it, I wouldn't be able to tell you."

Tally expected Meredith to chuckle at her self-deprecating comment, but she frowned instead. "You think Cash is too good for you?"

Tally shrugged. "Sometimes. Looks like I am my father's daughter. Pete told me Dad thought he was punching above his weight when it came to you."

Meredith's face crumpled, and she bent at the waist as though absorbing the pain of a blow to the stomach. "Your father was *not* punching above his weight. He was kind, funny, caring, a wonderful provider. He did everything for me and for you. It was me." She poked herself hard in the chest. "Me punching above *my* weight. You think because Cash is so handsome, that makes you lacking in some way?"

Tally ducked her head. "Not exactly model material, am I? You could have at least left me with your figure before you buggered off."

Meredith jumped down from the windowsill as blood rushed to her cheeks. "Don't." She gently nudged Tally's chin up until she had no choice but to meet Meredith's gaze. "Have you any idea how attractive you are? And I don't just mean physically, although you are pretty as a picture. I mean in here." She tapped four fingers over her heart. "Goodness pours out of you. I can see how you draw people in. They want a little piece of your warmth to touch them because then, they might feel worthy of being in your presence."

Tally's eyes widened, stunned at the strength of Meredith's outburst. The air caught in her throat, and she gulped through an airway that had closed over.

"It's Cash who's the lucky one," Meredith continued, seemingly unaware of Tally's struggle to breathe properly. "Sure, he's beautiful. I mean, you'd have to be blind not to see that. But so what? Beauty fades eventually. In the end, it's what's inside that matters. I know that sounds shit, like a trope of a line trotted out for effect, but it's not. It's true."

Hot tears pricked behind Tally's eyes, and she blinked several times. She didn't want to cry. Meredith's vehement support of her was exactly what she'd craved all those years. Because of heroin, she'd been robbed of a mother's love and that confidence building only a mother could give. It was time to tell Meredith the long-lasting impact of her choices, and then she could choose whether to stay or to leave. If she did the latter, well, Tally would be no worse off.

"I've struggled with a lack of confidence my whole life. I used to think there must be something wrong with me if my own mother didn't love me enough to stick around. Over time, that low confidence morphed into body-image issues."

Meredith gave her a horrified stare. "What have I done?" she whispered. She dropped to her knees in front of Tally and cupped both her cheeks. "My beautiful girl who now has a beautiful girl of her own. None of this is your fault. It's all mine, and I live with the reality of what I've done every day."

"It's okay," Tally said, her voice breaking as a rush of empathy for Meredith swam to the surface. "Really, it is."

Meredith shook her head vehemently. "No, it's not. But I promise you this. I'll spend every day of my life making it up to you if you'll let me."

Tally glanced down at her daughter. Darcey had eaten her fill, and her eyes began to droop. Tally laid a towel across her shoulder and gently patted Darcey's back before putting her back in her cot. She tucked the covers around her sleeping daughter. Darcey's full lips were parted, her tiny chest puffing in and out, her breathing slow and even. Leaning over, Tally kissed her soft cheek.

When she turned around, Meredith's eyes slid away, her head cast down.

Tally closed the gap between them and gently touched Meredith's upper arm. "Let's give it a try."

Meredith exhaled on a shudder, and she lifted her gaze. "I won't let you down."

There was an awkward moment where neither of them quite knew what to do next, and then Tally chuckled, breaking the tension.

"They'll think we've got lost. Ready to go back down?"

Meredith nodded, and Tally had one last check on Darcey before she quietly closed the door to the nursery.

When the two of them walked into the kitchen, all eyes turned to face them, and then everyone began talking at once. Tally frowned and caught Cash's gaze. His hand moved slightly towards the baby monitor, and she caught his drift. They'd heard every word.

Every. Single. Word.

Shit.

Meredith seemed to be none the wiser to the undercurrent swirling around them. Her shoulders were relaxed, and she'd struck up a conversation with Rachael, their heads close together as they chatted. It was only then Tally realised how on edge Meredith had been all evening. It had taken guts to turn up after years of absence and admit to her daughter that she'd been a drug addict and a prostitute.

Tally accepted then that she'd made the right decision to allow her mother to have a part in her life, but she knew by doing so, she was handing control of her fragile heart to someone who had already crushed it once in the most awful of circumstances.

She prayed Meredith would take care of it this time.

40

"Night," Tally said waving their guests off. She clicked the door shut and bolted it. Dead on her feet, she trudged back into the kitchen.

Cash was loading the dishwasher, a job he still hated and used as an excuse every time he told Tally they needed a housekeeper-cum-nanny. She was digging her heels in over that issue. Anna, their housekeeper in Northern Ireland, was different. She'd been with Cash for years and was a trusted member of their extended family. But the thought of having to put that trust in a stranger—well, she wasn't up for it.

"Thanks, ace," she said, pulling out a chair from the dining table and sagging into it. "So tell me, how much did you all hear?"

Cash switched the dishwasher on and turned around. He leaned against it, one foot crossed over the other, his arms casually folded across his chest.

"Everything."

Tally touched a hand to her neck. "Meredith would be mortified."

"No one will tell her." He held out his arms. "C'mere, baby."

She staggered to her feet and snuggled into the warmth of his embrace.

"I'm glad you don't look like a model," he said, chuckling in her ear. "You know how much I adore your curves."

Tally smiled against his neck. "Why didn't you switch off the monitor when you realised we were chatting?"

"And miss all that?" Cash said, a hint of mirth in his voice. "Not a chance. Besides, I'm glad I heard Meredith take full responsibility for what she did." He pulled back and studied her face. "She was right about one thing. I'm the lucky one. No contest."

Tally cupped both hands around the back of his neck and urged his mouth towards hers. She kissed him. His lips were so warm and comforting, taking her to a place of safety, a place where nothing could hurt her. As Cash deepened the kiss, those feelings of warmth and comfort ramped up into heat and desire. She moaned softly as his hands moved around her back, pulling her closer to him.

He broke off the kiss, and as his eyes met hers, he smiled.

"What are you up to?" she said, recognising that cheeky grin anywhere.

He showed her his watch. "It's past midnight."

"I know. That's why I'm knackered. And your daughter will be awake in three hours for her feed."

He wiggled his eyebrows. "Six weeks. She's six weeks old today." He leaned forward until their foreheads were touching. "How tired are you, sweetness?"

It took her a couple of seconds, but she finally caught on. "You can't remember we need milk or cereal, but you remember that?"

"Baby, *that* is way more important than either of those other things."

He bent his knees and swept her into his arms. She squealed

in surprise and then clapped a hand over her mouth so as not to wake Darcey.

He took off upstairs, holding her with ease. At the foot of their bed, he gently deposited her back on her feet. He set the baby monitor—which he'd somehow managed to carry as well as her —on the bedside table. Flicking her hair over her shoulders, he gazed at her intently.

"If this is too soon or you're too tired or it hurts, you have to promise to tell me. I know what you're like, and I don't--"

"Shhh," she said, placing her index finger over his mouth. "Stop talking. I want this. I want you."

Cash undressed so quickly, Tally couldn't help laughing, but when he took much more time removing her clothes, one piece at a time, her laughter faded. When they were both naked, his body skimmed past hers as he moved behind her, and she exhaled on a shudder as his erection nudged against her backside.

His hands settled on her abdomen, and she dredged up every bit of willpower not to react and pull her belly in. The skin across her stomach was still baggy from being stretched for nine months, and she doubted it would ever revert to its prebaby state, but after his reaction at the hospital, she owed him the respect of believing him when he said he didn't care.

His lips felt cool as he kissed across her shoulder blade, and her knees trembled as he worked his way down her back, his mouth warming as they absorbed the heat from her skin. Once on his knees behind her, he nudged her legs apart, and in that instant, she was swamped with fear and embarrassment. She'd pushed a baby out of her vagina and been stitched back together when Darcey's entrance into the world had torn Tally's tender flesh. And it didn't matter how good the surgeon was—she couldn't possibly look the same as she had before giving birth.

She clamped her legs together. Cash paused, one hand on her thigh.

"If it's too soon--"

She shook her head. "It's not that." She twisted around and sank to her knees until they were face to face. She met his gaze, and as she read confusion in the depths of his warm grey eyes, she dropped her chin to her chest.

"Baby, stop. You're scaring me." He clipped a finger under her chin. "Talk to me."

Heat flooded her face. Why did she still find it so difficult to talk about these things? After everything they'd been through, all the experiences they'd shared...

She took a deep breath. "What if it's not the same?" she mumbled in a barely audible voice. "What if it looks like Bride of Frankenstein or something?"

There was the briefest of pauses before a wide grin spread across Cash's face. "You crazy woman. Christ, I love the fucking bones of you." He slid his hands around the back of her neck and leaned in. He kissed her, softly at first, but after a few seconds, his mouth became harder, more insistent, and as she opened beneath him, his tongue surged inside, lapping at the inside of her mouth, taking everything she had to give.

Her heartbeat kicked up several notches when he lifted her so her thighs were on either side of his. He broke off the kiss, and as their eyes met, a spike of desire shot into her bloodstream.

"Lean back," he said, supporting her with his hands. She did as he asked until she was lying on the floor, her legs still on either side of his, exposing herself to him. He glanced down at the apex of her thighs before lifting his eyes to hers. They were sparkling with mischief.

"Baby, you've always had a pussy to die for, but now, it's like my daughter has given me a new pair of eyes, and I see everything so much clearer than before. You're *more* beautiful to me now. I wouldn't have thought it possible, but it's true."

A breath snagged in her throat as relief coursed through her. "So it doesn't look horrific?"

Cash burst out laughing. "No. It looks the same. Do you want me to get a mirror so you can take a look?"

"Ew, no," Tally said, giving him an appalled glance, which made him laugh even more.

He scooped her up and laid her on the bed. He bent her legs and pushed her thighs apart, and when he dipped his head, the sound he made, one of pure lust and longing, chased away every fear she had. She flung her arms over her head as Cash's hands and tongue began to stroke her slowly, rhythmically. Her stomach clenched, and her toes involuntarily curled. She was so close. She dug her hands in his hair.

"Cash, no," she muttered. "I want you inside me when I come."

He crawled up her body, his journey interspersed with sweet kisses. He paused at her breasts, taking turns laving each erect nipple and pulling it into his warm, wet mouth.

Tally arched her back, spasms of pleasure darting through her. "Don't make me wait."

He groaned and reached for a condom. After rolling it over his erection, he returned his mouth to hers and gently pushed into her, an inch at a time. She couldn't have felt more loved, more cherished. He stretched her slowly, no more than she could take, and when he'd completely filled her, she tore her mouth from his.

"I want to see you, ace," she said, holding his gaze without blinking.

A soft groan eased from his throat. "God, I love you," he whispered as his thrusts became harder, more urgent. "So much, baby. So much."

She cupped his face—his beautiful face that was so dear to her. But what they had was so much more than skin-deep. He was her heart, her soul, her very breath, and when he shifted position, hitting just the right point inside, pleasure overtook her.

"Jesus," she muttered as her climax powered through her,

making her body jerk as a rush of heat spread outward from her core. As she came, so did Cash. Their eyes locked, neither looking away as, in that moment, they became one.

THE PEAL of the telephone mingled with Darcey's screams. Tally groaned and rolled onto her side. She squinted at the clock. It was 2:40 in the morning.

The phone stopped ringing, only to start up again immediately.

"Cash, wake up," she mumbled, shaking his arm. "Get the phone. I'll see to Darcey."

Bleary-eyed, she threw on a dressing gown and staggered across the hall to the nursery. Darcey had managed to kick off all her covers, and Gary the Gorilla was squashed between the mattress and the sides of the cot, his face twisted at a weird angle.

"Oh dear," Tally said, lifting her out of the cot. "I'm not sure Gary is going to recover."

Darcey's wails turned to sobbing hiccups as Tally bent over to retrieve Gary. His face had been flattened on one side, making him look rather strange.

"At least Daddy will be happy," she said. "Although Auntie Kinga may be a little more put out."

She'd only just sat in the chair and begun feeding Darcey when Cash appeared in the doorway. His face was ashen, and she could tell he was barely holding it together. A cold chill swept over her.

"What's wrong?"

"That was William. Kinga's in hospital."

Tally's hand tightened on the stuffed toy Kinga had bought for Darcey, the stuffed toy that was now ruined. Somehow, it seemed like a prophecy.

"Is she... is she...?" Her words trailed off, and she struggled to hold back tears. Cash would need her to be the strong one, not to have her fall apart at the first sign of an emergency.

"She was taken in last night with breathing problems, and she's asking to see me. I can tell by William's voice that he's shit-scared. I told him we'd be right there, but I understand if you don't want to come."

"Of course I'm coming," she said, a little pissed he'd suggested otherwise.

He squeezed her shoulder gently. "It's because I know you're knackered. You've had less than an hour of sleep."

"So have you. Anyway, Kinga is more important. You get dressed and then pack a bag for Darcey in case we're at the hospital a while. I'll finish feeding her, and then we can go."

Cash nodded. He shoved a hand through his hair as he glanced helplessly around the room.

"Over there, in her wardrobe," Tally said, pointing even though he knew where the damn wardrobe was. "Nappies in the top drawer, and pack a couple of changes of clothes for her."

"Maybe we should ask Mum to take her."

"No," Tally said forcefully. "She stays with us. Besides," she added, in a gentler tone, "I'm sure Kinga would love to see her if she's well enough. And if she isn't, we'll figure it out."

Half an hour later, they set off for the hospital. Neither of them spoke on the way there, both deep in thought. What if this was the beginning of the end? Kinga had looked really well at the homecoming for Darcey, and that had only been a week earlier. How could so much change in that short a time?

The hospital car park was rammed, but they managed to squash the car into a space that turned out to be far too small when Tally realised she couldn't get out. Cash drove forward, waited until she'd got Darcey out of the car, and reversed again. He slid out of the driver's side as if he were limbo dancing.

"Fucking ridiculous." He picked up Darcey's car seat, being careful not to rock her, and slipped his arm around Tally's waist.

"Relax, ace," she said, applying light pressure to his back, enough to convey she was there for him.

"I'm not prepared, babe," he said, glancing down at her as they strode towards the hospital entrance.

Fear rolled through her, and the hair lifted at the nape of her neck. "What aren't you telling me?"

"Nothing. I'm just assuming the worst."

Cash swept them past the reception area and headed straight for the bank of lifts. He ushered her inside and pressed the button for the eighth floor. The hospital was deserted—not too surprising, given the early hour.

Exiting the lift, he took her hand, and they turned left and strode down the corridor. William must have told him which room they were in. Sure enough, Cash drew to a halt outside a door that bore a brass plaque that read, "The Elisabeth Mount Suite."

He rapped on the door once and then pushed it open.

Kinga was asleep, a couple of pillows propping her head up. Her skin was paper-thin, and there was a light sheen of sweat across her forehead. She was hooked up to two IV lines, one needle in each arm. She was so skinny. Tally wouldn't have been surprised to find out Kinga had lost a stone in the last week.

William glanced over his shoulder, a flash of relief sweeping across his face. "I'm so sorry," he said, waving at a couple of chairs. "I didn't expect you to come, Tally. Not with the little one."

Tally offered him a faint smile. "Don't you worry about it." She rubbed his shoulder, kissed Kinga on the cheek, and pulled one of the chairs closer. She took Kinga's hand in hers. It was cold, the skin pulled tight over her knuckles. Tally rubbed it between her palms, hoping to warm her a little.

"How is she?" Cash said, sitting in the other chair. He gently placed Darcey's car seat on the floor beside his feet.

William shook his head. "They had to sedate her because she was so distressed. She'll be out for a few hours yet, but it does seem to have settled her down. Her breathing is much more steady. They won't tell me anything about her long-term prognosis. It's all 'We have to wait and see,' and 'We're doing everything we can.' I want them to tell it to me straight."

"Fucking doctors," Cash muttered.

"It was the same when Cash was in hospital in Paris," Tally said. "They wouldn't tell me anything. Drove me crazy."

"Why don't I see if I can get anything out of them?" Cash said.

"No point. The consultant won't be here until nine."

"What the fuck is this?" Cash hissed under his breath. "Part-time medical care?"

A ghost of a smile flitted across William's face, even though Cash hadn't been joking. "Yeah. At full-time prices."

Cash smiled then. "I'll bet. Why don't you go and get a coffee or something? You look like you could do with the caffeine. We'll stay with her."

William hesitated, no doubt torn between knowing Cash was right and wanting to stay with Kinga in case she took a downturn. The seriousness of the situation weighed heavily on Tally, bringing back more memories of her dad. At least Kinga didn't seem to be in any pain, although Tally knew that would change. No matter how many drugs they pumped into her, in the end, it was a horrible way to go.

"Go on, William," Tally said. "As you said, she'll be out until morning."

The smile he gave her was so grateful that it made her heart clench painfully. He stood and then stretched out his back.

"Can I get you anything?"

Cash nodded. "Coffee would be good. Sleep is at a premium at the moment."

William glanced fondly at Darcey. "Worth it, though." Then his face fell. "I would have loved a family. Guess we don't always get what we want."

He dashed through the door before either of them could

answer, although what Tally could say to a comment like that when she had everything, and William would soon have nothing, was beyond her.

"God, baby," Cash said as soon as William was out of earshot. "She looks awful. I can't believe it. She was fine last week."

Tally could barely catch her breath as memories flooded her mind. Dad, full of energy, vibrant, handsome. A month after his diagnosis, he could barely walk to the bathroom on his own, his vitality gone, his face and body ravaged by cancer. An aggressive form, they'd said. Two months max, they'd said. Dad had stuck up two fingers to that. He'd held out for three months.

"Babe?" Cash brushed her arm, his fingers gentle as they made contact with her skin.

Her head snapped up. "Sorry."

"I shouldn't have let you come."

Tally covered his hand with hers. "Sometimes the memories hit me so hard I can barely breathe. They're probably more prevalent because of Meredith coming back into my life, but I'm not going anywhere, Cash. I want to be here for Kinga and for you. Besides, William looks like he's going to collapse at any minute. He's going to need us both to be strong for him."

"I want us to get married," Cash blurted out.

Tally met his gaze. "We are."

"No, I mean today, tomorrow, this week. As soon as we can arrange it. I know I promised you the whole big affair, but I don't want to wait any longer. None of us know what's going to happen."

Tally rested her head on his shoulder. "I'll happily marry you wearing a bin bag. I don't care about the big white wedding."

His body trembled as his arm came around her. "Then we'll do it as soon as we can."

When William returned with their coffees, the three of them sat in silence. Occasionally, a nurse would pop in to check Kinga's vitals, but mostly, they were left alone.

Cash and William eventually began to doze, their chins dropping to their chests, and when Darcey started to grizzle, Tally took her outside, loath to wake either of them or disturb Kinga.

She found a bathroom with baby-changing facilities, and after Tally had fed, burped and changed her, Darcey rewarded her with a smile.

"What would I do without you, baby girl?" she said, covering Darcey's face in kisses, which brought more smiles. She was such a good-natured baby. Sure, she cried like they all did, but once she was dry and fed, she tended to settle down, happy to kick her legs and wave her arms, pretty much entertaining herself. She and Cash were so incredibly lucky, especially with everything going on. A difficult baby would have added to the pressure they were under.

Tally's stomach growled, and she decided to find the hospital canteen and pick up some breakfast for herself, Cash, and William. Hopefully, the consultant would be around soon, and they'd be able to get a bit more information.

She grabbed bacon sandwiches and coffee, wishing she had the pushchair to carry all of it. She nudged the handle to Kinga's room with her elbow, impressing herself with her juggling abilities. Cash leaped to his feet when he saw her.

"Here," he said, lifting Darcey's carrier from her hand. "I wondered where you'd got to."

"I thought you might be hungry." She passed out the food and drinks. "What time is it?" she said with a yawn.

"Eight thirty," William said, giving her a grateful smile. He tucked into the sandwich with the ferocity of a man who hadn't eaten in far too long.

"Has she stirred yet?"

"No, although the sedative they gave her should start to wear off soon."

Tally quickly ate her sandwich and perched on the edge of the bed. She brushed away a stray hair that had stuck to Kinga's eyelashes. Kinga's hands were still cold, but Tally could have sworn she had a little more colour in her cheeks.

"She definitely looks better than a few hours ago," she said.

"I want her to wake up," William said.

His face was bruised with exhaustion despite the food and caffeine. He was clearly feeling the strain, and Tally's heart ached for him. She didn't want to tell him this was the easy part. When Kinga deteriorated, it was going to get a whole lot worse.

"She will. When she's ready."

He lifted his head wearily. "I have no idea how you coped when Cash was in a coma. Kinga is only sedated, and I'm falling to pieces."

She glanced over at Cash. "I didn't cope. Not at first. But I had to believe he would recover because the alternative was too awful to bear."

Cash came to sit beside her. He knitted their fingers together. "Kinga's tough. She'll come through this. I know it."

"Until the next time," William mumbled.

The consultant's arrival saved them from responding. Relieved, Tally picked up Darcey's car seat.

"We'll leave you to it, William." She cocked her head, signalling for Cash to follow her.

"You don't have to," William said.

"It's fine," Cash said. "We won't be far away."

Exhausted from lack of sleep and fear for Kinga, Tally managed to make it as far as the hospital coffee shop before gratefully sinking into one of the spacious couches. Cash joined the queue to grab a couple of coffees, but really, she could have had caffeine injected straight into her eyeballs and it wouldn't have made a difference. She was exhausted and anxious, and her stomach churned uncomfortably.

"Thanks," she said as Cash passed her a steaming cup of black coffee.

"Why don't you go home and get your head down. I'll get Mum to come across and stay with Darcey."

"No."

Cash made a frustrated noise. "You're so stubborn."

She smiled. "I know."

"At least promise me you'll shout if it all gets too much."

"I'm worried about William," she said, ignoring his comment. "He's not coping now, and it's only going to get worse."

Cash gave her a stern look but allowed her to change the subject. "I agree. Kinga's definitely the strong one in their relationship."

"When he falls apart, we have to make sure we don't, because Kinga is going to need someone to take the load."

"Even more reason for you to get some rest."

"I will. After I've seen her."

Cash gave a smile, but it didn't reach his eyes. "It's so strange how things work out."

"You mean me and Kinga?" she said.

"Yeah."

"She scared the hell out of me in the early days. Now I can't imagine what I'm going to do without her."

She swallowed past a lump in her throat and stared at her hands, only raising her head when Cash's fingers curled around hers.

"She got a hell of a kick out of scaring you then. She's changed so much."

"Yes, she has. But then, we all have." She finished her coffee and peered into Cash's cup, which was still half-full. "Come on, ace. Drink up. The consultant should have finished by now, and I'm hoping Kinga's awake."

When they returned to her room, Kinga was sitting up in bed, holding a cup of tea. Her face lit up, especially when she spotted Darcey.

"Hey," she said, putting the tea on the bedside cabinet.

"William told me you've been here all night. You didn't have to do that."

"Don't be silly," Tally said, giving her a kiss before stepping aside to allow Cash to do the same.

"How are you feeling?" he asked.

"I've been better." She nodded at the baby. "Can I hold her?"

Tally hesitated. She felt a slight nudge in her back from Cash.

"Of course you can," he said, lifting Darcey out of the car seat that had turned into her cot for the day. She didn't seem to mind the inconvenience.

Cash placed Darcey in Kinga's outstretched arms, and Tally had to bite her tongue to stop reminding him to watch the baby's head. She couldn't help her overprotective instinct kicking in every time someone wanted to hold her child. She kept telling herself it was because Darcey shouldn't have even been born yet, but there she was, six weeks old already.

"Oh, you guys. She's grown even from when I saw her last week." Kinga kissed Darcey's forehead, and right on cue, the baby woke up, her big blue eyes focusing right in on Kinga. "Oh, she's awake," she exclaimed. "She slept through the whole of last week, so I never got to see her eyes. Look how blue they are."

Kinga had perked up, almost as though Darcey was the precise pick-me-up she needed. Colour flooded back into her cheeks, and it was amazing what a bright smile could do. William flashed a grateful look their way.

"It's the only thing she's got from me," Tally said with a grin. "Everything else is Cash."

"Why don't we leave the girls cooing and get some fresh air," Cash said to William in a badly veiled attempt to get him alone. Tally knew he wanted to question William about what the consultant had said.

"Yes, go on, William," Kinga said. "The fresh air will do you good."

William reluctantly followed Cash outside, and Tally's skin

prickled at the way his shoulders dropped. Whatever the consultant had said, it wasn't good news.

As soon as the door closed, Kinga's bright smile fell. "He's not doing great."

"What about you?" Tally said. "What did the consultant say?"

She shook her head sadly. "It's spread. Fast. He reckons a few weeks at most."

"Oh God." Hot tears sprang to Tally's eyes. She dashed a hand over her face, annoyed at herself for not being stronger.

"Hey," Kinga said, gripping her hand tightly. "It's okay, Tally. I knew I didn't have long. I've made my peace with it."

"Cash wants us to get married as soon as possible," she blurted out. "He said it's because none of us know what's going to happen, but I think it's more to do with you. It wouldn't be the same if you weren't there."

Kinga's face lit up. "That's great news. I'll be there, even if I have to drag myself on all fours. Of course, if I do that, I'll still be rocking killer heels and an amazing dress."

Tally laughed. "I'll bet you will."

"Seriously, though," Kinga said. "I wouldn't miss it."

"I haven't a clue how I'm going to get everything done that quickly. Any ideas?"

Kinga nodded and pointed to her bag hanging over the back of a chair. "Fetch my phone."

41

Tally stood in front of the floor-length mirror in her hotel suite and gave herself a critical once-over. The off-the-shoulder floor-length fitted ivory-silk wedding gown clung to her every curve, but at least the control pants seemed to be working. She smoothed her hands over her stomach. No one would guess she'd had a baby eight weeks earlier. Of course, when the pants came off... that was a different story, but she wasn't planning on doing that in front of their guests.

Despite being critically ill, Kinga had performed nothing short of a miracle. Using every contact she had, she'd managed to secure the Dorchester, including rooms for all the guests. Even Cash had been astonished when she'd told him what she'd accomplished, but she'd just smiled demurely and refused to reveal her secrets.

Tally took a breath, enjoying a quiet moment to herself before chaos ensued, and taking in her last few minutes as Tally McKenzie. She'd said her new name out loud a couple of times but still couldn't get used to it. *Tally Gallagher.* Nope, didn't sound right, although every bride had to think the same. *And don't even get me started on the signature.*

Her phone dinged with an incoming text. She picked it up, her mouth lifting in a smile as she read it:

You're late.

Tally laughed to herself, her fingers shaking as she tried to type a text back. She kept making mistakes, and some of the suggestions from spellcheck were downright hilarious. Finally she managed to stab out a response:

I'm making sure my garter is in place. Something for you to peel off later—with your teeth.

She stepped over to the window and looked at the busy street below. People were going about their business, none of them knowing she was about to marry her soul mate. Even though the day was tinged with sadness because of Kinga's illness, Cash's suggestion to pull the wedding forward had been the right one. If she'd had months to plan their wedding, her nerves would have frayed.

Her phone dinged again:

Fuck, baby. What are you trying to do to me? I've now got a massive hard-on. Is that allowed in front of a man of the cloth?

She laughed and immediately replied, starting the text off with a shocked-face emoji:

Definitely not.

His reply came almost immediately:

Then get down here, woman. Otherwise, I'm coming up to get you, and given how turned-on I am, we'll be keeping the guests waiting for at least an hour!

Tally was about to type a reply, wanting to keep this fun game going, when a knock at the door stopped her.

"Come in," she called out, her head still buried in her phone.

"Well, aren't you a picture."

Tally spun around. "Nerissa!" She tottered across the room to greet her friend. She'd have run, but the skirt was too tight, so a totter was the best she could do. She pulled Nerissa into a tight hug. "What are you doing here?"

"You have a very special fiancé. He sent for me. Correction, he sent his plane for me." Nerissa grinned. "First time I've even flown in a private jet."

"I can't believe he did that," Tally said. "I'm so glad you're here."

"He loves you. You're a lucky girl."

"How's the café?"

Nerissa raised her eyes to the ceiling. "You want to talk business on your wedding day?"

"I want to know you're okay."

Nerissa gripped both her hands. "I'm fine. Life is good, Tally. Thanks to you."

Before Tally could reply, Pete poked his head around the door. "Showtime," he said, and then he stopped dead. "Wow."

Tally ran her hands over her hips. "Do I look okay?"

"Oh, Tally." He strode across the room and hugged her before holding her at arm's length. "Let me get a proper look at you."

Tears filled his eyes, and a shockwave hit her. She'd never seen Pete cry, not even when her father died.

"John would be so proud, and I'm devastated he can't be here. But I hope you think I'm a good enough substitute."

Tally's eyes began to sting too. "The best, Uncle Pete."

"Okay, well, there's a room full of guests all waiting to see the bride," he said in a gruff tone. "Ready?"

Tally gave Nerissa a quick hug. "You'd better go. Otherwise, you'll be following me down the aisle, and I'm sure that isn't the way it's supposed to go."

Nerissa kissed her cheek. "You deserve every happiness coming your way. You're a special person, Tally."

As Nerissa left her and Pete alone, Tally pulled back her shoulders and smiled nervously. "I'm ready."

Pete stuck out his elbow, and she tucked her hand inside.

When they reached the conference room where her wedding was taking place, Em was waiting outside. So many emotions rolled through Tally that she had to fight to hold back tears, the effort making the back of her throat burn.

"Oh no you don't, McKenzie," Em said. "I'm using you as an advertisement for my shit-hot wedding make-up. Think of the exposure in *HELLO!* magazine."

"I can't help it," Tally said, the words catching in her throat.

"Get her inside, Dozer," Em said. "At least the folks at the back might see her at her best. Pity Cash is going to be greeted by panda eyes, although I suppose he might still want to marry her despite that."

Tally laughed, and her tears receded, her friend's teasing having the desired effect. Em pressed a kiss to her cheek, and as the doors opened, Tally's breath caught in her throat, and she started to move forward, but Pete held her back.

"Make him wait," Pete whispered. "Let him savour the view. You're worth waiting for."

The guests' faces were blurred as she walked down the makeshift aisle, although she did spot Meredith brushing aside a tear. The only person she saw clearly was Cash, waiting at the front, Rupe by his side. No one rocked a tux like Cash, and that day was no exception. Their eyes met, and the look he gave her was so scorching she expected to find burn marks on her body when she removed her dress.

As she reached the altar, Pete placed her hand on top of Cash's outstretched one and stepped back.

"Sorry I'm late," she whispered.

"Sweetness, I'd wait a lifetime for you." He bent his head close to hers, whispering so only she could hear. "You look fucking hot in that dress. I can't wait to strip you out of it later."

Tally's face heated as the vicar began the introductions. She barely heard what he said until he invited Cash to say his vows. Rupe passed him a piece of paper, but Cash shook his head.

"I don't need that." He glanced down to where their hands were joined and then looked back up at her. "Nineteen months ago, I was in this very hotel, hosting a dinner for my tennis foundation, when my life changed forever because you blew into it. I wasn't looking for a relationship and certainly not with a journalist." He winked at her as a light ripple of laughter came from behind them.

"Everyone thought I had the perfect life, but I knew the truth. My life was empty, hollow, and I was desperately looking for something to fill the void. The strength of my feelings for you that night scared me to death, and I did my best to push you away. But you'd already burrowed under my skin, and the first time we kissed, I knew I was yours. All I had to do was convince you that you were mine.

"You saved me from myself on so many occasions with your unwavering love and support. You insisted there was good in me when all I saw was bad. You showed me the light when all I knew was darkness, and you helped me to forgive myself, because if someone as amazing as you could love me, maybe I was worth saving.

"And just when I thought it wasn't possible to love you any more, you gave me the most amazing and precious gift: our beautiful daughter."

Tally choked back her emotions as Cash continued, his gaze unwavering. "I will spend the rest of my life putting your happiness above my own. I promise to support you, respect you, and encourage you to be the best you can be. I love you, baby, and nothing will make me more proud than to be your husband."

He lifted her hands to his lips and kissed them both then dropped his gaze. His bottom lip trembled, and she knew he was trying like hell to hold his emotions in check.

Her knees shook as she tilted her head back, but as soon as their eyes met, her nerves disappeared.

"For so long, I watched you from afar, hoping that one day we'd meet and wondering what I would say to you if we did. But not even during the most extreme of dreams did I think I'd be standing here about to become your wife.

"We've had more than our fair share of challenges, but I know each and every one has brought us here, to where we are today, and has made us stronger together. You hold my heart in your hands, but I know it's safe with you, ace."

His lips curved upward, and his thumb brushed her knuckles tenderly.

"You make me feel so loved, so cherished, so special. You accept me for all that I am and all that I am not. You say that I saved you, but really, we saved each other. And that's how I know you're my soul mate, my best friend, my lover. I won my *ace*, and I'm never letting go."

Tally glanced over her shoulder to where Darcey was fast asleep in Rachael's arms. Her heart clenched, and despite fervent promises to herself, tears fell.

"I love you so much for giving me our baby. You're the most amazing father, as I knew you would be, and if I can be a fraction as good a mother, then our daughter will be the luckiest child in the world."

Tears began to slide down Cash's face too, letting Tally see his vulnerability, and she reached up to brush them away with her thumbs.

"I promise to be there for you when you need me and to step back when you crave space. I promise to keep challenging you, to laugh with you when you're happy, and to hold you when you're sad. Because of you, I'm living the life I only ever dreamed of, and for that, I give you my heart and soul. You're my everything, Cash Gallagher. You're the missing piece of me I sought for so long, and now, standing here, I know that the stitching holding me together will never break, because I have you."

She stood on her tiptoes and pressed a kiss to his lips.

"You're breaking the rules," he whispered when she stepped back.

She smiled. "You taught me well, ace."

They exchanged rings, and then it was all over. Cash tucked her hand inside his and began to walk down the aisle while their friends and family applauded. She caught Kinga's eye and smiled. As promised, Kinga was rocking a fabulous midnight-blue gown and killer heels, even though she'd had to succumb to using a wheelchair. But behind her bright smile, she was far too pale, and Tally felt a growing panic in the pit of her stomach.

"She shouldn't have come," she whispered to Cash as he swept her past.

"Would *you* have wanted to be the person to tell her that?"

"No."

"There you are, then. Look, baby, I know how worried you are about her. I'm worried too. But she'd be fucking furious if she thought for one minute we let her illness ruin our day. So for Kinga, if not for us, let it go for today."

She nodded in agreement while inwardly acknowledging that letting go wouldn't be easy.

As it turned out, it wasn't as difficult as she'd feared to forget her worries and enjoy her wedding breakfast, thanks to Rupe's best-man speech. He excelled himself, telling stories about their escapades from school days, and he didn't once mention Cash's rather colourful past with women. But it was how he closed out that made Tally cry.

"All I've ever wanted is for Cash to be happy. I'm not going to get all maudlin here, but despite how it looks to the outside world, he's had a rough time. It was only when he met Tally that he found true happiness. I know it's a cliché, but she really is the best thing that ever happened to him. And she's the best thing that's ever happened to me. She's like a sister, and I'll be forever grateful that she is in my life."

He walked over to her and kissed her cheek. "Love you, darling," he said, but as he moved in for another kiss, Cash barred his way.

"That's enough, Witters. We don't want the day to end with your face in the cake, do we?"

Tally laughed through her tears at Rupe's affronted expression, and when she stood and kissed Rupe on the cheek, Cash's expression made her laugh even harder. "Don't listen to him," she said to Rupe.

Rupe shot Cash a triumphant look and flounced back to his seat. He dusted off his hands as though saying, *That told him.*

Cash rolled his eyes and rose from his chair. "Come on, Mrs Gallagher. Let's get you on the dance floor before my ex-best friend tries to steal you away."

Pleasure rushed through her as Cash wrapped his arms around her waist and pulled her close.

"Thank you," he whispered, his warm breath brushing the shell of her ear.

She tilted her head back so she could look at him. "What for?"

"For making me the happiest man alive."

42

Cash managed to persuade Natalia to have a few days away after their wedding, but she'd only agreed on the proviso they stay in the UK. As neither of them could bear to leave Darcey behind, he'd booked a cottage on the outskirts of the Cotswolds, close to a small village with a couple of decent pubs.

He promised her a better honeymoon in a few weeks, although he omitted saying they would take it when Kinga was no longer there. He couldn't say *when she is dead*, not even to himself. It sounded too final, too brutal.

As he pulled into the driveway of the house he'd rented, Natalia began to laugh.

"You said a small cottage," she said, looking out of the window at the huge stone detached house, their home for the next week.

He stifled a grin. "I like space."

He jumped out of the car and unhooked Darcey's car seat. She'd slept all the way there, but now that the movement of the car had stopped rocking her, she'd woken. Her big midnight-blue eyes, the replica of Natalia's, were gazing up at him with the same adoration with which he was gazing down at her.

"Hi, baby girl," he said, nuzzling her nose with his. She let out the most adorable giggle, and his heart almost burst. "Oh my God, did you hear that?"

Natalia closed the car door, her answering smile wide. "Her first laugh."

Cash clapped a hand over his chest and sagged a little at the knees. "I'm so in love."

"I think the feeling is mutual. I shall be having a word with my daughter about the importance of sharing."

He leaned down and kissed Natalia, hard. "How about we go on a long walk, get lots of fresh air so she's knackered and sleeps right through?"

Natalia gave him an innocent smile. "Why, ace? What have you got planned?"

He carefully put Darcey's car seat on the floor and caught her hips, pulling her close. "You, me, a bottle of wine, and zero clothes."

A slight tremor ran through her body, and his stomach flipped. He still found it an enormous turn-on that she was so affected by him.

"Well, then," she said, lifting her eyes to his. "What are we waiting for?"

AFTER A FEW DAYS of country air, Natalia began to relax. She regained some colour in her cheeks, the worry lines across her forehead faded, and her shoulders spent a lot less time around her ears.

The countryside around the Cotswolds was some of the most beautiful in England, with green pastures and rolling hills. It was impossible not to feel carefree in a place like that. Their days were idyllic. They wandered around quaint little towns filled with thatched cottages and lunched at one of an abundance of cosy tearooms. Nights were spent locked in each other's arms.

"Maybe we should buy a place in the area," Cash said on their fourth day as they wandered hand in hand beside the River Coln. "Think how nice it would be to get out of London into all this. It's only a couple of hours' drive, and Darcey would love it as she gets older. We could even move the horses over from Marcie's place in Ireland. There must be loads of liveries around here."

She turned to him, her face flushed with excitement. "Really? I think that's a fantastic idea."

He returned her smile. "I'll get an estate agent onto it."

"Try not to buy a mansion, ace."

He flashed her an overly innocent look, to which she rolled her eyes and sighed.

"Why do I bother? You'll do what you want anyway. I give up trying to control you."

"Just as well, sweetness. It always was a waste of time."

CASH WOKE WITH A START, his phone blaring into the silence of the night. His eyes were stinging from too little sleep. He opened them a crack. It took a moment to figure out where he was. The shadows in the room were unfamiliar.

Beside him, Natalia turned over, but not before making a frustrated noise at being woken so early.

Cash closed his eyes again and felt around until his hand located his phone.

"Yeah," he mumbled as he answered.

"Cash?"

As he heard William's voice, he sat bolt upright. Fear congealed in his chest. "What's wrong?"

"It's time. Can you come?"

"Already?" he whispered, his stomach churning with an awful sick feeling. He didn't want to hear it. Shit, he wasn't ready to lose her. He'd had weeks to prepare for this moment, yet it could have been years, and it wouldn't have made a difference.

"I'm so sorry," William said, his voice breaking up. "Especially as it's your honeymoon and everything."

Cash fumbled for Natalia's arm and gave her a gentle shake. She stirred, but when he jolted her harder, she sat up. One look at his face and she read the situation. He shook his head, closing his eyes briefly as if that would make this horror go away.

"We're on our way," he said as Natalia leaped out of bed and began packing their things. "Where are you?"

"The hospice. I'll text you the satnav details."

"She didn't want to go into a hospice," Cash said.

"I know." William's voice broke. "She's suffering, Cash. She begged me to bring her here."

Cash dug his fingernails into his palm until he drew blood. The physical pain was a welcome distraction from the anguish in his chest.

"You tell her to wait for us. We're coming." He tossed the phone onto the bed, and for a minute, he sat there, stunned, unable to move.

"Cash." Natalia knelt in front of him, her face wet with tears. She rested her hands on his thighs. "Let's go, ace. Kinga needs you."

His head dropped into his hands, and he began to cry. Natalia climbed into his lap and wrapped her arms tightly around him. "I know, babe. I know."

He gave himself five minutes, not a second more. He'd have to do the rest of his grieving later. At that moment, he had to man the fuck up. The last thing Kinga needed was him falling apart in front of her. That would make him a dick, given what she was about to face, and he'd spent his life being a dick until Natalia had saved him from himself. He refused to regress.

He washed his face while Natalia changed and dressed Darcey, who was not impressed at being woken before her normal get-up time, and she was unusually grizzly as they put her in the car. He wouldn't have been surprised if she was picking up on their tension and letting it out the only way she knew how.

The roads were empty apart from the odd lorry whose driver was using the quietness to make headway. They didn't speak much, but on occasion, Natalia would touch his arm or squeeze his knee, her way of letting him know she was there, that she was feeling the same.

Two hours later, Cash turned the car in to the driveway of the hospice. After he reversed into a space, Natalia grabbed the door handle to get out, but Cash stopped her.

"I need a minute." He took a few deep breaths, trying to slow his thundering heart and the terrible churning in his stomach.

"Take as long as you need, ace," she said.

"Are you sure you want to come in?" He knew how hard she found it to be around someone with the same illness she'd lost her father to. Seeing Kinga would bring back all those horrendous memories.

She gave him a hard look. "Yes."

He nodded, her vehement response telling him he'd have no chance of persuading her otherwise.

"Okay. Let's go."

As he opened the door to Kinga's room, he realised no amount of preparation would have helped him cope.

It had been six days since his wedding—six days since he'd seen her, and the Kinga he'd known from the age of twenty was no longer there. The determined, tenacious, sparky, and sometimes downright annoying-as-fuck woman who had turned his talent for playing tennis into a money-making machine was gone, and in her place lay an imposter.

He slammed a hand over his mouth to stop the gasp of horror that clawed at his throat, desperate to get out. Natalia's tight grip on his arm told him she felt the same and was trying to hang onto her emotions, because if they lost it now, there was no coming back.

William glanced over his shoulder, but he could barely raise a smile. His face had sunken in on itself, the flesh baggy around his eyes, his skin tone grey. "Thanks for coming."

Cash had to force himself into that room when all he really wanted to do was run. He didn't want to remember Kinga like this. But he had no choice. She wanted him there, *needed* him there, and dammit, he *would* be there.

"Is she asleep?" Cash said as he fell into a chair.

Her breathing was uneven and shallow, and a horrible rattle sounded in her chest every time her lungs filled with air.

"For now," William said. "They've given her some pain relief."

Natalia placed Darcey's car seat on one of the chairs and went to hug William. His face crumpled as she put her arms around him.

"I'm so sorry," she said. "What do you need, William?"

"This. For you both to be here."

There was nothing more to say, and the room fell silent, but that made the terrible rattling in Kinga's chest seem even louder. Cash wanted to slam his hands over his ears, to make this all go away. The irony of his baby daughter beside him, her life journey beginning while Kinga's was ending far too early, was fucking awful.

Hours passed, and Cash began to fear Kinga would never wake up. In a way, he wanted that for her—to let her slip away without pain, without having to look at their faces, unaware of the terrible aftermath that would follow her death.

There, he'd thought it. *Death.* Because that was the fact of the matter. No point dressing the fucker up. Kinga was going to die. The finality of it all suddenly hit him, and he staggered to his feet, muttered, "Won't be a minute," and launched himself outside.

As he closed the door behind him, his legs gave way, and he

sank to the floor. For all their problems over the years, he fucking loved that woman. He wouldn't be where he was if it weren't for Kinga. Sure, since he'd met Natalia they'd had a lot of issues and said things that couldn't be unsaid, but the fact that he'd forgiven her time and again told its own story, even if it had been mainly at Natalia's insistence.

He expected Natalia to follow him, but he should have given her more credit. Her wedding vows had said it all. She knew when to bring him close and when he needed space. She'd always been able to tune in to his needs because she was inside his head and his heart. She knew him as well as he knew himself, and by leaving him alone right then, she was proving that once more.

After about ten minutes, Natalia poked her head around the door. "Cash, she's awake and asking for you."

He clambered to his feet, but before he could step inside, Natalia put her arm out. "I know you can do this," she whispered, low enough so her voice wouldn't drift into the room. "Be strong for her. Fall apart with me. That's the way this has to go down."

Jesus, what a woman she was. He brushed a hand along her jaw and forced a smile. "I don't deserve you."

"I know."

The smile he gave her then was genuine, and as she dropped her arm so he could pass, he took comfort in her strength.

A brief flicker of life appeared in Kinga's eyes as he walked over to her bed, but then the light faded. She tried to lift a hand, but the physical effort was too great.

"Hey," she said in a rasping voice that sounded nothing like Kinga's usual smooth, confident tone.

"Hey yourself." He wagged a finger at her. "The things you'll do to get your own way. You've wrecked my honeymoon. I hope you know that."

Her lips twitched in the beginnings of a smile. "My timing has always been impeccable." She winced then, and her body shifted to the side.

"Are you in pain?"

She nodded and squeezed her eyes together, her breath coming in short pants.

"I'll get someone, darling," William said.

"No. Don't," she said. "Not yet. I don't want to be out of it again yet."

Cash's lips pressed together in a slight grimace as he found himself stuck between two places, neither of which were appealing. But then his eyes softened, and he leaned across to kiss her cheek. "Stubborn old cow," he said, which forced a brief laugh from Kinga that sounded more like a cough.

"Have you brought the baby?" she said, trying to lift her head to catch Natalia's eye. When Cash nodded, she sighed. "Can you hold her up? I want to see her one last time."

Pain lanced through Cash, and he turned away before Kinga could see the tears that had welled up.

"Here she is," Natalia said, instantly understanding he couldn't speak right at that moment. She handed Darcey to him, and he gazed into his daughter's eyes as he tried to get a hold of himself.

"She's going to be a heartbreaker," Kinga said. "Like her daddy."

Cash met her eyes, and as he did, her face took on a peaceful look. She beckoned him to lean forward as her voice began to fade.

"I love you," she whispered. "Please don't forget me."

"Never." The tears he'd tried so hard to hold back broke free. "Never."

43

T ally made sure Meredith was comfortably seated before heading back to the entrance of the ballroom at the Dorchester. Two years had passed since the first time she'd entered this room on the night of Cash's foundation gala—a relatively short time, yet such a lot had changed. No longer was she on the periphery, hoping to catch a glimpse of her idol and at the same time dreading someone would discover the duplicity of hiding her press pass so she could get close to journo-phobe, Cash Gallagher.

Now she was Mrs Cash Gallagher, mother to a seven-month-old baby who made her remember every day how lucky she was.

The Dorchester had done them proud. The room was tastefully decorated but not too ostentatious, given the reason for the event.

"Memories, baby?" Cash said, curving a warm hand around her waist. He brushed her hip with his thumb, a habit he'd developed when they'd first met as a way to reassure her, and she loved it as much now as she had then.

"Yeah. Good ones."

"Do you think Kinga would like it?" Cash said, nodding inside the packed room. Every table was full of people anxious for a little piece of her husband.

Tally leaned her head on his shoulder. "She would. You've done her proud, Cash."

He heaved a sigh. She wasn't sure if it was relief that after six months of hard slog they'd achieved so much, or the realisation that he would be spending the next four hours making small talk —something he hated doing—in an effort to get people to donate to the cancer charity he'd set up in Kinga's name.

"Time to face the masses," he said, pulling a face.

"Don't worry, ace," she said, reaching up to press a kiss to his cheek. "You pay the penance this evening and get your reward tonight. Oh, and just to be clear, you're going to need to bring your A game."

She swept a hand over his arse and glanced up at him to see if her promise had had the desired effect. It had. Cash's mouth was parted, his cheeks tinged with a hint of red.

He bent down, and his lips touched the shell of her ear as he whispered, "Be careful, sweetness. I know I've matured over the years, but I'm not averse to deciding this event can manage without its host and hostess for an hour."

She laughed. "Only an hour? Slacker. Come on, you know how I love to hear you speak." She put on an exaggerated shudder. "Turns me on big time."

Before Cash could reply, she tugged on his hand and stepped into the room.

TALLY LAY in Cash's arms later that night, sated and happier than she'd ever thought possible. The event had been a huge success, taking an enormous weight off both their shoulders, and they'd secured enough funding to take them right through the following year, which was more than both of them had hoped for.

"Are you still awake?" Cash whispered after they'd been lying in the darkness for a few minutes.

"Mmm," she said, halfway between sleep and unconscious bliss.

"I wanted to talk to you about something."

"No more charities," she mumbled.

He chuckled. "I think two is enough. No, it was about me. Well, us. Well, tennis actually."

That caught her attention. Cash hadn't mentioned anything about playing again since he'd won the Estoril tournament at the end of April, almost eight months earlier. Since then, their lives had been overtaken by Darcey's birth, Kinga's passing, and then setting up the charity. She'd often been on the cusp of bringing it up, knowing he still had years ahead of him if that was what he chose to do, but in the end, she'd decided he had to make the first move.

And apparently, he'd just made it.

She reached over and switched on the bedside lamp. The lighting was subtle, but she still had to squint until her eyes adjusted.

"I'm all ears, ace," she said, sitting up and crossing her legs.

Cash turned onto his side, one hand propping up his head. "I think I want to go back on the circuit, but," he said, holding his hand up as she began to interrupt, "we have to make this decision together. Travelling with a baby is not going to be easy. I'm seriously out of shape, at least the type of shape I need to be in to achieve success on court, and if we decide I'm doing this, it's going to take up huge amounts of time, which will cut into the time spent with you and Darcey."

Tally motioned for him to sit up, which he did. She took both of his hands in hers. "See these? They're amazing. I've always loved your hands, but even more so now. They hold our baby when she needs comforting, they bathe her, dress her, play with her. And when you put them on me, they make me feel so good."

She glanced up for effect and saw that he was grinning, even though she could tell he didn't know where she was going with this yet.

"But you know what these do best, ace? They hold a tennis racket, which allows you to perform miracles on court. I miss watching you play—more than I have the words to explain. I understand it's not going to be easy, but we'll work it out. Plenty of others do. I won't be the first wife of a tennis player who hauls their kid around the circuit."

He raised his eyebrows and offered her a questioning gaze. "So we're doing this?"

She brought his hands to her lips and kissed every one of his fingers in turn. "We are."

EPILOGUE

Tally dabbed her forehead with one of Rupe's handkerchiefs with his initials stitched into the corner in cobalt blue. The edges of her mouth twitched as she tried to stop the giggle that threatened to break from her throat. Rupe and his *pretentious crap*, as Cash called his best friend's fondness for old-fashioned things, always brought a smile to her face.

"I can see you laughing," Rupe said, swiping back his hand-kerchief and stuffing it into his pocket. "I know I'm a dying breed."

"Dying?" Em said, giving him an incredulous look. "The chances of finding another one like you, my dear Rupert Fox-Whittingham, is as likely as a bloody dodo sitting at my feet and begging for a bone."

"No need to get personal," Rupe said, playfully sticking his tongue out at Em.

"Jesus," grumbled Brad. "Can't you two fuck and get it over with?"

"Ew," Em said. "Incest or what. Besides, have you forgotten...?" She waved her left hand in front of Brad's face, displaying a sparkling ruby-and-diamond ring. "Two months to the wedding."

"I pity David," Rupe said. "Poor bastard doesn't know what he's letting himself in for."

Tally tuned out their banter, her attention focused on the corner of Wimbledon's centre court as she waited for Cash to walk out. Despite promising herself she would focus on the future, she couldn't help her mind winding back three years to the last time she'd sat in the players' box on finals day, a day that hadn't turned out so well—the bad luck of Cash losing to Anatoly had been the start of almost a year of hell. And despite being in the dim and distant past, the pain of that time still cut deep. It could still make her wince if she thought about it for too long.

"Are you okay, darling? You look a little pale."

Tally rubbed Meredith's arm, an action meant to soothe and reassure. "I'm fine, Meredith," she said, still unable to call her Mum. She wondered if she ever would. Perhaps too much water had gone under the bridge. "A little hot, but other than that..."

Meredith's soft smile was full of love. "Here," she said, passing Tally a bottle of cold water. "Make sure you stay hydrated. Got to look after yourself and the little one."

As if knowing he was being spoken about, the baby gave an almighty kick. Tally glanced down, her hand automatically rubbing her belly. "Just my luck if he decides to make an appearance today."

Meredith chuckled, unaware of the pain that lanced through Tally as she remembered the last time she'd gone into labour with Darcey at Kinga's wedding. She missed Kinga. It was a little over two years since she'd died. The time had sped by, but not one day passed when she didn't think of her friend and the terrible set of cards she'd been dealt. It was so strange. They'd started out as enemies, but in the end, Kinga had become the older sister Tally never had. She missed her.

The gentle hum of the crowd gradually increased in volume

until everyone was on their feet, clapping and hollering and waving banners, hats, and giant tennis balls in the air. Tally's head turned in time to see Cash walk on court. A rush of adrenaline gave her a much-needed energy boost. It didn't matter how many times she watched the same sight. Cash sauntering on court, brimming with confidence, was something she'd never get sick of seeing.

He caught her eye and gave a quick wink before his face closed off, concentration overtaking his features, making his skin appear tighter over his cheekbones. It was all a front, a way to lull his opponent into thinking Cash might be worried about the upcoming match.

He went through a long-cultivated routine and then walked on court. He jumped up and down a few times, knees tucked tight, before he hit the racket against his open palm. After the coin toss and obligatory photographs, Cash jogged to the baseline and began warming up.

"He looks good, babes," Em whispered. "Gonna smash it."

"Yeah," Tally said. And she actually believed it. Cash hadn't put a foot wrong the whole fortnight, and his opponent was a wild card entry, a previous top-ten player who'd been out for a year with a nasty knee injury. The odds were stacked in Cash's favour, so much so that the bookies had stopped taking bets on him winning a seventh Wimbledon title the second he made it into the quarter final.

And as usual, the bookies had made the right decision. Cash stormed to victory in three straight sets, his win so emphatic Tally felt sorry for his opponent. Nobody wanted to lose six–love, six–one, six–two in any match, let alone the Wimbledon final.

As soon as Cash shook his opponent's hand, he flashed a triumphant look up at their box. All of Tally's jumping up and down had unsettled their unborn son, who was doing cartwheels inside her belly. Tally tried to soothe him, her hand making circular motions over the enormous bump. At least there was no sign of early-onset labour. She was determined this baby was going to term. *Two more weeks to hang on.*

"Shall I go and get Darcey?" Rachael said.

"Oh, yes," Tally said. "She should be part of this."

By the time Rachael returned with an exuberant Darcey, the red carpet had been laid out, and the Duke of Kent was making his way down the two rows of ball boys and girls, sharing an odd word with the lucky few.

"Daddy," Darcey yelled, her chubby little hands reaching down towards the court. Spectators close enough to hear her over the racket made murmuring sounds of approval, their smiles bright as they watched a little girl get excited about seeing her father, even though she couldn't possibly understand the momentous achievement he'd made.

"Yes, it's Daddy," Tally said, settling Darcey onto her lap. "Now, shush. You have to be quiet while the presentations are made."

Darcey pouted, looking exactly like Cash when he didn't get his own way. Tally chuckled and shared an understanding glance with Rachael, who clipped Darcey under the chin, bringing on a beaming smile. Darcey was so lucky having two grandmothers who doted on her and an extended family who were always around to spoil her rotten.

The duke had a quick word with the runner-up and handed over the silver plate, and then it was Cash's turn. He shared a few words with the duke before lifting the winner's trophy aloft.

Sue Barker appeared at the side of the court, ready to interview the winner and the runner-up. Cash patiently waited, a faint smile gracing his beautiful face as he stared into the distance, seemingly in a world of his own. Tally knew that look—he was overjoyed and overwhelmed in equal measure.

Eventually, Sue called him forward, and he sauntered over, gracing her with a warm smile and a kiss on the cheek. Tally was sure she could hear a collective sigh from the women in the crowd, regardless of age, and although she couldn't hear what Cash said, Sue's blush meant he was having the same effect on court. In the past, Tally would have been crushed by jealousy and worry, but nowadays, she simply felt incredibly fortunate Cash had chosen her—although whenever she told him that, he'd roll his eyes and tell her she'd got it the wrong way around. *He* was the lucky one for snaring her. And he'd never given her any reason to doubt him. If anything, she grew more and more trusting.

"Congratulations, Cash," Sue was saying. "Seven Wimbledon titles. How does it feel?"

"I'm not sure I can describe how I feel, Sue," Cash said. "I'd like to say thanks to Jim for a great match. He's done fantastically well to get this far after an injury that would have finished off a lot of players. I'm sure he'll soon be back in the top ten, and I wouldn't be at all surprised to see him in the finals again next year."

Cash paused as a ripple of applause broke around the stadium.

"And your whole family here to watch," Sue said. "That must be wonderful for you."

He nodded, his eyes flickering towards Tally. "Yes. It means the world to have them here, especially as my wife is so close to her due date. It's not easy for her in this heat, but I can't repeat what she said when I suggested she stay at home."

Laughter reverberated around the stadium as hundreds of people craned their necks to get a look at Tally. She ducked her head. She'd never liked the attention that came her way because she was married to Cash, but there was no getting away from it.

"And my daughter too. Hi, baby girl," he said, waving to Darcey, who struggled to get away from Tally's firm grasp.

A collective "Aaahhh" went up around the stadium.

"So what's next for you? I presume you'll be taking a bit of time off to welcome your new arrival, but I hope we'll see you back for the US Open."

Cash seemed to hesitate, as though he was in the middle of a decision but hadn't made up his mind whether to jump left or right. And then he leaped into the unknown. "Actually, Sue, today was my last match. I've decided to retire from tennis."

A composite gasp went up around the stadium. Tally sucked in a breath. "He did it," she murmured, a surge of pride swelling in her chest.

Rachael's eyebrows shot up in surprise. "He never said a word," she whispered to Tally.

Tally grimaced. "He's been back and forth for a few weeks. He didn't want to tell anyone in case he decided to carry on for a while longer."

When Em and Rupe began to fire questions at her, she shushed them and pointed to Cash, who was waiting for the crowd to settle before continuing.

"I want to spend more time with my family than the rigours of the ATP tour allow. Travelling around the world with a toddler and another one on the way isn't easy. My wife has sacrificed a lot to support me and my career, and now it's my turn to support her in her ambitions. My family will always come first. They'll always be more important than tennis.

"I also want to put more energy into both the Cash Gallagher Foundation—which, as you know, aims to help kids break the cycle of abuse through sport—and the Kinga Harrington-Bourne Cancer Trust."

"Wow," Sue said. "I thought as you'd won the Australian, the French, and Wimbledon, you'd be aiming for another career Grand Slam by playing the US Open."

Cash glanced up at the players' box. "I've already won the Grand Slam, Sue," he said, his eyes teeming with love as his gaze collided with Tally's. Her eyes pricked with tears as wave after wave of emotions raced through her. She glanced down at

Darcey, who was bouncing on the spot, and automatically cradled her belly. Her life was complete. She blew Cash a kiss.

"Well, I, for one, will miss watching you play," Sue said. "It's been a joy to watch you over the years. But thanks for giving the BBC the exclusive." She grinned. "Now, I'm sure this crowd want a chance to photograph you with this wonderful trophy."

She waved her hand for Cash to follow the tradition of carrying the trophy to all four sides of the court, to give ordinary people a chance to get a photograph of a lifetime, but Cash had always bucked rules and tradition. He picked up the trophy, carefully placed it next to his kit bag, and began the climb up to the players' box. Many had done the same climb in the past—it had become a bit of a tradition since Pat Cash paved the way in 1987—but they usually attempted it before the trophy was presented.

Cash received several pats on the back as he made his way through the crowd. On reaching his target, he vaulted into the players' box and threw his arms around Tally. "Love you, baby."

"I'm so proud of you," she murmured in his ear.

As Tally spoke, Darcey shouted, "Daddy, Daddy, up, up."

He did as she asked, swinging her into his arms and settling her on his hip. Then he kissed his mum and Meredith. Even Em was awarded with a brief peck before he shook hands with the rest of the team. The pictures would undoubtedly go viral in minutes, but for once, Tally didn't care.

"Hey, sweetness," he whispered in a voice so low only she could hear. "How about we get out of here and start our new life?"

Tally leaned into him as happiness swept through her.

"Ace," she said, "I can't think of anything I'd rather do."

FROM MY HEART

Writing the end on Grand Slam was bittersweet to say the least. I've lived with Cash and Tally for so long, they are my family and I'll really miss them.

I do hope Grand Slam met all your expectations. I know that I put you through the wringer at the end of both Winning Ace and Losing Game. Thank you so much for staying with me to the end. It means more to me than I'll ever be able to express. Love and hugs xx

Next up is Mismatch, where we follow Rupe's story. He certainly was a fun character to write. I hope you enjoy reading about him as much as I enjoyed writing about him. He can be terribly naughty sometimes! And of course, Cash and Tally make an appearance or two. After all, Rupe without Cash is like strawberries without cream!

As always, I'd love to hear from you. Please feel free to get in touch via email, Facebook, Twitter or by signing up to my reader group at www.traciedelaneyauthor.com

Would you consider helping other readers decide if this is the right book for them by leaving a short rating on Amazon? They really help readers discover new books.

ACKNOWLEDGMENTS

My thanks to my writing mentor, Beth Hill, a wonderful lady without whom, I wouldn't be where I am today.

To Incy—thank you from the bottom of my heart for your honesty and your generosity. This journey wouldn't be nearly as much fun without you.

To Louise just because...you know. Mwah!

To Mel Comley for her support, her advice, and her eagle eye! Really, lady, you are the bomb!

To my amazing street team who are tireless in their efforts to bring attention to an unknown writer. In no particular order - Loulou, Jules, Niamh, Lindsey, Del, Michelle, Kay, Dawn, Linda, Demei and Ana Irenea. We may be small, ladies, but we're fierce! Hugs and kisses to each and every one of you

And last but not least, to you, the readers. Thank you for being on this journey with me. Without you, I wouldn't be able to do the thing I love most in the world—write books. You have my eternal gratitude, love, and respect.

ABOUT THE AUTHOR

Tracie Delaney is the author of the *Winning Ace* series. She loves nothing more than immersing herself in a good romance, although she sometimes, rather cheekily, makes her characters wait for their HEA.

When she isn't writing or sitting around with her head stuck in a book, she can often be found watching The Walking Dead, Game of Thrones or any tennis match involving Roger Federer. Her greatest fear is running out of coffee.

Tracie studied accountancy, gaining her qualification in 2001. Her maths teacher would no doubt be stunned by this revelation considering Tracie could barely add two plus two at high school.

Tracie lives in the North West of England with her amazingly supportive husband and her two crazy Westies who filled the hole left by their predecessors, and who make her smile every day.

Tracie loves to hear from readers. She can be contacted through her website at
www.traciedelaneyauthor.com